Canter with a Killer

Canter
with a
Killer

A HORSE RESCUE
MYSTERY

Amber Camp

NEW YORK

Published in the United States by Crooked Lane Books, an imprint of The Quick Brown Fox & Company LLC.

Crooked Lane Books and its logo are trademarks of The Quick Brown Fox & Company LLC.

Library of Congress Catalog-in-Publication data available upon request.

ISBN (hardcover): 978-1-63910-180-1
ISBN (ebook): 978-1-63910-181-8

Cover illustration by Bruce Emmett

Printed in the United States.

www.crookedlanebooks.com

Crooked Lane Books
34 West 27th St., 10th Floor
New York, NY 10001

First Edition: November 2022

10 9 8 7 6 5 4 3 2 1

For Mom, I miss you every day.

Chapter One

I hit the ground with a meaty thud. I didn't have time to worry about what might be bruised or bent before I had to roll out of the way and escape the flying hooves. There seemed to be more of them than the standard four that horses usually had because it felt like I was dodging them from every direction. After what felt like forever, but was more likely just a few seconds, the hooves thundered away from me, leaving me splayed in the dirt gasping like a fish on a boat dock.

"Mallory! Are you okay?" Tanner's frantic voice came from above me, and I felt hands under my arms as he yanked me to my feet. The sudden change in position was enough to snap my diaphragm awake, and I sucked in a wheezing breath. I was glad that of my two volunteers who help at the rescue, it was Tanner's day. His large frame blocked out the early afternoon sun as he towered over me, and I doubted that Ashley, my other volunteer, would have been able to yank me off the ground like a sack of potatoes.

"I'm alright," I said breathlessly as I tried to dust off my jeans. I knew I was going to feel it in the morning. At forty-two, I didn't bounce back nearly as fast as I once did. "Where did he go?" I asked. I looked around the paddock and found it sadly lacking one very irate bay gelding.

"After he tried to stomp you into the dirt, he went straight for the back fence and sailed over it like a champion hunter jumper," Tanner said, using his hands to illustrate his point.

"Oh, great." I tried to capture the loose blonde curls that had slipped out of my ponytail and cram them behind my ears. "Just great."

I did *not* relish the idea of traipsing through my backwoods, through poison ivy, chiggers, and ticks to recapture a scared horse that had already tried to kill me once that day. But I didn't have any other choice, so I headed to the barn for a bucket of feed and a lead rope. Bribing a horse to be caught isn't the best training tactic you can take, but desperate times call for desperate measures.

The commotion had set off the other horses, and Biscuit, the donkey, was braying (or "honking" as Tanner calls it) so loudly that I couldn't hear myself think. With all the commotion, it took a few moments to realize that my phone was vibrating in my pocket. I answered it without looking at the caller ID.

"Just what do you think you're doing?" the male voice on the other end of the line loudly asked. I recognized it right away.

"Good afternoon, Albert," I said, impatience already creeping into my voice as I slung the lead rope over my shoulder. "What can I do for you?"

"You can stop this nonsense!"

"What *nonsense* is it this time?"

"You know full well what I'm talking about, *Ms. Martin*." He practically spat my name out like it tasted bad.

I took just a second to mentally lament the fact that I was now a "Ms." and no longer a "Mrs." before I let my exasperation get the better of me.

"I don't know, and quite frankly, I don't have time to play games. So if you could just get to the part where you tell me what you're mad about this time, I would appreciate it."

"I found your little flyer at the feedstore. You're planning to add riding lessons to that disaster of a rescue?"

"I think riding lessons would be a great addition to our rescue," I said, biting back both annoyance and amusement. I'm pretty sure that if Albert Cunningham lived in town, he would be one of those old men who scream at kids to get off his lawn.

The truth was that I needed some way to bring more money into the rescue, or I was going to have to scale back. The vet care alone had eaten into what I had put back for hay already. That didn't count the feed, basic supplies, fencing materials, dewormer, and about a million other things. The old saying about how to make a small fortune in the horse business came to mind. The answer to that is to start with a large fortune. I had neither.

"You'll have even more people bringing their *mongrel* horses in right next to my champions!" He continued to yell into the phone, and I clicked the volume down a few notches. "Your mess of a place has already affected my property value, and my buyers have to look at your eyesore every time I take them to the barn. I've put up with this since you moved back here two years ago. Enough is enough!"

I instinctively turned around to look at his farm nestled on the hill overlooking mine. The highline cut through the trees, and the electric co-op had cleared out a large swath of timber on each side. It made my house, barn, front paddock, and round pen all visible from his huge, fancy barn on the hill. And it made the contrast between his fourteen-stall show barn and my four-stall converted hay barn all the more stark in comparison.

Cunningham Performance Horses was a sprawling horse breeding and training farm known for champion quarter horses. His family had been here since the dawn of time to hear him tell it, and he felt that gave him the right to tell everyone else what was and wasn't acceptable. I was proud of the effort I had put into my "eyesore," and it was a needed resource. We had been at capacity, and sometimes beyond, since I had opened the barn doors. Besides, being here just felt *right*.

"I have a really hard time believing that my rescue has affected your property values." I kept a calm tone in spite of the fact that I was fast losing what little patience I had left. "And having a nice lesson barn in the area can only help the horse community."

"Well, it won't be a nice lesson barn if it's at your rat-infested place!"

He hung up before I had a chance to respond. Which was probably for the best since the response bouncing around in my brain was decidedly *not nice*.

"What's old Albert on a tear about now?" Tanner took the lead rope off my shoulder.

"He thinks lessons will cause more people to drive by his property, and I guess he thinks they might bring their horses. Which I can't figure for the life of me why that bothers him so much," I said and tried to take the rope back.

Tanner put up a hand. "I'll go get him. He's banged you up enough already. And Albert's just a cranky old codger."

"He's just scared," I said. "The horse, not Albert." I handed the bucket of feed over too. As much as I hated to admit it, I was

4

thankful Tanner was going to trek through the woods and hills and retrieve the gelding. His youth and athleticism were a welcome contrast to my *not youth* and less than stellar endurance.

"I know. But he'll have more trouble dragging around two hundred and fifty pounds of me than he will a hundred and twenty-five pounds of you." He grinned.

Bless him. I'm pretty sure my left leg weighs a buck twenty-five.

"Be careful," I said in my Mom voice.

He saluted me and headed out the back gate.

I busied myself tending to the other horses, and of course, our resident donkey, Biscuit. At present count, there were nine horses, including the new one. All of them had come to me in varying degrees of need, some of them neglected, some of them outright abused, as was the case with the current bay gelding. I had no doubt that we would bring him around like we had the rest. Tanner, with his gentle giant manner, instilled a sense of quiet calm in everything he did. And Ashley, my other volunteer, was as gifted a trainer as I'd ever met. Both of them were in their early twenties, like my daughter, and I hoped they would stay with the rescue for many years to come.

I tried to follow my then-husband, now ex-husband, to St. Louis, where his law practice had taken off. I tried to fit into that world, earning a master's degree and certification in forensic nursing, which had landed me a coveted position as a legal nurse consultant. But a square peg in a round hole can only fit for so long before it either falls out or its edges get rounded off. My edges never rounded off.

The decision to leave everything I thought I'd wanted hadn't been an easy one. It took a huge push for me to take the leap.

When Dad developed pneumonia and then sepsis, I took a leave of absence from work to take care of him. His weeks in the intensive care unit and then in the rehab unit afterward had left him too weak to even transfer himself into a chair. My marriage had already ended, and our only daughter was in college, so there wasn't much holding me down. My mom died a year and four months before Dad got sick, and we didn't have any other close family. It was an easy decision to come home and care for him. I've always adored my dad. Being home forced me to see things from a new perspective and reevaluate what I thought I wanted out of life. I was reminded nearly every day, everywhere I looked, of the blonde, curly-haired kid I used to be, the one who was obsessed with horses and desperately wanted to make a difference in the world.

It was in those days of doctor's appointments and physical therapy visits that the first ideas about opening a rescue crept back in. I'd wanted nothing more when I was a kid, but I hadn't entertained it as a serious option as an adult. After Dad decided that the farm, as he'd always called it, was too much for him to handle and moved into an apartment in town, I couldn't face going back to work as a legal nurse consultant, filling my days with chart reviews, time lines, and patient interviews. I didn't feel like I was making a difference anymore, not in any tangible way. Dad signed over the farm to me, and it just felt right to put it to good use. I cashed out my 401(k), tried not to think about the penalty or the fact that every financial adviser on the planet would tell me how stupid that was, and Hillspring Horse Rescue was born.

After I had put out feed and a few flakes of hay, scratched butts, and filled water troughs, I decided to go see if Tanner had managed to coax our escapee back into civilization. He met me at the gate. The big bay followed him quietly and without protest. A chorus of whinnies sounded from our residents at the sight of the new horse, and they were answered by Albert's champions on the hill.

"Good job," I said, impressed.

"He's just a big puppy dog once he gets to know you." Tanner patted him heartily on the neck. I could see the beginnings of infatuation there. Tanner had been looking for a horse to replace the one he had just retired. He had ridden pickup at all the local rodeos since he was a lanky teenager, and it needed to be a big, sturdy horse to carry him and do the job too. This bay definitely fit that bill. The problem was that the horse didn't belong to the rescue yet. We had taken temporary custody of him, but his owner would still have his day in court.

"I've fixed a stall for him. Better to keep him a bit more contained until he settles in," I said, pointing to the barn.

Tanner nodded and took the horse inside.

"He's going to need a name, you know," I called after them. "Why don't you give it some thought?"

"I'll do that." Tanner was positively beaming.

I stood for a moment and surveyed my place. Interactions with Albert always made me feel a bit more protective of the rescue than I usually was—kind of put me into "mama bear" mode, I suppose. The front paddock was attached to the barn's downhill side and opened up into a large, mostly cleared pasture. I was finally growing a good mix of Bermuda and fescue grasses, and in a year or two, I would be able to cut way back on hay in the summers if I rotated my grazing just right.

The barn nestled on the gentle slope at the front of my property had been a hay barn before I opened the rescue. A big chunk of my startup money had been used to convert part of the ground floor into four horse stalls where we could care for any rescues that needed monitoring or extra care. I converted the rest of the usable space to a feed and tack room, and a small corner was our makeshift wash rack. The loft still housed our square bales of hay, and I used one corner as an office space, although I kept most of the records and receipts at the house. It was still a nice area to work when my presence was needed at the barn.

My small white house was modest, but nothing here deserved to be called an "eyesore" in my estimation. I didn't have a full-time staff like Albert did, nor was I born into the county's wealthiest banking family, but everything was in good repair. I gave myself a pep talk and reminded myself that Albert must be a very unhappy person to spend so much time blaming others for everything. Forcing myself to see him as a miserable, flawed old man helped soften my anger.

I joined Tanner in the barn as he was settling the big bay in his stall.

"Hey, Boss," he said as he opened the stall door. "Is the camera in the loft?"

"Yes, but I can take the photos for the case file. You've gone above and beyond already."

"It's okay. I want to get some of his mane and get started on some bracelets for the shop anyway," he said over his shoulder as he climbed the steps to the barn loft.

I smiled. Tanner's mother, Rachel, owned a craft store in town. He made beautiful, intricate horsehair bracelets, sold them in his mother's store, and insisted on donating the profits back to the rescue. It was usually a modest amount, but I was touched more by the effort and gesture than any amount of money.

The late afternoon light cast a warm glow over the hillside, and I had the sudden urge to grab my DSLR and see if I could sneak in some wildlife shots before the sun set behind the hill. I was a total amateur, but I loved catching shots of songbirds, squirrels, and deer.

"Speaking of cameras, I'm going to grab mine and see if anything is stirring," I called up the loft steps.

"Sounds good, Boss."

It didn't do any good to tell him that he was an unpaid volunteer and not to call me "Boss." He would just give me a sheepish grin and tell me that I *was* the boss. I pulled my camera case out of my truck. I had gotten in the habit of bringing it with me since I had wished several times that I'd had it handy. Like when I spotted a mama deer with her speckled twins behind the bank parking lot in Hillspring. Or when the great blue heron caught a fish in the creek while I was stopped at the one-lane bridge on the road into town.

It didn't take long to get some great captures. I snapped a blue jay at the bird feeder, an adorable chipmunk at the edge of the woods, and a black vulture circling the valley below. Vultures aren't what most people consider beautiful, but they're an important part of the ecosystem, and I appreciate their place in the world, even if they aren't conventionally attractive. I looked forward to uploading them to my Facebook photography group. The members always had helpful suggestions about tweaking my settings to get better photos. Since I had started that hobby with no technical knowledge whatsoever, I appreciated any help that was offered.

I finished by snapping some shots of the horses grazing behind the barn. Tanner and Ashley kept offering to help me get a website going and boost our social media presence, and I thought a good place to start would be taking photos of our residents. We currently only had two that were suitable for adoption, and both of them were mowing the grass on the hillside, looking very photogenic. Molly, a bay pony, gleamed in the early afternoon sun, her dapples shining like new pennies. Beside her, River, a chestnut gelding, gently swished at flies while he sought out tasty blades of grass with his agile lips. With the forest framed behind them, they were a picture of tranquil beauty.

After taking a ridiculous number of photos—thank goodness for digital cameras—I checked in with Tanner before I went to the house for the evening.

"I'm gonna head home," he said as he met me at the paddock fence.

"Thanks for everything today."

"No problem." He shrugged. "I'm not sure when I'll be back this week, but I'll let you know as soon as I find out what Dad's plans are."

"Just whatever works with your schedule." Tanner split his time between the rescue and helping his dad on their own farm, choosing to follow in his dad's footsteps rather than pursue college or trade school. How he found time for rodeo and friends, I had no idea.

* * *

Evenings at the rescue are usually peaceful. The horses' soft murmurs and the sounds of munching hay were always the soundtrack to my soul. It was starting to feel like fall, getting cooler in the evenings as the sun set behind the hills. I wrapped my hands around the warm mug of hot chocolate and looked out over the farm. Although nothing was technically falling apart, there were a lot of things that could use some routine maintenance. The fences needed attention. The barn needed a coat of paint—its traditional red had faded over the years. The hay ring in the front paddock was hanging together by a prayer. The repairs were endless, and the money was tight, but my heart had never been happier.

I loved living just outside the city limits, but if I ever decided to go urban again, it would be here. Hillspring was about as quaint a little town as Arkansas had to offer. It sat nestled in the Ozark Mountains in the northwest corner of the state. There was something in the town for nearly everyone, from the bustling shopping district to the Victorian-style manors and cottages of the Historic District to New Bethlehem, the Christian-themed theater and art gallery. There were museums, a haunted hotel, cemetery tours, a train tour, and countless year-round festivals, which brought in tourists from all over the United States and abroad. It was truly one of the most eclectic places I've ever been, a fact that had been lost on me until I moved away.

We'd always had livestock growing up, even though Dad worked at the quarry and Mom ran a house-cleaning business. We kept chickens, goats, the odd pig or duck now and then, and, of course, the horses. We had three of the most wonderful, gentle babysitters you could ever ask for in a horse. Dancer was Mom's, a small palomino mare who loved carrots and chin scratches. Tug was unofficially Dad's. He was a red sorrel gelding that always looked annoyed, even though he was a total sweetheart. Dad would brush him down and have long conversations with him, but he only rode with Mom and me a handful of times in my whole life. There was always something more pressing he needed to fix, or so he said. And then there was Shadowfax, so named because twelve-year-old me was obsessed with Tolkien, and the horse happened to be a pale enough gray that I could pretend he was silver.

Frances and Jasper Hall, otherwise known as Mom and Dad, respectively, had me late in life, after years of being told they couldn't have children. Mom had been forty-two, the age I am now, when she'd had me. Being the only child of older parents can sometimes be lonely, even with devoted and loving parents. I think that's why Shadowfax was so important to me. I have no idea how many miles Shadowfax and I totaled in our years together. But I do know I spent those miles daydreaming about the horse rescue I would open and the lives I would save. I had planned to go to college, major in equestrian studies, and set the world on fire. What actually happened was that Shadowfax had a fatal bout of colic two days before my eighteenth birthday. I hadn't experienced heartbreak like that before in my sheltered life, and I couldn't face the thought of losing another one like that. I changed my major to nursing and pushed my childhood dreams to the back of my mind.

I settled into the rocker on the porch and pulled a blanket around my shoulders when I noticed the lights were on in the Cunningham show barn. It pulled me out of my nostalgia. It was odd at this hour. Albert never showed horses in the evenings. I had always been under the impression that he went to bed with the chickens. But that was just an impression. I couldn't see his house from my place, so I didn't really know how late he chose to stay up. I watched the barn for a little while and decided that it was none of my business, no matter what was going on over there. It was a constant struggle to not become the nosy neighbor.

Dad always told me that "curiosity killed the cat," which I would counter with my favorite teacher's often repeated Einstein quote: "The important thing is to not stop questioning."

By the time I turned in, I was thoroughly exhausted, and sleep came quickly. I actually felt refreshed when the sunlight shining through the crack in the curtains woke me the next morning. Stiff and sore from the previous day's brush with death, but refreshed. I fixed a quick breakfast and downed some coffee to knock off the last of the sleep and readied myself to start the morning chores. I threw back a couple of ibuprofen and thanked my lucky stars that it hadn't been worse.

I had just stepped outside when I heard the sirens.

"Hey, Boss Lady," Ashley called as I descended the porch steps. She had picked up Tanner's nickname for me. "What do you think is going on up there?" She pointed to the Cunningham farm. Her long, dark brown ponytail swung over her opposite shoulder when she raised her arm and turned her head.

"I don't know," I said, shielding my eyes from the morning sun with my hand. "Is that a police car?" I had just assumed the sirens I heard were from an ambulance. Working with horses can be a dangerous business, and I assumed that maybe someone had gotten hurt.

"It looks like it." Ashley squinted. "Let's go see what's going on."

"We can't just go get in the middle of whatever is going on up there."

"Of course we can! They might need help, after all."

"They have all the help they need," I said, even though I wanted nothing more than to go get *right* in the middle of it. Curiosity had always been one of my downfalls.

"Well, I'm gonna go," she said, hands on her hips. "We don't know who's up there this early, and the horses may need tending to."

I knew that was just an excuse. Albert Cunningham employed a full staff both at the barn and at the house, any of whom would be more than capable of caring for the horses. But it was a solid excuse; I had to give her that. What sort of rescue owner was I if I didn't offer my services to horses in potential need?

"Okay," I conceded. "I'll ride with you. Let me just put Banjo in the house."

I pointed to the house, and my goofy blue heeler mix ran to the door. I let him in and told him to stay. He looked disappointed but didn't try to make a run for the door. Behind me, Ashley pulled up in her silver Nissan Frontier. I climbed into the passenger seat.

"I already checked on ours. Everybody's good," she said as she pulled down the drive. "Tanner named the new one Zeus."

"Zeus?"

"Yeah," she laughed. "I hadn't pegged Tanner for the Greek mythology type."

"He's full of surprises, that one."

It only took a few minutes to get to the ornate entrance at the top of Albert's driveway. The massive wrought iron gates hung from colossal rock pillars, each one topped with an iron quarter horse. "Cunningham Performance Horses" was emblazoned across the archway. I'd bet that the gates alone cost more than my house.

I had always been curious about that place when I was a kid. The visibility afforded by the highline clearing was a relatively recent development, in the last few years. When I was growing up, you couldn't see the paddocks or the barn at all, so it had this mysterious air about it. Albert and his family had always seemed somehow foreign to me as well, even though they had much deeper roots in the community than we did.

The mansion sat nestled against the hill at the edge of an old-growth oak forest. To the left of the driveway was a picturesque paddock encircled with gleaming white vinyl fencing. Horses, which I'm sure had pedigrees that would make my head spin, milled about, grazing on the lush grass. To our right, overlooking my rescue, the show barn commanded our attention. The cream-colored metal siding reflected the morning sun and made the building look like it was glowing. The deep green of the roof complemented the surrounding pines. The structure was big enough to hold fourteen luxury horse stalls and a small indoor arena. It was the kind of barn that most equestrians only dreamed about.

There were two police cars and a sheriff's SUV parked in front of the main doors. There wasn't an ambulance. Ashley pulled in behind the SUV.

"What on earth?" she asked.

It didn't seem like she was asking me a question, so I didn't hazard a guess. We entered through the main doors, our boots crunching in the white gravel. It took a moment for my eyes to adjust after coming in from the bright morning light, and even longer to register that I was looking at two officers bent over Albert's body.

Chapter Two

Albert was lying face down in the main hallway of the barn. His characteristic white button-down shirt was marred with dirt like he had been rolled over. I didn't know if the police had done that or if they had found him that way. His head was turned away from us, thankfully. He looked like he could've been asleep if not for his head, which was at a decidedly unnatural angle to the rest of his body. I guessed that maybe his neck could be broken, which can happen in a fall sometimes if everything lines up just right to be wrong.

It would've been a fair assumption to think someone his age could have had a heart attack or fallen and broken the aging vertebrae in his neck, except that there was a smear of blood on the stall door across the hall and drag marks in the dirt. No one could have crawled that far after breaking their neck, and even if by some miracle they did, their hands and arms would have been dirty. From what I could see of Albert, his arms and hands showed no sign that he had crawled to his current location.

Ashley gasped and cupped her hands over her mouth. Both of the officers turned sharply to glare at us, and Sheriff Grady Sullivan appeared to our left.

"What are you two doing here?" he asked, glancing back at the officers.

"We just came to see if we could help with the horses," I said and instantly regretted it. What had seemed like a good excuse in my driveway now seemed rather flimsy in the presence of law enforcement and a dead body.

"The horses are fine," he said, trying to usher us back out through the doors we came in through. "Luis is taking care of them."

"Did Luis find him?" I asked. I'd been better acquainted with Albert's farm manager than with Albert himself.

"Yeah, he found him when he got to work this morning," Grady said and then looked like he wished he hadn't. Familiarity had likely made him more loose-lipped than he usually would have been. We had spent our high school years traveling in the same circles, and my rescue often had me working alongside law enforcement.

"Do you think he had a heart attack?" I asked as I absently patted Ashley on the shoulder. She was hugging herself and looked like she might cry.

"Mal, I can't talk to you about this." Grady took his Stetson off and rubbed his forehead with his sleeve. "Especially since we're going to need an official statement from you."

"From me?" My voice squeaked, and I cleared my throat.

"Yeah." He put his hat back on and stood a bit straighter. "He had your flyer in his hand, the one about lessons. And Luis overheard him arguing with you about it yesterday. I'll send someone over later to get your statement."

"Grady, do I need a lawyer?" I asked, suddenly feeling like all of the air had been knocked out of me again.

"As sheriff, I can't advise you one way or another." He shifted back and forth from one leg to the other. "But as a friend . . ." His voice trailed off.

But I understood. I nodded, turned, and got back into the little truck. Ashley got in a second later, still pale and shaken.

"He's dead," she said, her voice cracking as the tears finally let go.

"I'm so sorry, Ash." I patted her hand on the console between us. "I never thought this is what we would find."

She wiped her eyes and started the truck, just as someone knocked on my window. We both screamed before we could stop ourselves. I turned quickly to see Luis holding up his hands. I rolled down my window.

"I didn't mean to scare you," he whispered. "I just wanted to apologize, Miss Mallory."

"For what?"

"I heard what the sheriff said to you," he said, looking at his feet. "I was just inside, with Cleo's Top Cat, in the first stall. I didn't tell them I thought you had killed Mr. Cunningham. They asked about everything I had seen and heard before I clocked out last night. I just told them I heard him yelling at you again."

"It's okay, Luis. You told the truth. No hard feelings." I smiled. He didn't look convinced.

"I wouldn't do anything to hurt you, Miss Mallory."

"I know. Don't worry any more about it. It'll be fine. I'm innocent, so it'll be fine." I wasn't sure I was convinced either. Innocent people have gone to jail.

"Did you find him?"

"Yes, ma'am. Such a terrible thing." Luis shook his head and wrung his hands.

"What do you think happened?"

"I don't know, Miss Mallory. I came to work this morning and noticed that Mr. Cunningham's golf cart was already at the barn. He doesn't usually come down this early unless he's showing a horse, and I knew we didn't have any appointments today. When I opened the barn doors, I saw him just lying there."

"I'm so sorry, Luis. It must have been awful."

"It was. I don't know if I will ever get that awful image out of my head." He shook his head again as if he were trying to manually shake the memory loose.

"Has anyone notified Kathleen?" I asked. Albert may have been chronically angry, but I liked his girlfriend. Kathleen had always been polite and even friendly toward me, not that we had a great many opportunities to socialize. Still, I worried how she would take this. They had been together for years now, since just after his wife died. I knew the family would be notified, but I worried no one had thought to call his girlfriend.

"She's up at the house," Luis said, looking slightly confused. "She's waiting to give her statement."

"I didn't realize she was here." I glanced over my shoulder and looked for her car in the main driveway, which was silly, since Albert had what looked like a four-car garage.

"She stays here most of the time," Luis said, and then immediately looked like he wished he hadn't.

I admired Luis. He was always fiercely loyal to Albert, and in the few times I had seen them together, Albert had always been respectful and polite. I couldn't say that for Albert's interactions with most people, myself included. I suspected that Luis wouldn't do anything to paint Albert in an unflattering light, and while Hillspring had come a long way, old-fashioned values were still prominent in the community. Since Albert was also prominent in the community, I guessed that he might not want to advertise having a live-in girlfriend.

"Take care of yourself, Luis."

He nodded and went back inside.

"Can we go up to the house, just for a minute?" I asked as Ashley backed the little truck away from the barn. "I want to talk to Kathleen."

"Do you think we should do that?" Her voice was still somewhat shaky.

"She's always been nice to me, and I want to offer my condolences." That was true. But if I was being completely honest with myself, my curiosity was piqued. "She might know something too."

It might have been Ashley's idea to get in the middle of things, but since we were there, I wanted to know more. It was that curiosity that always fueled me in my former career. I wasn't responsible for the principal investigations as a legal nurse consultant, but I did conduct my share of witness interviews and sat in on most of the depositions. I didn't miss the hustle of that life, but my curiosity was a character trait I wasn't likely to shed as easily as I had shed pantsuits and briefcases.

"Grady is going to take her statement," she said even though she was already turning toward the mansion.

"She might be more likely to talk to me than the sheriff," I said. "And then I'll actually have something to say in my statement."

Ashley looked skeptical, but she pulled through the circle drive at the front of the house anyway. As she put the truck in park, she started chewing on her fingernails. The mom in me wanted to tell her to stop, but considering the shock we'd just had, I could understand reverting to nervous habits.

"I'm going to stay here," she said, anticipating the invitation to join me.

"I won't be long."

The fountain that took up most of the space in the circle was bubbling in a melodic, calming manner contrary to the circumstances. It wasn't until I had climbed several of the low, sloping steps in the walkway that I heard soft sobbing. Kathleen was sitting on the porch swing just to the left of the huge, intricately carved double doors. Her snow-white hair was pulled back in a low bun with wispy tendrils loose at the side. It was very flattering to her slender, heart-shaped face. She wore a pale yellow casual pantsuit that looked more fitting for a boardroom than a porch swing.

"Kathleen," I said softly as I approached, hoping not to startle her. "I'm so sorry for your loss."

She looked up and dabbed at her eyes with a tissue. "Mallory?"

"I heard the commotion and came to see if anyone needed help."

"That's very kind of you, but I'm afraid we're past needing help." Her voice choked on the last words.

"Is there anything I can do? Can I make any phone calls for you?" I asked, remembering how hard it had been to notify everyone when Mom died. I would have loved for someone to make those calls for me.

"No, dear. The staff is handling the notifications." She stiffened and I suddenly felt like I was intruding on her private grief, but my curiosity wouldn't let me leave.

"Do they know what happened?" I refrained from asking if *she* knew what happened, preferring not to draw attention to the fact that I knew she had been here last night.

"Not that they've shared with me," she sniffed. "Did you hear anything from your place last night?"

"No. Not until this morning when we heard the sirens. When did you last see him?" I took a seat on the rock ledge that circled one of the tall, white columns.

"We had an early dinner, and I was forced to retire early with a migraine. I didn't realize anything was wrong until the sheriff arrived this morning." Her eyes filled with tears again and she wiped them away quickly. She wouldn't look me in the eyes, instead talking mostly to my right shoulder.

"Is it normal for him to be gone when you wake up?"

"What?" She frowned and fidgeted with her watch. Her nostrils flared slightly.

"I just mean, was anything out of the ordinary this morning?"

"I don't think that's really any of your business." She sat up straighter and pulled her jacket around herself a little tighter. She flushed deeply, from her collarbones to her hairline, and I noticed that the right corner of her mouth had started to twitch slightly.

"Of course. I'm sorry, I didn't mean to be invasive."

She softened a bit, but she continued to spin her watch around her delicate wrist. "I'm sorry, dear. This has just been awful."

"No need to apologize." I smiled sympathetically. "I'm so sorry for your loss."

"Thank you."

As I walked back to the truck, one of the police SUVs pulled up on the other side of the fountain. I got in without waiting to see who it was. We drove back to the rescue in silence. Ashley pulled into the drive behind my F-150 and rubbed her eyes again.

"Why don't you take the day off?" I said as I watched Ashley chewing at her thumbnail again.

"No, I think I need to stay busy." She looked at me, determination replacing the fear. "Plus, I don't want you to be alone when they come to talk to you. Actually, the more the better. Can you call Lanie?"

"She's at the shop all day," I said, getting out of the truck. I was met with a symphony of whinnies and brays. The horses and donkey let me know that they were starving to death right before our very eyes since we were about twenty minutes late with their breakfast. "I can't ask her to come right now."

"She's got plenty of help, Mal."

I started to protest again that Lanie would be too busy with the last push of tourists coming nearly nonstop through her antique shop. But the truth was, I was scared, and having my best friend around sounded pretty good. And having her there for the other call I knew I needed to make sounded even better.

"You're right. I'll give her a call." I patted her on the shoulder.

"I'll get started." She patted me back and headed toward the barn.

I went inside to get my cell phone and thirty pounds of exuberant dog who clearly thought I had been gone for an eternity greeted me at the door. Once I finally convinced Banjo that I still loved him, I dialed Lanie.

"What's up?" came her cheerful voice over the line.

"I don't know where to begin," I said, still rubbing my dog's ears. "Is there any way you can get away for a little while today?"

"Yeah, I think I can duck out here in a bit. Is everything okay?"

"Not really. Albert Cunningham was found dead this morning."

She gasped. "I knew he would have a heart attack eventually. He was always wound up like an eight-day clock."

"Grady didn't say so outright, but I gathered that they think he was murdered."

"Murdered? That's impossible." Her voice rose several octaves.

"And they think I was involved."

"Forget ducking out later. I'll be there as soon as I can write out a list for Eve," she said, referring to the new manager she had just hired as part of her plan to take a more hands-off approach to the day-to-day affairs of her thriving antique store.

"I know you're busy right now; if you need to stay, it's not a problem at all."

"Nonsense. Eve has been asking for more responsibility. This can be her chance to shine. Do you want to come to my house?"

"I can't. Grady said he would send someone over to take my statement later. I guess I need to stay put until then."

"I'll be there as soon as I can."

We exchanged goodbyes and hung up. I felt better knowing she would be here. I looked down at Banjo and rubbed his ears again. He looked up at me with the complete and utter devotion that only a dog can manage.

"Let's get this over with," I told Banjo as I raised my phone to make the next call. I decided that I shouldn't wait for Lanie to get there before I called Ethan. She was not his biggest fan, out of nothing more than fierce loyalty to me, because he wasn't a bad person. Ethan hadn't cheated on me, and we didn't have a dramatic divorce. We just realized that we were both different people than we had been when we had gotten married, and these new people weren't compatible anymore.

I absently scrolled through my contacts, remembering the stupid, endearing line that Ethan had used when we first met. His family had moved to Hillspring during our senior year, and I developed a crush on him immediately. He was the opposite of my other teenage crush, who was blond, lean, and angular. Ethan was the epitome of tall, dark, and handsome. So, when he walked up to me, rose in hand, and said, "I just wanted to show this rose what beautiful really looked like," I melted into teenage bliss. The memory still made me smile.

I dialed my ex-husband's number and tried to settle my stomach, which was currently flopping around at the thought that his new girlfriend might be the one who answered. We had stayed civil, but I still didn't want to talk to Diane. I wanted him to be happy; I really did. But the intimacy of shared history makes it hard to welcome a new girlfriend. At least it did for me.

"Hello," Ethan said. Thank goodness.

"I'm sorry to call you out of the blue, but I need advice, and I didn't know who else to call."

"You can call me anytime, Mallory. You know that."

Perhaps that was the case, but I preferred not to if given the choice.

I relayed the morning's events with as much detail as I could remember, including Grady's implied message that I needed a lawyer.

"Keep it strictly factual, don't embellish, and only answer the questions they ask you. If you feel like anything is straying into territory that might entrap you, then refuse to answer. They can't force you to answer anything, even if they arrest you. You know all this, though."

"I guess what I'm really asking is do *you* think I need a lawyer?" I asked.

"It sounds like it might not be a bad idea, considering your history with the deceased. I'll make a few calls and see who might be available in the area to give you a consultation. In the meantime, don't volunteer any information. Keep it to just the verifiable facts, nothing else," he said. I could hear the gears turning as he spoke. He was like that about everything, thinking several steps ahead even when we shopped for groceries.

"If they get there before noon, you can call me during the interview. I don't have anything scheduled until later today."

"Thank you, Ethan."

"Of course. I'll be in touch."

I sighed heavily, drawing the attention of the dog again. He bounced up on the sofa beside me and washed my ear before I could escape.

"Come on, you goofball. Let's go help Ashley feed the beasts."

Ashley had most of it done by the time I got there. She was hardworking and efficient, and I wasn't sure how I lucked into getting two of the best volunteers anyone could ask for. I had hoped that I would be able to start paying them at least something this fall, but my fundraising efforts had been disappointing at best.

"I want to work with the bay some this afternoon if that's okay with you," she said as she tried to fend off Biscuit's insistent nose in her pocket. He was convinced that all humans carried goodies in their pockets and that he must investigate all the pockets even if he had already done so just a few minutes ago.

"Sure. But don't you go getting attached to him too. I think Tanner is already planning his rodeo career. He isn't free and clear just yet."

"I don't have any doubt that he will be, not after the mountain of evidence they collected at that farm. I just want to see if he knows anything or if we're going to have to start from scratch."

"You're more than welcome," I smiled. "I'm glad to have your expertise."

"I don't know about that." She looked embarrassed. Taking compliments was not one of her strong suits. I meant it, though—she was a great trainer, even at her young age.

Having her around helped with my rather intense case of empty-nest syndrome. My daughter, Ginny, stayed in Missouri to attend the veterinary program at the University of Missouri–Columbia. It was nearly a five-hour drive, so visiting each other in person was difficult. We settled for FaceTime and frequent phone calls. But for a former helicopter mom of an only child, the separation was difficult for me. Having Ashley and Tanner around helped, especially since they were both close to the same age as Ginny.

I busied myself mucking out the big bay's stall when I heard a car in the drive. I felt my pulse quicken as I thought it might be one of the officers coming to take my statement. But that was quickly dispelled when I heard Lanie loudly calling to Biscuit. She loved that donkey and had no doubt brought him carrots or apples or something else that would absolutely make his day. He always greeted her at the gate since she insisted on spoiling him even more rotten than he already was.

"It's been too long since I've visited, hasn't it?" she cooed at him, rubbing his big ears. She had brought him baby carrots and was feeding him in between scratches.

"I really appreciate you coming over."

"I wouldn't have it any other way."

"I feel kind of silly now that I've had some time to think about it. I mean, I didn't do anything, so why should I be scared?"

She gave Biscuit one last pat on the head and turned toward me.

"You watch enough true crime documentaries to know that innocent people get collared for things all the time."

"You're the crime documentary addict. Besides, this is Hillspring. Stuff like that doesn't happen here."

"Murders don't happen here either, and look where that got Albert Cunningham. And you're just as addicted as I am."

"Touché," I said. She had a point there, on both counts. "Why don't you go on in and make yourself at home, and I'll finish up out here."

"I'll get the coffee started."

Biscuit brayed when she walked away, causing her to double back and start cooing at him and scratching his ears again.

"You're spoiling him rotten."

"I can't help it. He's too cute for words."

I left the two of them and went back to the barn. Ashley was sorting supplements for the evening feeding. Joint supplements for the two seniors, weight gainer for one of the mares, and a skin and coat formula for the palomino that had come in with the worst case of rain rot I had ever seen. Rain rot is a fungal skin infection, and we had cleared that up nicely, which is why a good chunk of hay money had been diverted to the vet. But he still had bald patches and flaky skin. So, after addressing his nutritional needs, we added a skin and coat supplement.

"I'll finish that up. You can go work with Zeus if you want," I said.

"There's not much more. I don't mind."

"I can stay out here while you get started. We don't know that much about him, and he nearly trampled me yesterday."

"That would be great." She smiled.

I appreciated that she never mistook my concern for a lack of confidence in her ability. It was quite the opposite. I always found her to be more than capable, and I intended to keep her around as long as I could.

It didn't take long to see that Zeus was responding well to Ashley's efforts. Even as tiny as she was, she had a gentle authority about her that the horses all respected. She started him slowly in the round pen, not asking much but basic commands from the ground. He didn't appear to be mostly unhandled, as the owner had told the sheriff's deputy. My only guess was that was an excuse for how badly he'd treated the horse. Unfortunately, some people thought the only way to train a horse was to be as rough as possible with them, which was both inaccurate and destructive.

"I think we're good, Mal," Ashley called to me as she rubbed Zeus's neck. "I'm not going to do much more today. He needs to settle in more before I see if he's broke."

"Okay, sounds good."

"He's definitely been handled," she said as she extended her arm again and sent him around the round pen in the other direction. "He knows what I'm asking him to do."

"Yeah, I think Mr. Lawrence was full of it. He was abusive and neglectful, and he was grasping at straws trying to justify it somehow."

"There's no justification for that."

"Absolutely not. Be sure to add your notes to the log," I said as I turned to go back to the house.

"Sure thing."

Lanie had filled my house with the wonderful smell of freshly brewed coffee and cinnamon rolls. She had brought comfort food. I have the most perfect best friend in the world. Even my dog was curled up in his bed, happily chewing on a toy she'd given him. His wagging tail thumped against the wall, but he didn't get up to greet me. Loyalty only goes so far when you've been presented with a yummy chew bone. I bent over and scratched behind his ears, and he thumped even harder.

"It smells amazing in here," I called toward the kitchen. My kitchen sits just to the left of the living room, which is the first room you enter through the front door. My house's layout is a bit odd since it started as a one-room cabin in the early 1900s. Previous owners had built on in nearly every direction, including my parents, who had added on a laundry room when I was a toddler. They had bought the house to be a starter home, but they never left. It was times like this that I missed Mom so much it physically hurt.

"You're just in time," Lanie called back. "I just took the cinnamon rolls out of the oven."

"That sounds wonderful. I've apparently already burned through my breakfast."

"You know, Grady wouldn't have tipped you off if he hadn't thought this was serious."

"I hope the cinnamon rolls are better than your pep talk," I said as I plunked myself down at my table.

"Well, they are the only thing sugar-coated," she giggled at her own joke.

I couldn't help it. I chuckled too.

"I called Ethan. He's going to try to help if I need it." I took the coffee she offered.

"That was a brave move." She dished out two rolls and passed one to me.

"Not really. He sucks as a husband, but he's a great lawyer with useful connections," I said in between bites of one of the best cinnamon rolls I had ever put in my mouth.

"Did Grady give you any idea when they would be by to get your statement?"

"Nope."

She seemed to be considering that for a moment as she chewed.

"Why don't you come over to my house this afternoon then? Bill is going fishing with his brother this weekend, so I'll have the house to myself anyway. You can pack up Banjo, and we can have a sleepover and pretend we're in high school."

"I appreciate the offer, but I hate to leave the horses. They're very creative in all the ways they try to kill themselves." I would have loved to go to high school with Lanie. I bet she was wild, in the best way.

"Okay then, how about I stay here with you? Your neighbor was just found dead, likely murdered, and I don't like the idea of you out here alone."

She had a point. My immediate concern had been that I was a possible suspect, not that there was a killer on the loose. But I knew I hadn't hurt Albert, so there was definitely a killer out there in our little community.

"You know, that sounds like a great idea. I'll dust off one of the bottles of wine and we can relive the glory days."

"Whose glory days? I haven't had my glory days yet." She grinned. "Who could've done this?" she wondered out loud.

"Well, I found out this morning that Albert's girlfriend has essentially been living there. And she says she went to bed early with a migraine and didn't even know anything had happened until the sheriff showed up."

"Albert had a girlfriend?" Lanie asked with exaggerated shock.

"I think you're focusing on the wrong part of the story."

"It's always the girlfriend," Lanie said, punctuating her point with her fork.

"I don't think she's capable of something like that, though."

"That's the kind of thinking that got Lizzie Borden acquitted," she said.

I chuckled, but she had a point. And statistically speaking, the significant other was always a suspect until ruled out. I knew Grady would take a hard look at her. And as much as I hated to admit it, Kathleen had piqued my curiosity as well. She seemed overly defensive when I asked if it was normal for Albert to be gone in the mornings when she got up. At the time, I thought it was because I was being rude, asking invasive questions. And while that was probably still partly responsible for the way she responded, something about the interaction felt *off*. I had no idea how I would react to finding out my boyfriend had been murdered while I slept off a migraine, so I was willing to give her the benefit of the doubt, at least until I'd heard whether Grady ruled her out or not. But I couldn't get rid of the nagging feeling that she was hiding something.

I motioned for another cinnamon roll since I had inhaled the first one. She cut another and flopped it unceremoniously onto my plate. I was about to dig in when Banjo barked one of those barks that has a question mark at the end. I turned to listen and then heard Biscuit start his "honking." The donkey was honestly a better watchdog than the actual dog.

I glanced at the clock—1:29 PM. Too late to call Ethan, which was probably for the best anyway. I would take a referral, but it would be better if he weren't directly involved, just for the sake of keeping things uncomplicated between us.

I got up and went out onto the porch. Sure enough, it was a sheriff's department SUV. I could just make out the driver as he pulled in behind Ashley's little truck. I didn't recognize him, which was a rarity in our small town. He was square-shouldered, with thick brown hair. He didn't waste any time getting out and coming straight to the porch where I stood. Lanie was planted firmly behind me.

"Mallory Martin?" He said with a voice devoid of any accent that I could place. If he was a local, he had either spent a long time away from here or was actively working on speaking without the usual Arkansas drawl.

"That's me," I said, extending a hand. "And who are you?"

"Corporal Darrin Bailey, ma'am. I need to talk to you about your neighbor."

I gestured for him to join me on the porch, and I took a seat in my rocking chair. Lanie sat to my left on the bench, which left the Adirondack for the corporal. He didn't sit, choosing instead to stand over the two of us.

"I'd like to speak to Ms. Martin alone," he said, looking from Lanie to me.

"You can like whatever you want. I'm not leaving," Lanie said and flashed him one of her most dazzling smiles.

"Ma'am, I need . . ."

"You can talk to her with me here or not at all."

"Are you Ms. Martin's attorney?"

"Does she need an attorney?"

"I think maybe we got off on the wrong foot here," he said, backing up and taking the seat I had initially offered him.

"I think maybe we did," I said, leaning forward in my chair as Lanie leaned back in hers. She crossed her arms across her chest and eyed him coolly. She had already decided he was the enemy, but I hadn't made up my mind yet.

"How well did you know Albert Cunningham?" He pulled out a notepad and pen.

"Not well. We were neighbors, but I didn't socialize with him."

"Would you characterize your relationship with him as hostile?"

"It's no secret that Albert didn't like the fact that I started the rescue here next to his property."

"So you two didn't get along?"

"Would you just stop beating around the bush?" Lanie stood up. "She didn't kill him, for goodness sake!"

"Why do you think someone killed him?"

"Because you're here asking questions that make it sound like you think she killed him."

"Lanie," I said in the gentlest tone I could muster. "Would you get Corporal Bailey a cup of coffee?" And then, turning to him, "Do you take cream or sugar?"

"Black, please."

Lanie wasn't stupid. She knew I was asking her to shut up. But she took it well, putting her hand on my shoulder as she turned to go inside.

"I'll give you a written statement," I said. "How far back do you want me to cover?"

"I still have a few questions." He gave me a kind of half-smile that conveyed more about his annoyance than anything else.

"No, you don't. I'm not answering any more questions. Just tell me how far back I need to cover, and I'll give you my written statement."

"We need to know your whereabouts from yesterday afternoon until this morning. And we need to know what you discussed during your conversation with Mr. Cunningham," he said. His smile disappeared completely.

"Do you have a form, or do I need to go get some paper?"

"We have a form." He stood and slapped his notebook shut before retrieving the form from the SUV. He was clearly unhappy with how things had gone. On the one hand, I didn't want to make enemies of the law enforcement officers I needed to work alongside on neglect and abuse cases. But on the other hand, I didn't want to set myself up as an easy scapegoat so they could close a major case.

"I don't want to be difficult." I tried to soften my tone and demeanor. "But this is all quite a shock in our little community, as I'm sure you know."

"It *is* a shock, Ms. Martin." He, however, had not softened at all. I was afraid that I had already made an enemy of Corporal Bailey.

It didn't take me long to write out everything that had happened since yesterday morning, mainly because not much had happened. I debated about including details of my phone call with Albert in the statement. I figured they had already heard about his side of the conversation from Luis, so I ended up adding it in. I also hesitated to include that Tanner had overheard my side of the conversation because I hated to cause him any trouble. But omitting a detail like that would just add to their suspicion that I was guilty, or at the very least hiding something.

I made a mental note to let him know when Corporal Bailey left. After I signed and dated the bottom of each page, I handed it over to the corporal, who said a terse goodbye and warned me that the sheriff himself might want to follow up with me.

"He must be new," I said to Lanie as he drove away. "I don't recognize him from any of the rescue cases."

"Well, Grady could do a lot better if you ask me. He seemed like a jerk."

"He was just doing his job. And he doesn't know me."

She made a disapproving "humph" noise. "I'm going to head home and grab an overnight bag, and I'll be back in a bit."

She stopped at the fence to rub Biscuit's ears again before she left. I pulled out my phone and sent a text to Tanner, giving a quick rundown of what happened and that I had mentioned him in my statement. He responded with "K," which, in light of my years as a nurse, I always interpreted as "potassium" instead of an abbreviated "okay."

Chapter Three

Ashley came up from the barn shortly after Lanie left.

"How did it go?" She scrunched up her nose as she asked. "I hung out close to the fence. I thought it would be weird if I got in the middle of it."

"I have no idea," I lied. I was pretty sure they considered me at least a "person of interest," if not the prime suspect. I wondered what Luis had told them about Albert's side of the conversation that had made them decide I might be capable of murder.

"There's bound to be people who have more to gain from Albert's death than you do, right?" Ashley brushed some horse dirt off of the front of her jeans as she spoke. "Like Heather. She nearly decked him at the fair."

"You didn't tell me about that," I said, imagining tiny neo-hippie Heather Rogers getting mad enough to punch someone.

"He walked by her booth, and she just started tearing into him about his pesticide use and manure runoff ruining her organic farm. It was crazy."

"There's a chance that he wasn't even murdered. He wasn't exactly a spring chicken," I said, although I didn't really believe it. Grady wouldn't have warned me, and they wouldn't have needed a statement if anyone thought it had been natural causes.

"We both know that he was." She pulled her keys out of her pocket. "I have evening classes, but I can come back after if you want. I worry about you out here by yourself."

"That's very sweet of you. But Lanie is staying with me tonight."

I thought about all five foot three of Ashley acting as my protector. Granted, she could be a little stick of dynamite when she needed to be. I was reminded of the reason she came to volunteer at my rescue in the first place. She'd been ordered to do community service after getting arrested at a protest. Ashley's mother, Danielle, told me she had called several places in the area and they had turned her down. I got the impression my newly formed rescue had been a last resort.

Danielle told me that the protest was a doomed attempt by a few high school kids to keep a favorite teacher from getting fired. The story touched my heart so much from all sides that I couldn't refuse. The teacher had been battling breast cancer but wanted to finish out the year with her class of seniors. Someone reported to the school board that she was using medical marijuana to manage the negative symptoms of chemotherapy. As a nurse I'd seen how awful those side effects could be, but I also understood why the school board had to uphold the state laws at the time since it was not legal then. I also understood the passion behind Ashley's protest and why she had pushed the officer who tried to remove her. It was just a horrible situation for everyone involved.

"Are you sure?" she asked, pausing before getting into her truck.

"I'll be fine. Besides, I have my guard dog," I added.

We both laughed at that. Banjo was a lot of things, but guard dog wasn't one of them. We said our goodbyes, and I wished her well in her classes. She was majoring in social work and hoped to have a hippotherapy practice someday. I couldn't think of anything that suited her more; her natural talent and empathy were perfectly suited to that vocation. She had mellowed in the last year, finding a direction to channel her passion, and I didn't worry about her getting into shoving matches with the police anymore, but her commitment to fairness and equality were completely intact.

I went back inside and finished my second cinnamon roll that I definitely didn't need. It had gotten cold but no less delicious. Banjo was still working on the chew bone that Lanie had brought him, holding it between his front paws and chewing like his only job in the world was to destroy that bone.

I tried to focus on lining out the feed and supplement order, but I couldn't quit thinking about Albert. Sure, he was a cranky old codger, and our only interactions consisted of him calling my place an eyesore or some other colorful name. But he didn't deserve to be murdered. I had seen more than my share of death as a nurse and read a lot of awful things as a nurse consultant, but I hadn't been to crime scenes, and I hadn't personally known the victims. I couldn't shake the image out of my mind. Albert lying there, head at an awful angle. I shuddered.

Since I couldn't get it out of my mind anyway, I decided to look at it analytically, like I had as a consultant. Even though my cases were mostly malpractice suits and insurance fraud, investigation techniques are similar for all crimes. I turned the page in my notebook to a clean sheet. I made a column for things I knew, labeled "facts," things I didn't know, labeled "questions," and one for things I wanted to follow up on, labeled, appropriately, "follow-up." It didn't take long to have several items in every column. The last thing in my "follow-up" column was to pay a visit to Heather Rogers. I had interviewed enough witnesses in my capacity as a consultant to develop a knack for sensing when people are hiding things.

The first thing in that column, however, was talking to Luis again. I needed him to tell me exactly what he had told the sheriff about Albert's end of our conversation. I had no idea how long it would take them to catalog everything at the scene, and it wouldn't look good for me to just show up again. So I decided to see if I could find my old set of binoculars and find out if I could see anything at all from my place. That was no small feat. I had torn through half the house when I finally found them tucked away in a box in my closet.

Next on my "follow-up" list was to talk to Kathleen again. I had nothing tangible to make me suspicious of her, but I kept circling back to how odd she'd seemed when I spoke to her. Grief looks different for everyone, and I knew better than to make assumptions. I thought about our short interaction over and over, and I kept coming back to the fact that she seemed more nervous than grief-stricken, despite the tears.

I headed outside to test the binoculars. I could see the driveway that led from the barn to the mansion just fine, but I couldn't find anywhere that would allow me to see the entire parking area in front of the barn. It didn't matter since I could see a sheriff's cruiser by the fountain that sat in the middle of the circle drive in front of the house. I couldn't see the mansion itself either, but they were likely looking over the entire property. It could take days. I wondered if Grady would call in the state police or keep the investigation in his department. That would probably depend on whether they needed the extra manpower or received political pressure to do so. I had no idea if Albert had any political connections or not, but with his money, it was likely that he did.

I was trying to figure out how to talk to Luis without barging back into a crime scene when I heard the unmistakable crunch of gravel in my driveway. Thinking it was too soon for Lanie to be back, I crossed the paddock and was standing at the front gate when Tanner pulled up in the Dodge pickup his grandpa had given him for graduating high school with honors. It was pre-owned, but it had been slick and well taken care of, with leather seats and not a single chip in the glossy black paint. Tanner continued to take excellent care of it, and it was rarely even dirty. That's why the yellow splash of road striping paint behind each wheel was so noticeable.

"Oh no!" I pointed at the paint.

"Tell me about it," he said, looking wistfully at the glaring blemishes. "I was mad enough to fight when I noticed it. There weren't any signs on the road at all last night, just the wet paint. I tried to wash it off, but most of it stayed put."

"Did you call the highway department?"

"Yeah, but they said the supervisor would have to call me back. I'm still waiting on that particular call."

"Hopefully, they'll have some suggestions."

"I have a few *suggestions*." He gritted his teeth. "I watched some videos online, but nothing has worked to get it all off. It dried too much before I noticed it."

"I'm so sorry." Even though it wasn't my fault, I hated that it had happened, especially since it wouldn't have happened if he hadn't been out on my road yesterday.

"I'll get it off eventually."

"What are you up to today?" I asked since he wasn't on the schedule, although I had my suspicions that it had to do with a certain big bay horse.

"Ashley texted and said that she had worked with Zeus some today." He looked at his feet while he talked. He still acted like a little boy when he asked for something, even though he wasn't even a teenager anymore. It was very endearing. "I was hoping that maybe I could throw a saddle on him and see how he does."

Suspicion confirmed.

"I don't mind," I smiled. "I just hate to see you get attached to him before we know if he's staying or not."

"I think it's too late." He grinned, still looking at his feet as he kicked gravel with the toe of his boot.

"Yeah, I think you're right. I think you were a goner the minute we unloaded him."

"Well, I wasn't too happy when he tried to run you over. But when I went to get him, after he'd calmed down some, he was just so willing and responsive."

"Ashley put him back in the barn. Be careful," I said, Mom voice again. I couldn't help myself.

"I will," he said as he opened the back door of his truck and pulled out his roping saddle. "I plan on taking it real easy."

"Lanie will be back later, so be on the lookout since we don't know how he does with traffic."

He grunted an acknowledgment as he turned to go through the gate.

"Bird watching?" He nodded toward the binoculars I was still holding.

"Not exactly," I said. "I was trying to see if I could tell if the police were still at the Cunningham farm."

"Yeah, it was a shock to hear about old man Cunningham," he said, shaking his head. "Can't hardly believe that happened. And I sure can't believe they think you had anything to do with it."

I appreciated the vote of confidence.

"Like I said in my text, they'll probably want to talk to you since you heard my side of the conversation," I said, feeling bad that he had to be involved at all.

"I already gave them a call, and I have an appointment tomorrow afternoon to give my statement." He threw the heavy saddle over the paddock fence.

"Thank you very much," I said, touched that he had taken the initiative to call them on his own.

He just shrugged and gave me an "aw, shucks" look and then changed the subject. "I'm not going to get him out of the round pen today."

"That's probably a good idea."

"Hey there, bud," he said as Biscuit presented himself for treats or attention, whichever he could entice someone to give him. Tanner didn't have treats, so he scratched behind the insistent donkey's ears, which was received with great enthusiasm.

Biscuit was my first rescue. He had been used as a roping dummy, which meant that they had used him instead of a calf to practice for rodeo events. I'm not anti-rodeo, but I am anti-cruelty, and Biscuit had been in really rough shape by the time he was found. We don't know for sure why he was dumped at the Hartman Campground on Mill River, but I guessed it was because he had been injured so badly that he was no longer useful and dumping him was cheaper than vet care. He had severe rope burns on his neck and back legs, and his jaw was broken. It had taken every penny of startup money I had put back to invest in the rescue for his vet care, but it had been worth every cent.

Thankfully, he had been less than a year old, so he had the healing capacity of youth to help in his recovery. He warmed up to positive attention easily and quickly became our unofficial mascot, since his charms instantly won over nearly everyone who came to the rescue. He was a great ambassador for the newcomers, showing by example that we mean well and are not to be feared. He was also a great security guard, as donkeys are natural protectors.

"I'm going to grab an iced tea and a book. I'll just be on the porch if you need anything." He gave me a thumbs-up, and I headed to the house.

I settled onto the bench with my tea, a blanket, and a good book. The scents of horses and hay carried on the gentle breeze. It's almost impossible to describe the way horses smell, an earthy aroma that stirs something in my soul. The sun would be settling behind the hills soon, and I could think of no better way to spend the evening. Cicadas and numerous other bugs serenaded us from all over the mountain, but it wouldn't be long before it was too cold in the evenings for them. I missed the whip-poor-wills' songs, my absolute favorite sound of summer. Banjo curled up under the bench with the remainder of the chew bone Lanie had brought him. It was a good one; he usually demolished them in no time flat.

I found myself watching Tanner more than reading my book. He had started on the ground, letting the horse get used to him and putting him at ease. Zeus had settled far more quickly than

I thought he would after the initial explosion. I find that's the case sometimes. Once the chaos of whatever situation they were in is removed, they settled in without much of a fuss. That's not to say that they were magically "fixed" just by being here, but a calm routine helps.

Tanner had just saddled the big bay when I heard a car coming up the drive again. I was expecting Lanie, so when the white sheriff's SUV rounded the curve and came into view, I instantly bristled. Biscuit started braying, sounding the alarm that a stranger was coming. I couldn't see the driver since the sun reflected off the windshield at that hour of the day. I pulled the blanket back and stood at the top of the steps. I didn't want to be too welcoming to someone who suspected that I had murdered my neighbor. Except it wasn't the corporal from earlier, it was Grady.

Zeus danced around briefly at the sudden commotion, but Tanner settled him quickly. He was still patting the big bay on the neck when I turned to face the sheriff.

"Evenin', Mallory," he said as he shut the door.

"Hello, Sheriff Sullivan. What can I do for you?"

"Corporal Bailey said you weren't exactly cooperative earlier." He paused at the bottom of the porch stairs. "And what's with the 'Sheriff Sullivan' stuff? I've known you since junior high."

"I guess I'm not in the mood to be super friendly to people who think I'm capable of murder."

"Oh hell, Mallory," he said as he took his hat off and leaned on the railing. "You know I've got to follow the evidence. You know that as well as I do."

I knew he was referencing my background as a legal nurse consultant.

"Did you just come here to tell me again that you're following the evidence to me?"

"No, I came here to tell you to cooperate so we can clear you and get on to catching the real killer."

"That sounds a whole lot like the 'tell me what happened so I can help you' tactic that the police are so fond of," I snapped.

"I'm not the enemy here, Mallory."

"I *did* cooperate, Grady. I gave a full statement of what happened, my entire conversation with Albert, and where I was all night long."

"Home alone is hardly a rock-solid alibi."

"Well, it's the only one I have. I didn't know I would need an alibi, and I live alone, so . . ."

"And you didn't address your entire conversation, either. Leaving out details just makes you look guilty even when you're not."

"What are you talking about? Our *entire* conversation was in my statement. Did your deputy lose it?" I raised my voice more than I'd meant to. My anger got the best of me.

"I'm going to need you to come to the station tomorrow and clear this up." He put his hat back on and straightened up.

"I'll call my attorney, and we will make an appointment," I lied. I didn't even have an attorney yet, beyond my ex-husband, and I sure didn't want *that* conflict of interest beyond how much I had already involved him.

"If you feel that's necessary." He stiffened.

"Yeah, I think it's necessary. You've as much as accused me of lying in my statement. I don't think I need to talk to you any more without someone looking out for my interests."

"See you tomorrow," he said as he tipped his hat and turned back to his car.

I hugged myself as I watched him turn around and leave. I was shaking, more from anxiety and anger than the chill creeping into the evening air. I waved at Tanner, who had stopped at the paddock fence. He patted the horse on the neck and gave me a thumbs up again. It looked like the horse was doing well.

I pulled my phone out of my pocket and typed out a message:

I have to go to the police dept tomorrow. They think I lied in my official statement. I don't know what evidence they have.

I sent it to Ethan. I didn't want him to represent me, but I hoped he would hurry up and refer me to someone else. I had to admit it; I was scared. There would be a lot of pressure to clear the murder of a prominent, wealthy citizen. I was essentially a nobody. Sure, I had grown up here, but I wasn't a member of the country club, and my family didn't have a wing of the little local hospital named after us.

I wanted to call Dad, hear him tell me everything was going to be okay, but I didn't want to worry him. I was also afraid he might cut his cruise short to come home and stay with me. Since this was the first vacation he'd taken since Mom died, I wasn't going to interrupt it because I needed parental comforting. There would be plenty of time to fill him in when he got back.

I sat back down and pulled the blanket around my shoulders again, but I didn't return to my book. I wanted to be within earshot if anything happened to Tanner, but I needed to make notes of my conversation with Grady while it was still fresh in my mind. I opened the Notes app on my phone and jotted down everything he had said to me. While I was at it, I noted everything I remembered about my conversation with Albert, since that seemed to be a point of contention. I realized that it was even more critical for me to talk to Luis since he was the one who had overheard Albert's side. I needed to know what he'd told them and why they thought I was lying.

After I had entered my notes into the app, I sat there staring at the screen, my mind wandering to the cinnamon rolls Lanie had left in the kitchen. And then a wild idea hit me. It was a great southern tradition to bring food for the family when they lost a loved one. People from all over Hillspring had brought food for Dad and me when Mom died. We had to freeze most of it. I yanked the blanket off my shoulders and ran inside. I could use food as a great excuse to talk to Luis and Kathleen and still be neighborly and polite at the same time.

There was still an untouched pan of cinnamon rolls, which I quickly covered with plastic wrap. I threw together a pot of homemade chicken noodle soup, the quickest dish I could think of that I had everything I needed to make. I tapped my fingers on the counter as I waited for the broth to boil, thinking of the old adage about a watched pot.

Banjo wandered into the kitchen, proudly carrying a huge stick that he had brought through the open front door. I left the door open so that I could hear any commotion at the barn, since Tanner was still working with Zeus. I hadn't expected my goofy dog to bring in half a tree. He thought we were playing a super fun game of Chase the Dog Through Every Room in the House, and he took his role in the assumed game very seriously. I finally caught up with him when he tried to take it through the doggy door into the backyard. He found that it was too big to fit through the opening and came to a stop long enough for me to take the log and toss it into the backyard. He bounded after it, tongue lolling out the side of his mouth.

By the time I got back to the kitchen, the soup was boiling nicely, and the vegetables were just about perfectly cooked.

"I'm gonna head home," Tanner called from the open front door.

I peeked around the doorframe. "Okay, see you next time. I'm so sorry about your truck."

"It'll be alright, one way or another." He shrugged. "That sure smells good."

"Do you want a bowl? I'm taking over some food for Albert's girlfriend, Kathleen."

"I think the sheriff is still up there. You probably ought to steer clear. Don't want to give them more reason to look at you." He glanced at my notebook open on the coffee table, my notes clearly visible to anyone with even moderately decent vision.

"It's the neighborly thing to do," I said, not willing to concede that he had figured out my real motives.

"I'll go with you," he said as he removed his baseball cap and ran his fingers through his mop of curly hair. "We can represent the rescue together."

"You don't have to do that." I smiled, unsure if he was planning to derail my plan to question Luis and Kathleen or just keep me from looking suspicious.

He followed me back into the kitchen, where I transferred the soup into a large, disposable plastic bowl. "Last chance, did you want some?"

"No, thank you. It sure smells good, though. I'll carry it to the truck. Not gonna take 'no' for an answer." He looked at me sheepishly as he said it. He was so rarely assertive that I'm sure it seemed foreign to him. I nodded and handed over the soup.

I pulled up to the house first, thinking it would be less suspicious than taking food to the barn. I would try to catch Luis on our way out. Tanner got out, still holding the soup, and I followed him with the cinnamon rolls. About halfway up the low steps, he slowed and let me take the lead. I had just raised my hand to knock on the door when it opened, revealing a middle-aged woman wearing a dark blue polo shirt and beige pants.

"May I help you?" She smiled coolly and tucked a strand of ash-blonde hair several shades darker than mine behind her ear.

"We're from Hillspring Horse Rescue, just down the hill. We wanted to extend our condolences." I held up the cinnamon rolls. She glanced from the rolls to Tanner behind me.

"I have soup," he said awkwardly.

"This way, please." She opened the door.

We followed her into the biggest kitchen I've ever seen. There were two of nearly everything, two stainless refrigerators, two in-wall ovens, and a double-sized gas range. The center island was nearly as big as my entire kitchen. The one pan of cinnamon rolls and bowl of soup looked small and out of place on the marble counter.

"Is Kathleen up to seeing anyone?" I asked when we had deposited our meager offerings.

"I'll check. Please follow me," she said and led us back to the foyer.

We had only waited a few moments when she returned with Kathleen.

"I didn't expect to see you again." She glanced at my jeans and T-shirt and frowned. She went full sneer as she looked at Tanner's dusty boots.

"We brought over some food," I said. "We are just so sorry for your loss."

"Thank you," she said, her delicate mouth drawn into a thin line.

She didn't appear to have been crying this time, and I had to wonder if earlier had been a show for the deputy. Then I felt guilty for jumping to conclusions.

"I know I already asked, but is there anything I can do?"

"Maybe you can ask his family when they get here because they've asked me to leave," she said, standing a little taller and straighter as she said it.

Tanner and I exchanged uncomfortable looks, and then Tanner realized he was still wearing his baseball cap. He snatched it quickly off his head and smoothed his hair down with his other hand.

"We're sorry about that, ma'am," he said, looking at the floor. I was surprised he spoke up at all since he had a shy streak a mile wide. "Bein' such close neighbors, though, we were wondering if the police think this was a random thing or if they suspect someone close to Mr. Cunningham?"

I caught my jaw before it fell open, but I did stare at Tanner for a moment before I composed myself. I had told Ashley that he was full of surprises, and clearly that was proving to be true. Kathleen seemed to be taken off guard too.

"Nothing was stolen, so it doesn't look random. But they didn't share their theories with me. If you'll excuse me, I need to finish packing, and since I have to be supervised while I do it, I need to be finished by the time the housekeeper leaves." She looked back over her shoulder at the woman who had let us in. She looked uncomfortable but didn't respond to the barb.

"Of course," I said, taking a step back toward the door. "Thank you for your time. Please accept our condolences."

She didn't respond. She turned on her heel and disappeared back down the hall.

The housekeeper seemed torn between seeing us the few feet to the door and following Kathleen, so I let her off the hook. "We can see ourselves out."

We descended the front steps side by side, and I reached out and gently punched Tanner on the shoulder. "You've been holding back on me. You're a born investigator."

He blushed ever so slightly and grinned. "I saw your notebook. And I thought it might be better for me to ask the questions since the sheriff thinks you might be involved."

"You never cease to surprise me," I said. I wasn't sure if his asking the questions would help or not, since Grady seemed to have his mind made up, but I appreciated his initiative nonetheless.

I'd hoped that the last sheriff's SUV would be gone from the barn parking area by the time we left the house. As we climbed into my truck, I noticed it was still there.

"I'll catch Luis another time," I said as I followed the circle drive around the fountain. "No need to borrow trouble."

Chapter Four

Lanie brought enough food and drink to last us a week. We had settled on the sofa surrounded by sweet and savory snacks and a good bottle of red after Tanner left for the evening. I still felt apprehensive, but I hoped the wine would help with that.

"So what happened? You're twitchy and restless," she said as she pulled her legs up underneath her.

I recounted Grady's visit and touched on my ideas about finding out more information on my own, feeling shaky and sick all over again.

"How can he possibly think you would have anything to do with this?"

"I don't know what evidence they think they have, but it must be pretty convincing." I took a gulp of wine.

"Oh, stop. They don't have anything because you didn't kill him. He was horrible to everyone. If having an angry conversation with him gives you motive, then most of Hillspring has a motive."

"Speaking of motives, Tanner and I had a really weird conversation with Kathleen."

"I told you, it's *always* the significant other."

"She told us the family asked her to leave. Don't you think that's odd? I mean, they've been together for years. She would've attended family events and been acquainted with everyone, wouldn't she?"

"It's probably not weird to tell the girlfriend to take a hike if they can't stand her."

"I guess so." I took another sip of wine. I rarely indulged, and it was a nice treat. "She said that she was required to be supervised while she packed, though. So it seems like they don't trust her."

"I've never met the woman, and I don't trust her. It's always the girlfriend."

"So you've said," I laughed. "I'm going to try to talk to Luis in the morning."

"What? Why? You can't go back over there!"

"He's the one that overheard Albert talking to me on the phone, and whatever he told them made them home in on me. I need to know what he said because nothing Albert said to me is suspicious at all."

"I don't think you should go back there." She leaned in and put her hand on my arm. "You don't need to be seen poking around his place."

"I'm not. I'm planning to try to catch Luis on his way in to work."

"So, you're going to stalk him? Yeah, that's a great way to look innocent."

"It's better than poking around a crime scene!"

She shook her head. "Mal, I really think you should focus on getting an attorney and staying away from the investigation."

"Duly noted."

"But you're not going to, are you?"

"I definitely need an attorney."

She sighed. The fact that I hadn't committed to staying out of the investigation wasn't lost on her. That reminded me that I had never heard from Ethan after I texted him earlier. So much for relying on him for help. I'm not sure what I expected, he was my *ex*-husband, after all.

"There's Andy Hannigan. He just moved to the new building behind the post office," she said.

"Oh yeah, I saw his ad in the paper. I think he just handles family law, divorces and adoptions and such."

"Well, he might be able to tell you who to call."

"That's a thought. I'll see what he says tomorrow."

We chatted for hours, giggling and carrying on like a couple of teenagers before we finally turned in for the night. I dreaded setting my alarm for the break of dawn, but I knew that Luis got to work just after six every morning and I would definitely have to be an early bird to catch that proverbial worm. I went to sleep feeling hopeful in spite of the situation.

* * *

As I was afraid it would, it felt like my alarm sounded about five minutes after I went to sleep. I hurried and dressed as quietly as I could, hoping to let Lanie sleep on the sofa until I returned. I had forgotten to ask her last night in between wine and cookies if she had planned to work today, so I didn't want to let her sleep too long.

I tiptoed out into the living room, acutely aware that every move I made sounded much too loud in the quiet house. Why does everything seem louder when you're trying to be quiet? I stopped at the door to the kitchen and paused briefly, trying to decide if I could make coffee silently or if I even had time.

"Let's go."

I screamed and whirled around toward the voice. Lanie held up her hands in the universal gesture for surrender. Banjo let out a confused "bork?"

"You scared me half to death!"

"Sorry." She stifled a giggle. "I thought you knew I was up."

"Clearly, I did not," I said, trying to catch my breath and slow my heart rate.

"Well, let's go stalk Luis. I don't want to get up this ridiculously early for nothing." She reached down and scratched behind Banjo's ears. He looked up at her adoringly.

I nodded and grabbed my keys off the hook by the door. Banjo did a few excited circles and wagged his bushy tail. I'm not a fan of tail docking in companion animals, so my goofy dog had one more appendage to knock things off tables and get covered in mud on a regular basis.

"Load up," I told him to let him know he could go. He bounced a few times on his front legs and bounded out the door. He hurriedly peed on every plant between the porch and my truck and then waited at the passenger door. Lanie opened the door for him and climbed inside. She's about four inches shorter than me, so it was an effort for her to climb into my lifted F-150. It had been the last thing I had done to say goodbye to my old life and embrace my new one: trading my sensible Prius for the truck.

The trip to the Cunningham driveway was a short one. We stopped to wait by the mailbox. Since the road dead-ended at my place, we didn't have to worry about traffic. Banjo wasn't sure why we had stopped so soon after starting out, but like the good boy he was, he settled in quickly and climbed into the back seat for a nap. As I sat there trying to stay awake, I felt like joining him.

"Why didn't one of us get up early enough to make coffee," I said with a yawn.

"I don't know, but we will definitely plan our stalking better next time."

"Will you stop calling it 'stalking'?" I laughed in spite of myself.

"Okay, fine. We will plan our *investigation* better next time."

"I think that's him," I said, pointing to the blue sedan rounding the corner. I got out and stood beside the truck, which prompted Banjo to assume his watchful position in the driver's seat.

Luis pulled in next to us and rolled down his window.

"Good morning, Miss Mallory," he said, friendly enough, but there was an air of skepticism in his expression. "Is everything okay?"

"Yes, everything is good. I just need to ask you a few questions about what you told the sheriff yesterday."

"I don't know what I can tell you," he said, squirming in his seat. "And I need to get to work."

"I won't keep you long. I'm so sorry to have to do this." I leaned forward and put my hand on his window, hoping that would keep him from driving off, since he looked like he might bolt. It made me nervous that he was nervous.

"I just told them what I overheard Mr. Cunningham say while he was on the phone with you, that's all," he said, looking at my hand.

"Would you tell me what you heard?"

"With all due respect, Miss Mallory, you were on the phone with him. You know what he said."

"I do, but I didn't hear it from your perspective."

He seemed to be considering that for a moment, looking from my hand to the driveway.

"I heard him telling you that he wasn't happy about the flyer, you know, for the lessons. And then . . ." His voice trailed off.

"Yes?" I mentally ran through the conversation again in my head as he paused.

He looked again from my hand to the driveway.

"I really need to get to work."

"And then he told me he thought my place was affecting his property value and called it 'rat-infested.' And then he hung up."

He squirmed in his seat.

"He told you that you weren't in a position to ask him for anything and that he wouldn't regret a damned thing," he said quietly.

"What? No, he never said that to me."

"I heard him, Miss Mallory. I don't think you would do anything to hurt Mr. Cunningham, but that's what I heard. I really have to go now."

He looked apologetic, but he still nearly rolled my hand up in his window, and he sped off, causing me to jump out of the way.

"What the hell was that?" Lanie asked as she got out of the truck. "He nearly ran over you!"

"He said that he heard Albert tell me that I wasn't in a position to ask for anything and that he wouldn't regret a damned thing. Only he never said that to me. I've gone over that conversation again and again and I *know* what he said to me. And I sure didn't ask him for anything."

"Did anyone else hear your conversation?"

"Tanner heard my side of it, and he made an appointment to give his statement today."

"Okay, good. That's good," she said, nodding. "He can clear this up then."

"I hope so," I said, but I didn't feel as confident as she sounded.

I had been so focused on Lanie and calming myself after nearly getting run over that it hadn't registered that another car was approaching. It had slowed to turn into the drive by the time I noticed it. It was a white BMW coupe, but beyond that I had no idea. Luxury car models were a breed I was not familiar with. The car pulled in slowly beside us and the very darkly tinted driver's window rolled down.

"Are you guys broke down?" the man behind the wheel asked, taking his sunglasses off to reveal the same piercing blue eyes as Albert.

I recognized Braydon Cunningham instantly even though it had been years since I had seen him at the last reunion. Most of the girls at Hillspring High would probably still recognize him since he had been the subject of many a teenage crush. He still had the same sandy blond hair, cut in that way that looks both tousled and carefully styled at the same time. He still looked like he was in the same great shape that he had been when he dominated both the football field and the basketball court.

"No, we're fine. Thank you," I said, blushing, even though I had no reason to blush. I had no idea what to say to him. Surely he had been notified, right?

"Mallory?" Recognition started to dawn on his face. "What are you guys doing here?"

"Hello, Braydon," I said, suddenly feeling self-conscious. "I'm so sorry about your dad." I hoped beyond hope that he had been notified.

"Thank you," he said. He looked up the driveway and clenched his jaw. "I came as soon as I could."

"It's all so awful," Lanie said. "We wanted to catch Luis on his way to work and see if he was okay, but we didn't know if the sheriff was still at the barn and we didn't want to interfere."

The ease with which she was able to fabricate an excuse on the spot was either really impressive, or really disturbing. Or both.

"Do they have any idea who would do something like this?" he asked, nodding as he looked from Lanie back to me.

I cringed. I couldn't very well say, *Oh yeah, they're pretty sure I murdered your dad.* So I just shook my head while Lanie squeezed my arm.

"If you guys are okay, I'm going to go on and face this," he sighed. "But let's have lunch soon and catch up."

My face must've looked like I felt, because Lanie kicked me gently to respond.

"Sure," I croaked. "I would like that."

He managed a smile that didn't reach his eyes, but under the circumstances, who could blame him? He pulled away and I watched the car disappear up the driveway.

"He is *hot*." Lanie punched me in the shoulder. She was a transplant to our area. She didn't grow up watching girls fawn all over Braydon Cunningham.

"Elaine Harris! His father was just murdered." I *tsk-ed* to emphasize the point.

"I'm aware of that, but it doesn't change the fact that he's smoking hot and he was interested enough in you to ask you to lunch on the way to take care of his father's affairs."

"Isn't that weird, though?" I crossed my arms. "Why would he be worried about catching up in the middle of all of this . . ."—I searched for the right word—"awfulness."

"I didn't think it was weird." She grinned as we climbed back into the truck.

My focus, though temporarily derailed by my high school crush, was elsewhere. I started the truck and drove home on autopilot. My thoughts were spinning like the Tilt-A-Whirl at the fair. I couldn't figure out why Luis had heard a conversation that hadn't occurred. That did explain why suspicion had been cast on me, though. If the police thought I had told him he would regret something and then he turned up dead . . . I didn't follow that thought through. I couldn't start thinking that I was going to get blamed for murdering my neighbor.

Back in my kitchen, Lanie made us coffee and toasted some cinnamon bread she had brought with her. I swear she had brought enough food for an army. I made a mental note to figure out how to repay her. I really did have the best friend in the world.

"I forgot to ask if you were going into work today," I said in between bites of buttered cinnamon toast.

"Yeah, I'm going to work on the clearance stuff today. I have a few consignors who want to mark down some stuff and I can't really leave that for Eve."

"That's no problem. I hate for you to have to babysit me all weekend, but I have really appreciated you being here."

"I've enjoyed being here. We need to do this more often." She patted my hand. "And I think Bill likes the idea that I'm not home by myself too." She looked wistful as she said it. I knew that she and Bill had been trying to have children their entire marriage, though Lanie didn't like to talk about their fertility struggles. It certainly wasn't too late for her. She was only a year older than me and plenty of people have children in their early forties.

"How does he feel about you being so close to the scene of the crime?"

"The same way that I do, that it's highly unlikely for anyone else to be in danger. Someone was after old Albert, and they don't have any reason to come after anyone else."

"I worry that it was random," I said, thinking about the senseless drug-motivated crimes I had seen in St. Louis.

"Even if it was, the crackhead is probably long gone."

"Yeah," I said and crammed the rest of my toast in my mouth. After I was finished chewing, I added, "I'd better go feed the beasts or they'll be coming in after me."

"No problem. I'm not planning to open up until ten. That'll give me time to play with my favorite donkey in the whole wide world," she said with a grin.

"How many donkeys do you know?"

"That's irrelevant," she said, gathering our dishes. She put them in the dishwasher and leaned against the counter. She was beginning to spoil me. "I had no idea they were such wonderful creatures."

"They're pretty special," I agreed.

* * *

The time I spend with the horses always feels like it flies by, even though a lot of the work is manual labor. I enjoy all of it, from feeding them to picking their hooves, to cleaning the stalls. It all has a certain Zen to it, a state of calm attentiveness where my natural intuition and love for the animals drives my movements and allows me to connect. When I had finished most of it, and was checking the outside water troughs, I noticed that there were more police vehicles at the Cunningham estate.

"They've been there about thirty minutes now," Lanie said when she noticed where I was looking.

"I guess they didn't finish everything yesterday," I said, wondering how much evidence they could possibly find. "I'm going to go clean up and follow you into town. I'm going to see Andy Hannigan in person."

"Sounds great," she said. She gave Biscuit another hearty scratch behind his long ears and followed me inside.

I showered in a hurry and threw on some clothes that were suitable for public presentation. I thought I might as well surprise everyone in Hillspring and show up in clothes that didn't smell like a barn. I paused in front of the full-length mirror that hung on the back of my bathroom door. Even with the extra pounds I was carrying around, I thought I looked decent in my faded jeans and Dunder Mifflin T-shirt. My curly blonde hair hung loose to my shoulders. I usually wore it in a ponytail, but I thought I would let it finish drying instead.

Lanie had settled on the sofa with my goofy dog flopped across her lap.

"Why don't you have pets?" I asked, something I had wondered for a while now.

"It's easier to just love on yours. That way I don't have to worry about walking them, vet visits, or general upkeep. I just get to play, and scratch, and enjoy."

I laughed as I grabbed my purse. She followed suit, telling Banjo she would be back tonight. I gave him a kiss on his head, and he pouted from his perch on the sofa. Normally, I would have just taken him with me, since the places I usually go allow dogs. But I hated to take him to the lawyer's office, especially since I hoped to make a good enough impression to get a referral. Ethan, after acting so helpful and concerned, still hadn't bothered to answer my text, so I didn't want to count on him to help out.

I followed Lanie the best I could. She drives like she's competing in a rally race most of the time. My big truck was built for work, not hugging the curves of Ozark highways. Don't get me wrong, I love my truck, and it is definitely what I consider a luxury ride, but it doesn't corner at the same speed as Lanie's plum crazy purple Challenger.

The short drive into town is one of the most scenic in the area. One side of the road is dominated by the ubiquitous Ozark limestone bluffs, crowned with old-growth oaks, cedars, and some wayward pines. In the fall you can make out the vibrant foliage of hickories and maples, and in the spring the evergreens are punctuated by the bright purple blooms of redbuds. White Oak Creek winds along the other side of the road on its way to Deadwood Lake, and since it's spring fed, it runs year-round. It alternates between low, rocky rapids and deep, gently flowing pools. Incidentally, it's also home to some of the best smallmouth bass fishing in the area.

I pulled up behind her at the intersection of Highway 123 and Memory Spring Road. There aren't any stoplights in Hillspring, but there are plenty of stop signs. She waved like a maniac and tore off up Memory Spring Hill. I continued straight, where

Highway 123 turned into the historic Main Street. I was determined to go straight to Andy Hannigan's office before I did anything else so I wouldn't lose the nerve I had worked up.

I was encouraged that the small lot was empty when I pulled up in front of the log cabin-turned-office. Parking is a continual issue for most everything in Hillspring. And during the tourist season our population of nearly two thousand swells considerably, adding to the parking problems. Hillspring is nestled in a valley surrounded by a series of natural and mineral springs. As the reported healing properties of the mineral springs grew in the early 1900s, the town exploded. Mining didn't really take off in this particular area of northwest Arkansas, but in addition to the mineral springs, there are numerous limestone quarries that supplied building materials for surrounding cities, some of which are still in operation today.

Due to the topography of the area, everything is built on the side of one hill or another, which makes parking a challenge. There are also strict restrictions on what can be built in the Historic District, so that means we don't have parking garages or sprawling asphalt parking lots. It also means that you can spend most of the day trying to find somewhere to park. Luckily, that wasn't the case this Friday morning. And realizing it was Friday morning made me panic a bit that the offices were closed and that's why there were free spaces. But I could see lights on and a woman on the phone who I took to be the receptionist.

The interior of the log cabin looked more like a lodge than a law office. Across from the reception desk there was a large native stone fireplace, and while it was still too warm for a fire, I could imagine it roaring in the winter months. They hadn't covered the rough-cut timber that was used for the walls, and it just added to the rustic feel. Overhead, the open ceiling featured a large skylight that let in the warm afternoon sun. It was a stark difference from the cold metal and glass law office where I used to work.

I presented myself in front of the reception desk and smiled my most confident smile. The receptionist, or assistant, I couldn't be sure since she didn't have a name tag or plaque, looked me over like she was trying to place me.

"Good morning," she said, her perfect brunette hair framing her perfect makeup. I really envied women who looked like they walked out of a fashion magazine. I usually looked like I had walked out of a prison riot. "Do you have an appointment?"

"No. But I was hoping Mr. Hannigan could fit me in for a brief consultation. I really need an attorney today, and I was hoping he could point me in the right direction."

"I'm so sorry, but Mr. Hannigan doesn't see clients without an appointment."

"I can understand, but as I'm in kind of a fix, I was hoping he could make an exception. I won't take up too much time."

"There are no exceptions." She was still smiling, but any warmth had officially drained out of it. I was envying her less and less by the moment.

"Sherry, can you get Mr. Adamson on the phone for me?" Andy Hannigan poked his head out of his office and glanced at me.

"Good morning, Mr. Hannigan. I'm Mallory Martin. I run Hillspring Horse Rescue, north of town," I said, practically jumping forward to shove my hand into his.

"Oh yeah," he said, recognition dawning on his face.

"I will put Mr. Adamson through on line two. Ms. Martin doesn't have an appointment," Sherry said.

"Sheriff Sullivan thinks I killed Albert Cunningham yesterday and I need an attorney. I know you don't do criminal law, but I need a referral to someone who can help me, and fast," I said, barely taking a moment to breathe.

Mr. Hannigan looked me over, his kind expression reminding me of Mr. Rogers. In fact, his entire demeanor and appearance reminded me of Mr. Rogers, right down to the tan sweater he was wearing. He looked to be about my age, but he had kind, knowing eyes that made him seem older somehow.

"Hold off on that call to Mr. Adamson, Sherry," he said, opening the door to his office. "Come on in, Ms. Martin, and tell me more."

It didn't take long for me to tell Mr. Hannigan, who insisted I call him Andy, everything I knew about the murder and why the sheriff thought I had something to do with it. He listened intently, taking notes on a yellow legal pad as I spoke. When I was finished, he leaned back in his chair and laced his fingers across his chest. He was still looking at his notes with a furrowed brow.

"Unless they're holding back some critical piece of evidence that puts you at the crime scene, all they have is circumstantial at best," he said finally. "But I can understand why you would be worried. I don't have anything that can't be rescheduled this afternoon, so I'll go to the sheriff's station with you."

I was temporarily struck speechless as he got up from his desk and went back out to Sherry.

"Sherry, please clear out my afternoon," he said. "I will email Mr. Adamson myself."

"Sure thing," she said, and then glared at me through the open doorway.

"Mr. Hannigan—Andy, I didn't mean to burst in here and disrupt your entire day. I was just hoping you could point me to someone who would be willing to represent me on short notice." *And someone who knows what they're doing*, I didn't add.

"Granted, it's been a few years since I actively worked a criminal case, but I'm fairly certain that we can navigate this initial interview together. If I see that things progress beyond my capabilities, I will make sure you're represented well."

It felt a little like he had read my mind.

"That's very generous." I squirmed in my chair. I wasn't sure how to politely bring up money. Having been married to an attorney, I knew they don't come cheap, and the horse rescue business isn't exactly a lucrative one.

"I just need to discuss your fees," I said, unable to look him in the eyes. I was as broke as I had ever been and prospects for fundraising weren't looking good if I was named suspect number one. My leather work wasn't moving at Lanie's shop either.

"How much cash do you have on you?"

"What?"

"How much cash do you have on you right now?"

I hesitated for a moment, trying to decide if he was serious or not. He looked serious, so I dug my wallet out of my purse and found that I had exactly $43.78.

He reached over and pulled a twenty out of my hand.

"I'll have Sherry write out a receipt." He put the twenty in his pocket. "You've just hired an attorney."

Chapter Five

I rode to the sheriff's office in Andy's immaculate silver 2010 Lincoln Town Car and felt awkward and self-conscious the entire time. While I appreciated his grand gesture with the twenty-dollar bill, I wasn't sure I liked the loosey-goosey terms we had regarding his future fees. Looking like Mr. Rogers didn't guarantee that he was trustworthy and altruistic.

Even the sheriff's department in Hillspring looked like it was from another era. It was built from the same cut limestone as the courthouse and some of the other historic buildings. It was ornate for a law enforcement office. The additions to the building had been added below the main floor, extending down the hill like chambers in a rabbit warren. The grounds were xeriscaped in matching limestone gravel, with a few manicured shrubs and native prickly pears.

Andy pulled his briefcase out of the trunk, a lovely old leather case that looked like it had probably seen him through law school. I hoped he wouldn't need anything in it. I hoped we could give my statement, answer a few questions, and be on our way.

"Mallory Martin here to give her follow-up statement," he announced to the clerk, "and Andrew Hannigan, her attorney."

"Does she have an appointment?" the clerk asked. That was the second time I was asked about having an appointment.

"Sheriff Grady asked me to come in today," I said, remembering that I had told him I would, indeed, make an appointment and that I had failed to do that.

"I'll let him know you're here."

It only took a few minutes for Grady to appear at the front desk.

"You really did hire an attorney," he said, shaking his head.

"Why wouldn't I?"

"Because it makes you look guilty."

"Let's not get off on the wrong foot here, Sheriff," Andy said, with a warm smile and an outstretched hand. "Andy Hannigan. And you know as well as I do that having an attorney is not an admission or suggestion of guilt. I am here strictly to make sure that Ms. Martin's best interests are upheld."

Grady took the offered hand, and the men shook as Andy spoke. Grady continued to grimace as he took us to a back room, which I took to be the interrogation room. It didn't look like the intimidating rooms you see in movies. It was just a small, plain room with off-white, almost yellow walls and absolutely no decoration at all. There were also no windows. A single camera jutted out from the corner opposite the doorway like an intrusive eye. In the middle of the room was a heavy wooden table surrounded by four chairs. Andy and I took the chairs with our backs to the door. Grady disappeared for a moment before returning with a folder and a legal pad.

"I forgot to tell you that I saw lights on in the barn later than usual the night Albert died," I said as soon as he sat down.

"When did you remember that bit of information?" Grady wrote as he talked.

"I don't know, Sheriff. I've been a bit frazzled since you and your deputy seem to think I murdered someone."

"You're familiar with the hours that were usually kept at the barn?"

"Albert's barn is clearly visible from my porch and paddock. I'm often out there in the evening and I'd never noticed lights on in the barn that late except once before."

"When was that?"

"About a year ago when Albert had a mare that had trouble foaling. I didn't know at the time what was going on but found out about it later."

"Tell me again about the conversation you had with Albert the afternoon before he was found dead."

I recounted the conversation again.

Grady seemed to be following along as he skimmed my written statement while I talked.

"You're not leaving anything out?"

"No," I said, glancing at Andy. He nodded, which I took to mean that I was answering in ways that wouldn't land me in jail.

"You know we have a witness to the conversation, right? And we're going to get his phone records."

"You have three witnesses to the conversation," I countered.

"Oh? How do you figure that?"

"Me, Luis, and Tanner Blake. Tanner heard everything I said to Albert. And the phone records aren't going to matter because we all know he called me that day."

"Tanner gave his statement this morning. It seems that he doesn't recall hearing the whole conversation. But Luis does. And Luis heard Albert reacting to what sounded like threats," Grady closed the folder and leaned on his elbows.

I cursed to myself. I really thought Tanner had heard my side of the phone call, or at least enough of it to clear me.

"My client has told you what she said to Mr. Cunningham," Andy said before I had the chance to respond. "Do you intend to charge Ms. Martin with anything at this time?"

My stomach did a little flip-flop. Just the thought of being arrested made me sick.

"Not at this time," Grady said. "But we will want to talk to you again soon. If you think of anything else, please let me know."

"Are you looking at Kathleen Clark? She claims she had a migraine the night Albert died. But isn't it a bit far-fetched that she wouldn't notice he was gone until you showed up?" I blurted out before Andy had a chance to shush me.

Grady paused for a beat. "We're investigating all relevant information. And you would do well to steer clear of playing amateur detective."

I opened my mouth to say something, but Andy bumped me with his elbow.

"Thank you for your time." Andy got up abruptly and extended his hand again.

I followed his lead. I couldn't get out of there fast enough. When we got back out to Andy's car, I realized I had been holding my breath and let it out in a "whoosh."

Andy opened his car door for me, and I glanced into his warm, brown eyes. There was something so comforting about him, and I thought for just a moment that he would make a better therapist than an attorney. But I also had to admit that he had done a fair job of handling the interview and keeping me from blurting out things that might hurt my case.

"It's going to be okay," he said, glancing at me as he turned out onto the main road. "They don't have anything, or they would've charged you with something."

It wasn't *they*. It was *him*. It was Grady Sullivan, a man I had known most of my life. Someone who shouldn't think I was capable of hurting an old man, no matter how disagreeable that old man was.

"Thank you for saying that, but I'm not so sure. This is a small town and if word gets out that I'm a person of interest in the murder of one of the wealthiest men in the county, I might as well just go ahead and close the rescue because I'll never be able to get another red cent donated."

"Don't borrow trouble," he said, using a phrase that had been a favorite of my mother's. "Nothing has happened yet. They're just following leads as they come to them. And that was sound advice in there. Keep your nose clean."

I nodded, but I didn't feel that confident, either in being ruled out as a suspect or in my ability to stay out of the investigation. I felt like my entire foundation was crumbling.

When we got back to Andy's office, I didn't follow him inside. I asked him to send me an invoice and an estimate of future costs, and he argued with me a bit but finally caved when I told him that with everything being unsure, I needed to have a game plan and needed to know how to start budgeting for potential legal fees. He gave me a gentle pat on the arm and promised me that Sherry would email the invoice and estimates.

I'm sure Sherry would appreciate that. We exchanged numbers and he assured me I could call him anytime with questions or concerns.

I was just pulling into the employee lot behind Lanie's antique store when my phone jingled its text alert.

Ethan.

> Sorry. Something came up, will explain later. I have a few feelers out on a referral for you. Delicate question, but what can you afford?

I felt briefly annoyed, but I didn't have the energy to sustain it, not when nearly everything I had was fueling a constant loop of worst-case scenarios in my brain.

> No problem. I have an attorney. You can stop worrying about it.

I thought about adding a "thank you" at the end but decided against it. I wasn't super thrilled with how long he had left me dangling. I was just about to shove my phone in my purse when it chimed again.

> Who did you retain?

I stared at it a minute and then decided not to reply. I pulled up his contact and selected "block this caller." I figured I could always turn it off later. I am fully aware that this was not the most mature response I could have had, but for better or worse, Andy Hannigan was my attorney, at least for the time being.

And I knew that Ethan had very elitist views when it came to other attorneys, so he wasn't likely to have anything nice to say about him, if he knew him at all. And not knowing him at all would have been worse for Ethan, because that would have meant that Andy had never done anything noteworthy to have gained a reputation.

I rounded the building to go in through the front doors, because even though I totally take advantage of being Lanie's friend and park in the back, I don't have a key to the employee entrance. I stopped for a second and admired her new sign. *Junk & Disorderly Antiques & More* was emblazoned in dark blue lettering against a pale cream background. It looked very professional and certainly beat the heck out of the old hand-painted one.

Her antique and consignment shop occupied what had once been the Country Cupboard Buffet, a Hillspring favorite until the original owners retired and no one else had been able to capture the appeal that had put the place on the map. It changed hands several times in the early 2000s and finally sat empty for about five years until Lanie took the plunge and opened her store. She painted pale blue over the pukey yellow, ripped out the booths, tore out most of the kitchen equipment, and now you would never know it had ever been a restaurant.

I was happy to find the store had multiple customers milling about and two in line to check out. Lanie had taken as big a gamble as I had, putting all her eggs in the antiques basket, and I wanted her to be successful. Eve was the one checking customers at the counter, and she waved at me enthusiastically. I didn't see Lanie anywhere, but Eve pointed to the door to the back room. I nodded and headed through the "employees only" doors.

"Hey!" Lanie called cheerfully from behind a mountain of boxes. "That was fast. They must've not wanted to know much. That's a good sign, right?"

"Not exactly," I said, picking up a spare box cutter from the worktable. "I'm definitely suspect number one."

"What the hell is wrong with them?" She put her hands on her hips. "You and Grady go way back. Surely he can't think you would murder someone."

"Oh, but he does," I said, anger bubbling to the surface.

"Okay, let's look at this calmly then." She took a deep breath. "Did you talk to Andy Hannigan? Did he recommend anyone?"

"Actually, he's representing me." I rubbed my eyes with the back of my hand.

"I didn't think he took criminal cases."

"He said it had been a few years." I used the box cutter to open one of the boxes piled in front of Lanie, maybe a little too enthusiastically. It felt good to rip into something at that moment, though. "But he also said that if he gets in over his head, he will consult another attorney. He went to the interview with me, which wasn't really an interview. It was just Grady telling me what Luis already told us, that he overheard me threatening Albert. Oh, and that Tanner didn't hear everything that I said to Albert."

"So, they essentially have nothing other than suspicion."

"Pretty strong suspicion."

"What are you going to do?"

I looked up from my box destruction. My chaotic thoughts came screeching to a halt as I considered what *exactly* I was going to do.

"I'm going to do everything I can to keep my butt out of jail," I said, feeling resolute and focused for the first time since all of this started. "Someone killed Albert, and since I'm not focused on the wrong person like the sheriff's department is, I'm in a good position to figure out who that was."

Lanie seemed to chew that over for a bit, her dark eyes cast downward.

"Okay," she said. "We'll figure it out."

"I can't ask you to get involved. After all, we are talking about a killer."

"You didn't ask. And I'm not about to let you go through this alone."

I crossed the distance between us and pulled her into a fierce hug. I loved her for being so loyal and for the sentiment behind her words, but the words themselves stung a bit. Being alone isn't how I had envisioned my life at this point. The truth was, I had been on exactly two dates since my marriage had ended. The first, a blind date set up by a colleague from the law firm where I worked in St. Louis, had been comical it was so disastrous. He had been an hour late, arriving just as I was getting up to leave. He spent the entire dinner talking about his ex-wife and wanted us to take selfies to send to her because I was attractive enough to make her jealous. Yes, he actually told me that.

The second was a date with a man I had met just after moving back home. He'd been in the feedstore when I went to get my first load of supplies for the rescue. He seemed nice enough when he asked me out. When we met for the first date, he thought it would be a good idea to take me home to meet his mother. She had expected me to help her cook the meal for us, which was okay, just odd. But it got weirder from there, complete with a rousing discussion of whether or not my hips were suitable for childbirthing. I wish I was joking. I'm not.

I guess I sort of gave up after that. There had been some harmless flirting here and there, but no one that had intrigued me enough to take a chance. Or I hadn't given them the chance to intrigue me.

"So, how do we do this thing?" she asked as we separated.

"I'm going to go home and outline everything we know up until this point. I actually already have a head start on that. I started keeping notes right after I talked to Grady at the crime scene."

"Smart girl."

"We can go over it tonight and figure out a game plan."

We hugged goodbye and I waved again to Eve, who was still busy at the register.

* * *

Back in my truck, I took a deep breath and tried to steady my nerves. I had meant what I said to Lanie about taking matters into my own hands, but the enormity of it was overwhelming. The cases that I had assisted with were investigated by an entire team, and I had just been one member of that team. I had relied on law clerks and paralegals for research and the police to interrogate witnesses and suspects. I told myself to take it one step at a time, one detail at a time. Since the firm I worked for dealt primarily with malpractice claims, I would start my portion of the investigation by reviewing the medical records and witness statements and preparing a detailed time line. That was as good a place as any to start with my murder investigation.

I was mostly on autopilot on the way home. I felt an extreme urgency to get things set up the way I used to in my former office. I hoped slipping into that old routine would kick-start my brain into investigative mode. I needed all the help I could get.

Banjo met me at the door absolutely covered in mud. He looked as if he had been buried and dug up, like that cat in *Pet Sematary*. Only he was anything but evil, as he bounced and wagged his stumpy tail, quite proud of his excavation efforts. I followed his muddy tracks all the way to the back door, where mud was caked on his doggy door, and out into the fenced back-yard. He has free run of my place when I'm home and can super-vise him, but when I'm not, I prefer to keep him more contained. He had managed to dig a fairly impressive hole near the back fence, likely spurred by his intense hatred of moles.

He ran over to the hole and looked back expectantly, like he just knew I was going to tell him what a good dog he was. I couldn't bring myself to scold him, but I sure wasn't going to praise him either.

"Come on," I said. "Let's get you in the bath."

Luckily, Banjo doesn't mind baths too much. I don't think they're exactly his favorite activity in the world, but he is coop-erative at least. It felt like it took forever to get the dog and the house back in order. When I finally did, I went straight to work.

I use one of the three bedrooms in my house as a home office of sorts, just somewhere to keep all the records and paperwork for the rescue. Since I already had a desk and computer set up in there, I figured that was the logical choice to set up my inves-tigation. I took down the large painting of a field of horses that Lanie had gifted me two Christmases ago and stashed it safely in the closet. I pulled out a pack of Post-it notes from the desk and grabbed my notebook from the kitchen. I spent the rest of the afternoon transcribing the notes onto the Post-its and organizing them on the wall in the space where I had removed the painting. By the time I needed to feed the horses again in the evening,

I had a great start on my evidence board, pulling on memories of the ones we used at my former firm.

What I knew about the case so far was easy enough. Albert was murdered. There was no obvious cause of death, like a gunshot or knife wound. Nothing had been stolen from the barn or house. There were two viable suspects so far: Kathleen Clark and Heather Rogers. Kathleen had the opportunity to commit the murder. She was physically on the property all night and claimed she didn't know anything was wrong until Grady and his deputies showed up the next morning. But she didn't have a motive, at least not one that I had uncovered yet.

Heather, on the other hand, had plenty of motive but no obvious opportunity. She was convinced that Albert's farm was polluting her organic farm and was even seen in public yelling at him about it. At my former firm, we didn't usually have to worry about motive and opportunity because we specialized in medical malpractice. That's where my expertise came into play. I would comb through the patient's medical record and look for inconsistencies and deviations from established evidence-based standards.

I told myself that it was that attention to detail and being able to step back from the minutiae to see the whole picture that would help me figure this out. I added a few sticky notes in a different color, green to be precise, outlining my next steps. It felt like a solid plan to talk to Heather Rogers and find out who else had a strong motive to kill Albert. I added a final note to the board reminding me to ask Grady if he'd found out anything about Kathleen. I would shift focus and priorities as I learned more.

* * *

I took my time in the barn as a reward for all the work I had put into organizing my notes. Biscuit was always ready for attention, but several of the others were feeling social as well. Goldie, one of our seniors, particularly loved being groomed and would stand untethered for as long as someone was brushing her soft palomino coat. After I'd groomed her from one end to the other, I braided her mane and told her that she would rival any show horse.

River, Stormy, and Ace, three of the geldings, had wandered up the hill to graze with Tunie by the time I'd finished brushing Goldie. Tunie, or Fortune in Iced Tea as her registered name read, was a leggy off-the-track Thoroughbred that had come to us after she'd been removed in a puppy mill investigation. The local Humane Society had been prepared for numerous dogs, but they hadn't expected the starving horse and other livestock. Tunie was wary and standoffish even after being here for nearly a year, much to Tanner's dismay.

I had finished the evening feeding and the obligatory scratches and treats when Lanie pulled into the drive. As usual, she went straight to Biscuit and then joined me on the porch.

"What a day," she said, flopping down heavily on the bench.

"It sure looked busy when I was there."

"It was steady all day, which is a good problem to have."

"True that."

"So how is your organization coming along?"

"Pretty well, I think. I got everything so far up on the evidence board."

"Any ideas about who might have done this? Anyone jump out at you?"

"A couple, actually," I said. "Kathleen certainly had opportunity. I don't know anything concrete about what motive she might have yet. But I don't want to get tunnel vision this early. I need to talk to Heather Rogers before I decide where to focus more energy."

"Who is that?"

"She owns the organic farm down the road, Heather's Happy Organics. She should be at the farmers market tomorrow. Ashley told me that she went off on Albert at the fair. I want to find out what she was so angry about."

"I remember her now. She wrote that opinion piece last spring about how the livestock farms in the area were polluting her creek." She leaned forward. "She totally could've done it."

"Maybe," I said. I wasn't convinced. I didn't want to make assumptions or jump to conclusions, but I couldn't imagine Heather Rogers killing anyone. Of course, people always say that, don't they?

"Wanna go all good-cop, bad-cop on her?" Lanie kicked me gently with the toe of her stylish boot.

"You're insane."

"That's the pot calling the kettle black." She got up and tugged on my sleeve. "It is definitely time for wine and chocolate."

"That sounds fantastic." I followed her into my house.

After a bit of wonderful, mindless chitchat, we found ourselves standing in front of my wall of Post-it notes. Lanie read each one, leaning over the lower row.

"This is impressive," she said, standing back and gesturing toward the wall with her wineglass. "You didn't miss anything, did you?"

"I hope not."

She sat down in the desk chair, still studying the wall.

"You know, we should check public records and see if there have been any complaints or suits filed against Albert or the estate recently. That could be a motive, right?"

"People have definitely killed for less. I'll go to the clerk's office Monday."

"I'll go. Bill's niece, Jennifer, works there. She might be able to tell me something that isn't in the public records."

"Great, thank you."

It felt good to have a solid plan, even if I didn't have a lot of confidence that it would turn up anything.

"Now for more important things." Lanie got up, physically turned me around, and started marching me back to the living room.

"What's more important than being suspected of murder?"

"Albert's hot son, of course. Who would've thought? I mean, Albert wasn't exactly movie star material."

"You're awful." I laughed in spite of myself. "He looks like his mother. She was gorgeous too."

"You *do* think he's hot." She looked like the cat that ate the canary.

"Well, of course I do. Everyone thought he was hot. He was the quintessential high school catch. And then he grew up and moved away to be some big shot somewhere else."

"So, go have lunch with him."

"He isn't going to want to have lunch when he finds out Grady thinks I murdered his dad."

"We'll get you out of those crosshairs soon enough." She reached over and patted my knee.

* * *

After Lanie left for the antique shop the next morning, I made quick work of feeding the horses. Ashley joined me about halfway through. She was in a great mood, chattering about her classes and how proud she was of her younger sister who had just made the gifted and talented program at her high school. I hated to leave her alone again, but I had to get to the farmers market as soon as possible. Booths tended to close down if everything sold, and I didn't want to risk missing Heather. I felt like our conversation was best suited for neutral territory and I didn't want to have to go to her farm.

Ashley waved enthusiastically from the paddock as I turned my truck down the driveway. I drove slowly past the Cunningham driveway, which was stupid since I couldn't see anything from the road. I wondered if Braydon had found out that I was a suspect yet. And then I wondered why I cared. It wasn't like I was really on his radar. He had just lost his father and he wasn't going to want to reconnect with someone he had never noticed before.

On my way into town, my phone rang. I was ecstatic when I glanced at the screen on my truck dash, and it displayed my daughter Virginia's nickname: Ginny. She had made a habit of calling me every Saturday morning since she'd started college. She often called through the week too, but I always knew I could count on the Saturday call even if she got busy.

"Mom, you're never going to believe what happened," she launched right in right after I'd said "Hello."

"What?"

"I got in! I got the internship at the vet clinic!"

"Ginny, that's fantastic!"

"I don't know when I start yet, but I'm hoping to come home for a visit before I get started."

"I would love that."

"What's going on with you?"

"Oh, not much," I didn't want to worry her about any of my potential legal issues. "I'm just headed into town for the farmers market."

"That sounds like fun," she said absently. I wasn't sure how much fun it was going to be, but I hoped it would be productive.

We talked all the way into town about her studies and her new roommate, who apparently had a bad habit of making very smelly fish dishes. Talking to Ginny had been just the distraction I needed as I pulled up to the farmers market, which was held in the old Coldstone Bank parking lot. The bank had moved to a new, bigger building on the east side of town, and nothing had been done with the old one yet. There were rumors all the time that it had been sold for this or that, but none of them had panned out. So, for the time being, they allowed various events, like the farmers market on Saturdays.

It was positively bustling. There were numerous booths, and I had to park nearly two blocks away and walk in, which was uphill. Because everything in Hillspring is on a hill. As I passed the first booth, gasping like I'd just scaled Everest, I made a vow to start exercising more. I passed booths for honey, goat milk soap, quilts, and several resale vitamin vendors. I hadn't seen the cheerful rainbow sign that marked Heather's Happy Organics yet, and I thought she was usually set up closer to the road. But there aren't assigned spots, so I decided to look around before I gave up.

I got distracted by a pottery booth with the most amazing collection of stoneware and decorative pieces. The pieces were pricey, but they were clearly well made, and I had no doubt that they were worth it. I took a flyer. If I ever had any extra money, I planned to pick up a few pieces for the house.

I turned around and shoved the flyer in the pocket of my faded hoodie. I spotted Heather's sign several booths away, on the side of the parking lot that bordered the urban forest occupying the heart of the town, where the craggy hollers were too steep to build. She was talking to a young couple using animated gestures, clearly passionate about what she was telling them. I couldn't hear what she was saying, but she picked up a carrot to illustrate her point. To be fair, it *was* a good-looking carrot. I inched my way over, stopping at a booth where a young woman was selling knitted dishcloths. To me, it looked like a lot of work to sell them at two for five dollars. But I can't crochet or knit to save my life. I picked out a couple in colors that would complement my blue and yellow kitchen décor and handed over the five bucks. Farmers markets are my kryptonite. I adore handmade crafts and locally sourced foods and veggies.

The couple at Heather's booth finally moved on and I made my way over before someone else stopped there. She had an impressive selection of vegetables and a few fruits, and they all looked delicious. She had displays next to each type of vegetable that showed them growing on her farm. From what I could see in the photos, her farm was just as bright and immaculate as her booth.

"Mallory?" She leaned over at the waist and looked up at me from the awkward angle.

"Hi, Heather," I said as enthusiastically as I could muster.

"One of my closest neighbors and I haven't seen you in ages." She smiled, but it didn't quite reach her bright brown eyes. She threw her long, brunette braid over her shoulder. She took off her gloves, which were very cute. They didn't match, but I think they were designed that way. I couldn't be sure. The left one was soft-looking leather dyed in a rainbow pattern with each finger a different color. The right hand had flowers dyed into the leather. I wanted to ask her where she got them, but it didn't seem to be the time.

"The rescue takes a lot of time," I said, still looking at the stupid gloves on the table. They really were cute.

"Yeah, the rescue." Her voice trailed off. She reached under the table and pulled out a binder. She opened it and put it on the table next to the onions. "I would love for you to look at these graphs of the nitrate levels over the last three years."

She turned the binder around and pointed to the graphs.

"The runoff from the livestock farms in the area is killing White Oak Creek. The algae bloom this year has been the worst yet," she said as she flipped the page to photographs of the creek.

I wasn't sure how to respond. The photographs showed slimy green, stringy algae choking the narrow waterway. And her graphs illustrated a steady line pointing upward.

"You have more horses this year than have ever been at that location, don't you?"

"I do, but . . ."

"And you have absolutely no runoff management in place either, do you?"

"I do. The paddocks do not extend entirely to the property line and I've left the native vegetation intact in the buffer zone," I said calmly. I had been required to prepare an environmental impact statement and have my place inspected when I applied for the nonprofit status. "And I've seeded even more native grass on the downhill side of the property as well."

"Well, I have to say that's more effort than your neighbor has put into it." She crossed her arms, leaving the binder open to the photos of the creek. "But I'm afraid that your livestock numbers are outweighing the efforts."

"I'm actually here to talk to you about my neighbor," I said, ignoring the last bit. "Was that what you talked about with Albert Cunningham at the fair? The runoff?"

"What? Did he say something?"

"No." I was surprised that she didn't know. Albert's death had been all over the local Facebook pages and was on the front page of the weekend edition of the *Hillspring Herald*. "One of my volunteers said that your conversation looked a bit heated. I was hoping you could give me some insight into what made him so angry." I didn't tell her Ashley said that *she* had been the angry one.

She seemed to be considering the question for a moment before she said, "Yes. I tried to reason with him about the runoff from his farm. He has refused to see me or take my calls, so when I saw him at the fair, I took the opportunity."

She closed the binder and put it back under the table.

"He has a history of being rather difficult to deal with," I said, though I was sure I wasn't telling her anything she didn't already know.

"I am preparing to send these Monday, but since you're here, I will give it to you personally." She reached under the table again and pulled out her backpack. She retrieved a manila envelope addressed to Hillspring Horse Haven and handed it to me.

"What is this?"

"You need to read it in its entirety, but it's a letter asking you to reduce the number and type of livestock on your *rescue* and to consult with the state agriculture department to establish an approved runoff control system," she said, putting her backpack back under the table. When she straightened back up, she crossed her arms again.

"If you don't," she continued, "I'm prepared to take you to court. I have a similar letter for Mr. Cunningham."

"Heather, I can assure you, my place has been inspected. It was part of the application process with the bank." My heart sank at the thought of more legal issues.

"It's not enough." Her mouth drew into a thin line. "Read the letter. My intentions are clear. I'm going to save my farm by any means necessary."

"Does that include murder?"

"What?"

"Albert Cunningham was murdered in his barn."

Her eyes widened and she opened her mouth to say something, but abruptly shut it again. Finally she said, "I don't believe you."

I pulled out my phone, entered Albert's name and our city in the search field, and then turned the screen over to her.

"You need to leave." She took a step back.

"Have you ever been to the Cunningham farm?"

"I told you he wouldn't see me or talk to me," she said, pulling her phone out of her back pocket.

"You seem to know a lot about his lack of runoff management for someone who has never been there."

"If you don't leave, I'm calling the police."

I held up my hands in surrender and backed away. I had no idea if she was bluffing or not, but it had worked if she was. I didn't need another encounter with the police. I stalked back to my car, disgusted with myself for letting the interview get so out of hand. I had planned to be much more subtle and cunning. I did learn a few things, though. Heather was more desperate than I had thought, and even if she hadn't murdered Albert, she planned to murder my rescue.

Chapter Six

After adding my notes to the investigation board, I went out to the barn, where Ashley was still working with the big bay. On Monday I would have to talk to Andy Hannigan about more potential legal trouble with Heather's lawsuit, and I wanted to distract myself. Watching Ashley work with horses was like watching poetry in motion. I had been around and ridden horses my whole life and I like to think I have a special knack for dealing with them. But nothing compared to Ashley's natural talent. She always seemed perfectly in sync with them.

"Hey, Boss," she said as she sent the horse in another circle around the round pen.

"He looks good. Much more relaxed."

"He's settling in nicely. The farrier came while you were out. He trimmed Zeus here, Molly, and Goldie. I knew they needed it, but I forgot to ask you about the others."

"I forgot to update the schedule. Sorry about that." I cursed under my breath. "No one else is really pressing right now, thankfully." Farrier work is hard work and this one would be my third since starting the rescue. I hadn't met him in person, and I was hoping to do so on this visit. But I had actually forgotten he was coming, with all of the other chaos going on. I also hated to leave things like that for my unpaid volunteers.

"It's no problem. They were all sweethearts."

She held up her hand to signal the horse to stop. He did and then turned to face her, his sides gently heaving after the exertion. Although he needed to put on a little weight, he wasn't as thin as some of the other horses that had come to the rescue. His body was peppered with scars, both old and new. I hated to think about what might have caused them. Acknowledging the benefit of the doubt, horses are very accident prone and hard on themselves. So I hoped that his road map of scars were just bad luck, even though it was hard to imagine that he could have done all that damage to himself.

He watched her with big, alert eyes, ears pricked forward awaiting her next command. She walked up to him and rubbed his neck.

"You're a good boy," she said to him. "I will never understand how people can mistreat animals."

"Me either." I shook my head as I felt a familiar warm snoot rooting around in the general vicinity of my right pocket. I looked down at the very determined donkey mining for whatever goodies he thought I had stashed there.

"I don't have anything, bud." I scratched the ear closest to me and he abandoned his search. He turned his head sideways, pushing his head into my hand.

"Did you run by the feedstore on your way back? We're out of senior feed for Goldie, and the joint supplement probably won't make it until Monday. I'm not sure what else."

"Crap! No, I didn't. I'll run back into town."

I left Biscuit, who looked hurt that I hadn't devoted the rest of my day to hunting down every single inch of itchy donkey hide. I quickly made a list of the things we needed. I kept a mental tally of how much it was all going to cost and prayed that I had enough in the general account to cover it. Things had been tight before, but they had never been this bad. I reminded myself that worrying about it wouldn't solve anything, so I took a deep breath and shoved my list in my pocket.

"I'm finished for today," Ashley said as she led Zeus through the barn doors. "Do you want to try to turn him out with the boys or put him back in the stall?"

"In the stall for now. I want to be home when we try to turn him out."

"I can stay if you want me to."

"That's sweet." I smiled. "But go have some fun on your Saturday."

"This *is* fun."

"You're always welcome, but you don't have to stay."

"I think I will see how he does. I brought my laptop with me, so I can write my paper from the barn loft and still watch him."

"I don't know what I did to deserve you, but I sure am thankful."

"Oh, stop it," she said, her freckled cheeks flushing.

She had her thick brown hair pulled up in a high ponytail so she couldn't do that thing where she lets it fall around her face and hides behind it.

"I won't be long," I called over my shoulder. I patted the seat and Banjo happily jumped in, my copilot at every opportunity. I was just about to leave when a car pulled in behind me, to Biscuit's honking announcement.

I looked in my rearview mirror and watched Braydon get out of a black SUV. It took a minute to register that he had traded his BMW for Albert's Cadillac Escalade. He came up to the window of my truck with a crooked grin. I turned the engine off and opened the door.

"I caught you at a bad time." He gestured generally toward the truck.

"No, I'm going to the feedstore, but I have a few minutes."

"I just wanted to come by and let you know that Dad's remembrance is going to be Wednesday at eleven. We'll have to wait until the state crime lab finishes the autopsy to have the actual funeral, but Aunt Mae thought that we needed to do something sooner, you know, him being who he was and all." He shuffled from one foot to the other. It was odd to see him uncomfortable. I'd always known him to be confident and sometimes cocky and arrogant.

"I'm so sorry, Braydon," I said. I wanted to say more, but I didn't know what to say or how to say it.

"Thank you," he said. "Dad and I have never been exactly close, and we haven't gotten any closer since Mom died." He looked over my shoulder toward the Cunningham farm.

I wondered if he would still want me to come to the service if he knew I was a suspect. I felt guilty, with him clearly grieving, and keeping that from him.

"Braydon, I need to tell you something." I got out of my truck and left the door open for Banjo.

"I know you didn't have anything to do with my dad's murder." He looked me straight in the eyes with such intensity that I felt a little weak-kneed. "Luis told me what he said to the sheriff and I know there has to be some other explanation."

I suddenly found myself speechless. I had expected to defend myself and to proclaim my innocence, but I hadn't expected this. It caught me completely off guard.

"Are you okay?" he asked.

I felt my cheeks burn red. I must have looked like an idiot, standing there staring at him.

"Yeah, I'm sorry. I just didn't expect that," I said, truthfully.

"You expected me to think you murdered my father?"

"Well"—I flushed again—"I guess I did. The sheriff has known me since high school, and he seems to think I could be capable of something like that. I didn't figure it would be much of a stretch for someone who didn't know me as well."

"Let's fix that then." He flashed that smile again. "Let me take you to dinner. I'll pick you up at eight, unless you have plans. I really need a distraction."

"No, I don't have plans."

"Perfect. I'll see you later then." He backed away a few steps and then got back in the SUV before I collected myself enough to argue.

I leaned against my truck, trying to figure out what had just happened. My biggest teenage crush had just asked me out to dinner. I suddenly panicked. I had nothing to wear to dinner. I had donated most of my "business" clothes when I moved back home, and I had worn nothing but jeans and a T-shirt for so long, I wasn't even sure how to dress up anymore. Was my makeup even still good? Does makeup expire?

"Mal, are you okay?" Ashley asked as she closed the paddock gate.

"Yeah, I'm fine," I lied.

"Who was that?"

"Braydon Cunningham. Albert's son."

"Wow. I didn't realize he had kids. He never seemed to be the nurturing type."

"I don't think he was."

"Did he say something to you? You're really pale." She put her hand on my shoulder.

"Yeah." I smiled like an idiot. "He asked me out."

* * *

I flew into Lanie's shop, waved absently at Eve, and barged into Lanie's office, Banjo on my heels. He curled up at Lanie's feet and went to work on the chew toy she kept for him.

"Come right in," she looked around her monitor.

"Lanie," I said breathlessly, "he asked me out. To dinner. Tonight."

I don't know if it was the fact that my high school crush had asked me out or what, but I felt like I *was* back in high school, all giddy and reckless.

"Mr. Hottie with the BMW?"

"That's the one."

"Good for you!" She pushed her chair out from behind the computer as I flopped into the chair opposite her desk.

"Is it? Good for me? I have no idea how to do this anymore." I ran my hands as far through my curly hair as I could. "I don't have anything to wear on a date, and especially on a date with Braydon-freaking-Cunningham. And why am I even considering going out with the son of the man I'm supposed to have murdered?"

"Take a deep breath. You have the dress you wore to Ginny's graduation. You looked great in that."

"That was almost two years ago! I have no idea if it still fits." I leaned back in the chair, feeling like I couldn't catch my breath. You'd think I'd never been on a date before.

"It will still fit," she said calmly, like she was some sort of hostage negotiator.

I sighed heavily and let my purse fall to the floor beside me.

"Stop overthinking this," she said. "Just go, have a nice dinner, and enjoy yourself."

"But overthinking is what I do."

"No joke! But you need to take a step back and just go with it. It's one dinner. One night. You know you want to go, so just figure out how to get it done."

I nodded. Lanie always had a way of jerking me back to reality. We all need a friend like that.

"Okay, you're right." I kept nodding like a bobblehead.

"Want me to come by this evening and help you get ready?"

"You've babysat me for days. Take tonight and have some time to yourself."

"I might just do that. If you're sure," she said.

"I'm sure. I appreciate the offer, though."

After freaking myself out about the date, I had almost forgotten to tell Lanie about my visit to the farmers market. I recounted all the details, and after I had finished Lanie crossed her arms over her chest and leaned back in her chair.

"She sounds like she might be desperate enough to kill someone," she said.

"I don't know. She's certainly passionate, but kill someone?" I shook my head. "And killing him doesn't really solve her problems—the horses are still there. And she's planning to take me to court too. Unless she's planning to kill me too." I shuddered as I said it. That particular thought hadn't occurred to me until I'd said it out loud.

"Maybe you can casually work it into the conversation tonight and see if Mr. Hottie knows anything about it. You know, if she threatened Albert or anything like that."

"I don't think Braydon was that close with his dad. He may not know anything."

"Well, it won't hurt to find out."

I nodded. I didn't know if I wanted to talk about Albert during dinner, but if it came up in conversation, I might try to work it in.

We hugged our goodbyes and I headed to the feedstore. Hillspring Feed and Hardware occupied one of the older buildings in town, a massive limestone storefront that had been at various times in its history a tomato canning factory, a bathhouse, and a flea market. When the current owners, Bob and Janet Peterson, purchased it, it had been vacant for several years, just like Lanie's building. But they had managed to scrape by those first few years and build up a steady and thriving business.

I backed my truck up to the loading dock and climbed the stairs to the front doors. The weekend spit and whittle club had taken up residence on the benches that sat under the wide front awning. I nodded a "hello" as I passed them, but no one seemed to notice, as they were too enthralled in the current discussion about riding lawn mowers.

I cracked my windows and told Banjo to keep watch. That was an accurate request since *watching* was all he was likely to do. He would probably greet any potential truck thief like a long-lost relative, threatening with nothing more dangerous than drool and a wagging stumpy tail.

Inside, the front of the store was the hardware section, which blended into the feedstore on the lower level. They also carried a nice assortment of tack and pet supplies. It took no time to find the supplements I had come for, and I took my place in line to put in my feed order. Bob Peterson was working the counter that morning in his usual unhurried way. I had no idea how old he and Janet were, but she had mentioned one time that this was their retirement endeavor. They had both left their corporate finance jobs up north, moved here, and opened the store as a way to slow down. Running a business didn't seem like a relaxing retirement to me, but then again, I had never worked in finance. Bob's hair had already started receding considerably when they had opened the store, and he was nearly bald now. He was one of those guys who wore bald well, though, and thankfully he didn't feel the need to try to compensate with a combover. He was about my height and very squarely built.

"Mornin'," he said when it was finally my turn, without looking up.

He didn't have his usual wide grin, but I chalked that up to his being busy. I put my items on the counter and gave him my feed order. When he told me the total, I did a quick mental calculation and decided to put the balance on my tab, praying that I could pay it off at the end of the month.

"I'm so sorry, but we can't add anything on your account right now," he said quietly.

"Have I reached my limit?" I asked, panicking. I had thought I was a long way from reaching the allowed limit of a thousand dollars.

"Maybe this is best discussed some other time," he said, nodding to the people behind me.

"Bob, I've been shopping here for years, and unless I've really miscalculated, I still have plenty of credit," I said as quietly and calmly as I could manage.

He leaned over the counter so he could lower his voice.

"If you go to jail, who is going to pay your bill?"

I gasped before I could stop myself. My cheeks burned, and I knew that my fair skin was probably blazing red.

"I haven't been arrested for anything," I said, my voice shaky in spite of my best efforts to remain collected.

"Janet's cousin works at the sheriff's office, Mallory. We both know that it's just a matter of time."

I gasped and my pulse pounded in my ears.

"Well, Janet's cousin should mind their own business. In the meantime, unless you plan on altering your policy, I suggest you put my order on my account and let me be on my way."

He drew his mouth into a thin line, but he didn't argue further. I stood there, shaking, while he readied the receipt for me to sign. When I was finished, I hurried for the door and avoided looking at anyone as I went. I did notice on my way out that all of my flyers had been removed from the community bulletin board. I ran to my truck and slammed the door, barely able to breathe. I felt like I had run a marathon and there wasn't enough oxygen getting into my lungs. I nearly jumped out of my seat when the first bag of feed hit the bed of my truck. I looked in the rearview mirror and saw one of the warehouse workers loading my feed. I waved out the window to signal my thanks and pulled out of the parking lot as soon as I could.

Tears stung my eyes and threatened to escape as I pulled out onto Main Street. And that made me mad all over again, that my default reaction to just about every strong emotion was to cry. The repercussions had already begun, and I hadn't even been arrested. I managed to hold it together long enough to find a parking spot, and then I pulled over and grabbed a napkin out of my console and dabbed my eyes, determined not to give in and cry.

I sat up straighter and decided, with new resolve, to figure out as much as I could about Albert's murder. This was *my* home, and I wasn't going to let a criminal take that from me. When I had something substantial, I would take it to Grady.

And speaking of Grady . . .

I stoked the ember of anger that was burning through the self-pity until it was a raging fire. And I decided to rain that fire down on Grady's head. I jerked my truck into drive and made a beeline for the sheriff's office. I was getting out and slamming the door to my poor truck before I realized it was Saturday and Grady likely wouldn't be in the office. I did a quick once-over of the parking lot just to make sure, and I was glad I did. Grady's SUV was parked in its assigned spot.

I stalked up to the front doors and yanked them open. The deputy at the desk jumped and dropped his pen. He looked like he was barely out of high school and still had a good dose of acne riddling his chin.

"I need to talk to Sheriff Sullivan. Now."

"Do you have an appointment?"

"I am getting really tired of that question."

"It's okay. I'll see her," Grady said, and the deputy jumped again. I was beginning to wonder if this line of work was the best choice for him.

Grady gestured to his office, and I led the way. I squared my shoulders and took the seat he offered me across from his desk.

"What brings you here today? Should we wait for your attorney?"

"What brings me here today is your gossiping staff." I cleared my throat to keep my voice from shaking.

"What?"

"I just came from the feedstore, and Bob threatened to close my credit account because I might go to jail. He heard it from someone who works here. Janet's cousin." I may have been able to keep my voice from shaking, but my hands were another story. I was practically vibrating with anger.

Grady's eyebrows formed a V and his jaw visibly clenched.

"Where else should I worry that my name is getting dragged through the mud?"

"Nowhere if I have anything to say about it," he said, pushing himself back in the chair. "I can assure you if those rumors did come from this office, I will handle it."

"You know," I plowed on, "I really hoped to continue to have a good working relationship with law enforcement, given that a lot of my horses come to me from legal seizures, but my trust is eroding pretty rapidly."

"I hope that we can keep a good working relationship too. I will deal with any information leaks we might have in this office."

"Is it true then?" I asked.

"Is what true?"

"Bob said that it was just a matter of time before I was arrested."

"I can't talk to you about an open investigation. You know that. You were around enough lawyers to know that I can't share any of this with you. Just know that we will follow the evidence," he said with a heavy sigh.

"That's easy for you to say," I snapped.

"Nothing about this is easy." He pinched his eyes with his thumb and forefinger.

I felt a momentary pang of sympathy. I could imagine that he was under tremendous pressure to solve this case. We hadn't had a murder in our county in years, and then it had been a crime of passion committed in the heat of an argument over infidelity.

"I've asked the state police to assist in the investigation," he sighed again. He looked exhausted. "I don't want there to be any accusations of leniency since we have a shared history, and we've worked so closely on the animal cruelty cases. They'll be here Monday. And they may want to talk to you again."

"Leniency?" I crossed my arms. "If you think what you're doing to me could be seen as leniency, I guess I should be glad you aren't being hard on me."

I didn't know if bringing in outsiders was a good thing or not. I hoped that they would be more objective than Grady had been, but I was afraid they would be swayed by his tunnel vision.

He looked like he was about to say something else, but I cut him off. "Thank you for your time," I said and got up to leave.

"You're welcome here anytime, Mallory."

I nodded and hurried back out to my truck. My initial anger had faded, and I just felt shaky and emotional. All the things that I had been afraid would happen were slowly coming true, so it was imperative that I get things sorted out sooner rather than later. I pulled my truck out into the street and pointed it toward home. I was glad Banjo was with me. Stroking his soft fur and scratching his ears as I drove was just the comfort I needed.

Chapter Seven

I sent an email to my new lawyer as soon as I could after I unloaded the feed. I told him that the rumors were already flying and that the state police were coming on Monday. I knew Grady was right. They would want to talk to me in person. I definitely wanted my lawyer present for *that* interview. I hoped that my drama wasn't disrupting Andy's practice too much, but in my defense, I had only asked him for a recommendation.

My phone rang seconds after I put it down.

"Do you know for a fact the rumors came from the sheriff's office?" Andy didn't bother with a greeting.

"Yeah," I said, chewing my cuticle and then mentally scolding myself for the bad habit. "Bob told me his wife's cousin works at the sheriff's department. There's really nowhere else it could've come from." As much as I hated that Grady suspected me, I knew he wasn't one for gossip.

"I'll call Sheriff Sullivan. This is unacceptable."

"I already talked to him."

Andy paused for a beat.

"When?"

"I went straight there from the feedstore." I hesitated for a moment before adding, "I was really mad."

He sighed quietly. "I know you and the sheriff go way back, but you need to look out for your own interests, and right now that means not talking to anyone in law enforcement alone."

"I understand. I won't do it again," I said, feeling a bit sheepish.

We briefly discussed the probability that I would have to rehash everything with the state police and then ended the call.

I reluctantly dug through the dark recesses of my closet and found the garment bag that held the dress Lanie mentioned, the one I had worn to my daughter's graduation. It was really more of a summer style, but I doubted that anyone would pay attention to that. It was a short-sleeved chiffon dress with a fitted waistline that fell nicely to my calves. The pale gray-blue complemented my blonde hair and blue eyes. Lanie was right, it really did look good on me, and I was beyond thrilled when I pulled the zipper up and found that it still fit. It hugged in all the right places and hid all the right places. I turned to look at myself from every angle I could manage and ended up feeling pretty good about myself.

I wasn't sure when I had shaved my legs in recent history, so I decided to do that before the evening chores. My daily uniform consisted of old comfy jeans and a T-shirt, so I hadn't put forth the effort to shave in ages. I grabbed a peel-off mask from the medicine cabinet and slathered it on so it could dry while I shaved. I wasn't sure when I had exfoliated either. Maybe I should make more of a daily effort . . .

After I finished and washed the remnants of the mask off, I grabbed a banana and headed back out to the barn. Ashley waved from the loft window. I smiled as I thought about all the countless hours I had spent up there as a kid. When the weather wasn't suitable for riding or hiking the woods around our house, I would hide away in the barn loft and read or draw. I planned my whole life up there, and I was happy that it finally looked like the life my heart had always wanted.

The big bay was lazily grazing on the hill with the other geldings. River, a sorrel, had come to us after being abandoned, you guessed it, on the river. Some kayakers found him, scratched up and skinny, but otherwise fairly healthy. They called the sheriff's office and stayed with him until I came to get him. When no one came forth to claim him, the court awarded him to the rescue. He was one of the ones that I had hoped to use as a lesson horse. He was as calm as they come.

The oldest horse at the rescue was Stormy, named so by Ashley because he's gray. We didn't really know how old he was, but our vet estimated him somewhere in the neighborhood of thirty. He was shaggy and cranky and wonderful. He had been voluntarily surrendered to the rescue when his owner became too frail to care for him anymore, and I vowed that he would have as comfortable a life as he could for as long as possible.

Ace and Buck had come together, another neglect case. We were able to rehab Ace, a bay like Zeus, but Buck had remained lame. He did alright when left to pasture, but if he was ridden at all, he would limp for weeks. So he was our resident companion horse. Aptly named, Buck was a pale buckskin, what the old timers called a "buttermilk buckskin." Zeus seemed to be integrating easily into the herd.

I climbed the steps and poked my head into the loft.

"Looks pretty peaceful out there," I said.

"They squealed and acted a fool for about five minutes and then everyone settled down and started grazing," she shrugged.

"That's good," I said. "How's the paper coming along?"

She gave a little snort. "If I was even remotely interested, it would go a lot faster."

"Yeah, I can't say that I miss that about college." I smiled as I noticed Banjo was curled up at her feet. "I think he would just go home with you, if you'd let him."

"I'm a good substitute when you're not around." She reached down and rubbed his ears. He yawned and stretched.

"Come on up to the house if you want a snack. Lanie brought enough food for an army."

"I'll probably just pack up here before long. Mom texted a bit ago and we're going to the Mill River Steakhouse for my brother-in-law's birthday tonight."

"Oh, I'm jealous," I said. The Mill River Steakhouse was probably the best restaurant in the area.

"Don't be. I don't think even the food there is a fair trade-off for listening to Ian drone on and on and on about his latest gaming obsession." She rolled her eyes.

I laughed. "Well, if you change your mind, just come on in."

"Hey, I have a favor to ask," she said tentatively.

"What do you need?" It would be nice to help her out for a change.

"There's a commercial farming group, Agri-Dyne, that is trying to put in a large-scale hog farm on the mountain above Heritage Valley," she said, sounding as if she had rehearsed this spiel. "The ecological impact study indicated that it could have a significant negative effect on the area, but they have obtained the necessary permits anyway. I don't have to tell you how devastating it would be for Hillspring to lose Heritage Valley and all the tourism dollars it brings to the area. And perhaps even more importantly, there has been a sighting of a potential breeding pair of red-cockaded woodpeckers, which are critically endangered, in the pine forest below the proposed hog farm. I've drafted a petition to halt any further construction until we can get someone in from Fish and Game to investigate the sighting," she continued. "I would love to add your signature, if you're willing."

"Of course!" I said.

"Thank you! Would you be willing to talk to Lanie and Bill too? I have a pamphlet I've put together."

"I would be happy to." I took the pamphlet and looked it over. She'd done a nice job. It was very compelling while not demonizing the farmers.

*　*　*

I busied myself straightening up the house while I waited until time to feed again. Battling dust and dog hair was a constant struggle. I wasn't sure how Banjo wasn't bald at the rate he shed. It didn't take as long to finish the chores in the evening as it did when there were horses in the barn. Mucking out the stalls was always time-consuming. It only took a mild skirmish for the horses to figure out a new lineup at feeding time to accommodate Zeus. And for all his bluster that first day, he was settling in to be a very docile and easygoing guy. I could definitely see why Tanner wanted to claim him. I hoped it would work out for him to do just that.

I still had about an hour before I needed to get ready, so I curled up on the sofa with my laptop and uploaded some of the photos I hadn't had a chance to work on yet. I don't do much editing on my captures, just a crop or slight adjustment here and there. Mostly because I'm a complete amateur, and I lack the skills to do much editing. Banjo hopped up beside me, thoroughly washed my face, and curled up to sleep. I hoped dog slobber was as good a facial as my peel-off mask. I set an alarm on my phone so I could lose myself in the work without worrying about the time, and that's just what I did. I jumped like I'd been shot when the alarm went off.

* * *

By the time I had finished getting ready, my initial nerves and panic had completely subsided, and I was just looking forward to having dinner and the prospect of getting to know Braydon better. I did a final once-over in the full-length mirror and then sat at the kitchen table to wait, which was the safest place to ensure I didn't get covered in dog hair. I had just opened my book again when there was a knock at the door and Banjo barked his customary one bark, but a little louder than usual. He beat me to the door and sat staring at the doorknob.

I opened the door and Banjo started wagging. He's a great dog, but he loves everyone. As long as I had opened the door to reveal a human and not some sort of monster, he was convinced that we were safe, and his job was done. At that moment, I tended to agree as I stared up into Braydon's piercing blue eyes. He looked almost like he did in high school, tall and broad enough to fill up nearly the entire doorway and still lean and muscular. His hair looked effortlessly tousled, the sandy blond highlighted with streaks of platinum that looked so flattering that I wondered briefly if he had it professionally done. My own almost platinum blonde hid my gray really well, but nearly every-one else we'd gone to school with had some salt sneaking into the pepper, unless he had won that genetic lottery as well.

"You look stunning, Mallory," he said with a smile that made me weak in the knees.

"Thank you. So do you."

"I hope you don't mind a bit of a drive," he said as he took my arm and escorted me to his car. "I made reservations at a great restaurant in Fayetteville."

"I don't mind at all."

Like a gentleman, he opened the car door for me. He had brought Albert's sleek, black Cadillac Escalade again. I was used to tall vehicles that required climbing into, but I felt a bit awkward in the dress. If he noticed he didn't react.

"I hope you don't mind the SUV. These roads are beating up my BMW," he said as he got behind the wheel.

"Not at all."

"How long have you had the rescue now?" He made polite chitchat as he turned down my rocky drive.

"About two years. I had hoped to be better established by now, but I'm still working on ways to bring in some steady income."

"Oh yeah," he said, as we pulled out onto the paved county road. "Luis told me that you were planning to start giving lessons and that was what set Dad off the day he died."

"Braydon, I'm so sorry about that."

"Don't worry about it. Something was always setting him off. He was a miserable old man."

I wasn't sure how to respond to this blunt assessment of his dad. It was accurate, but it was unsettling to hear it coming from his son so soon after his death.

He must have noticed my expression, even in the dark car, because he added, "It's not that I didn't love Dad, but I don't have any illusions about him. He was difficult. That doesn't mean he deserved what happened, of course, but I know he was hard to get along with."

"Does your Aunt Mae live close by?" I asked, trying to gently change the subject a bit. And I was curious. I wasn't aware of any of Albert's family, but we weren't exactly traveling in the same social circles either.

"No, she lives in Illinois. She's flying in Tuesday for the remembrance," he scoffed. "What a stupid name. It's a funeral without a body, which I'm sure we will just have to repeat when the crime lab releases it, or do a graveside service at the very least. I wish she would've just let us all wait."

"That has to be difficult," I said. "Was she his only sibling?"

"She's the last one left. Uncle Del was the oldest. He died two years ago. Dad was the middle child, and then Aunt Mae was the youngest. Dad always said she was spoiled rotten, being a girl and the baby to boot."

"What have you been doing all these years?" I hoped at this point to change the subject completely. I wanted him to be able to grieve, but hearing intimate details of their family dynamics felt unnecessarily invasive given that I didn't know him that well yet. "I heard you were doing something in finance, but I'm afraid I don't know much about that field."

"I've bounced around a bit. I get bored easily, and when a job becomes too routine, I feel it's time to move on to something else. Right now, I'm working for a small venture capital firm. Our current project centers around securing funds for a stem cell startup. It's really exciting."

I decided not to tell him what I thought of most of the stem cell companies, which was that they were barely better than snake oil. They promised a cure for everything from sprained ankles to autism while spouting junk science and preying on the desperate. But there was some legitimate research being done too, and I hoped his startup was one of those.

He spent the entire rest of the hour drive describing the daily details and subtle nuances of venture capitalism. I tried to pepper the conversation with nods and sounds of acknowledgment at appropriate intervals, but honestly, I'm not sure if he even noticed. I was relieved when we finally pulled into the parking lot of Jordan's. I had only eaten there once, for an anniversary dinner with Ethan, but it had been fantastic, and I was looking forward to something upscale and fancy for a change.

Braydon opened the car door for me and offered me his arm on the way in. He smelled amazing. I couldn't place the cologne, but it was earthy in the best way. We had a great table next to the floor-to-ceiling window that overlooked Clear Creek. It was dark outside, but the creek was illuminated by floodlights mounted on the side of the building and the rope lights in the trees. It was almost ethereal.

Braydon ordered a bottle of the house white after consulting me, and we both opened our menus. I was starving and would have gleefully ordered one of everything on the menu. I finally narrowed it to the quail and wild rice. Our server, a very quiet and polite young man, waited patiently while I agonized over what I wanted to order.

"It's nice to dine with someone who isn't afraid to eat," he said after our server left.

"Um, thanks?" I laughed.

"I just mean that a lot of women just order a salad."

"I've never been afraid to eat." I shrugged.

"Before I forget to ask, do you know that woman who has the organic farm down the road from Dad's?"

"Not well," I admitted. "But she's threatening to take me to court over runoff from the rescue." I inwardly celebrated that he had taken care of how to bring up Heather Rogers.

"Yeah, she sent a letter to the farm too. She had to have put it in the mailbox herself because it didn't have postage."

"That sounds about right."

"Is she a nutjob? Could she have, you know?" He leaned closer across the table even though there was no one seated close enough to hear. "Killed Dad?"

"I really don't know. And I don't want to speculate. I've already felt what it's like to be on the receiving end of that."

"I'm so sorry about that." He reached across the table and put his hand on mine. "Do you think it would help if I made a statement? You know, telling them that I don't believe you had anything to do with it."

"I wouldn't ask you to do that. Besides, I doubt if it would make any difference. Grady has set his sights on me, and I don't think he's even considering anyone else."

"I'll talk to him anyway. It can't hurt."

I smiled. It was touching that he was willing to do that, especially given the circumstances.

Our conversation meandered about a bit, covering why I had left St. Louis and briefly touched on my daughter and finally landed on everything Braydon had done since high school. His monologue, and it really was a one-man show, carried us all the way through the meal. My eyes were starting to glaze over when I finally excused myself to the restroom for a breather. As I reached into my bag to retrieve my lipstick, I noticed my phone had several unread texts. I swiped it open and found a series of messages from Lanie and one from Ginny. Lanie wanted details, and Ginny was just checking in. I responded to both of them and took a deep breath.

I was more than a little disappointed in the evening. Braydon was still as self-absorbed as he had seemed to be in school, and I couldn't kindle any sort of connection with him, in spite of his devastating good looks. I had always been on the periphery of his group in high school, so I didn't know him intimately then. I dreaded the long trip home, and I made a mental note to keep all future first dates closer to home, or better yet, meet at the restaurant in separate cars.

I went back out to the table and found Braydon on the phone. He didn't end the call as I sat down but did hold up one finger to signal that he would be a minute. After a few seconds of listening to him talk about accounts and acquisitions, I decided that it was a work call. It must be hard to be "on duty" 24/7, as it was pushing 10 PM. I quit paying attention as I perused the dessert menu. Again, I could have ordered one of everything they offered, even though I was pretty full from the main course. It just all looked *so good*. I chose the chocolate cake because you can never go wrong with chocolate cake. Braydon pointed to something on the menu and the server nodded.

I waited for him to get off the phone for several more minutes, finally gave up, and dragged my phone out of my bag. I occupied myself scrolling through social media until our desserts arrived. I wasted no time devouring my cake, which was so good it was ridiculous. I was ready to just get up and walk out when Braydon finally ended the call.

"Sorry about that," he said as the server brought the bill.

"No problem," I lied. "What's my share?"

"It's on me." He flashed that dazzling smile again. It was less effective this time.

"I appreciate that, but I don't mind covering my own meal."

"Call me old fashioned," he said as he tucked his card into the folder and waved our server over.

"Well, thank you. It was a lovely meal."

Back in the car, Braydon picked up right where he had left off in the restaurant, outlining for me why he had left his fiancée in Thailand when he found that he couldn't embrace her culture as fully as he thought he could. I think he took my polite nods and grunts as invitations to continue, so he did, on and on *and on*. About fifteen minutes from the house, he finally ran out of steam.

"I feel like I've talked all night," he said. "You're just so easy to talk to, and the last few days have been so stressful."

And I suddenly felt intensely guilty for my unkind thoughts that evening. I had been judgmental and impatient with a man who had just lost his father under horrible circumstances.

"If there's anything I can do to help, I'm just next door." I had no idea what that would be, but I felt terrible for being so judgmental all night.

"Thank you," he said and reached over to let his hand rest on mine. I'm not ashamed to admit that I was conflicted about that. I *wanted* to be attracted to him—I mean, the man looked like he had walked out of *GQ* magazine, but I just wasn't feeling it. But I also didn't want to kick a man when he was down, so I planned to be as nice as possible without leading him on.

At my house, he opened the car door for me again and walked me to my porch. I lingered on the steps, trying to figure out how to avoid inviting him in. He took my hand and kissed the back. That was probably the most endearing thing he had done all night.

"Good night, Mallory."

"Good night."

"Come over tomorrow," he said, walking back to his car. "I'd love to get your opinion on a couple of the broodmares. I'm going to downsize a bit and I want to keep the best stock. I'm a little rusty on everything equestrian."

"Are you sure that's a good idea? I mean, Luis isn't exactly my biggest fan right now."

"I'm not worried about what the hired help thinks of you," he said, laughing.

"Tomorrow then," I said coolly. "I'll be there around eleven."

He waved as he drove away. I took off my heels as I climbed the last three steps. Banjo barked half-heartedly from behind the front door.

Chapter Eight

I paused in the late morning sun as I got out of my truck in the Cunningham driveway. In true Arkansas fashion, the day had started out foggy and chilly and had warmed as the day wore on. I closed my eyes for a moment and let the sun warm me.

"Good morning," Braydon said behind me.

I turned to face him. He was wearing jeans that accentuated everything in all the right places and a denim shirt that hugged everything else. He looked like the cover model for a western romance novel. I hadn't dressed up, but I did brush my hair.

"I had Luis bring the mares to the barn corral so we could take a close look at them, and I pulled their papers this morning."

"Great. Let's get started then."

I enjoyed sorting the mares more than I had enjoyed the dinner the previous evening. Braydon was attentive and seemed genuinely interested when I pointed out when one pedigree was better than another and when I showed him which mares had the best conformation. And getting to interact with the horses was a delight as well. Luis and his team took great pride in gentling and training them, and they did an excellent job.

Luis had taken one look at me and made himself busy as far away from me as he could get. I hated feeling guilty, especially since I hadn't done anything to warrant the guilt. I knew that Luis thought I was involved, though, and I was afraid that if I tried to talk to him it would just make it worse.

"Come up to the house and have some lunch," Braydon said as we finished evaluating the last of the mares.

"That sounds great," I said. After he mentioned it, I realized I was starving.

*   *   *

We walked up to the house together. I had never been inside the main house before I brought Kathleen the soup and cinnamon rolls. I had been to the barn a couple of times. First, when I moved back home and had tried to be friendly with my closest neighbor. And then again when one of our rescues had escaped and found his way to Albert's herd.

The house could only be described as a mansion, and that was how I usually referred to it. I don't know architecture, but I know it was massive and looked like it belonged on a plantation in Georgia rather than nestled in the Ozarks. Inside, it looked more like a museum than someone's home. It felt cold and impersonal, which I guess suited old Albert just fine. I wondered if it had felt different when Marion had been alive, although Kathleen hadn't left any feminine touches that I could see. I had seen Marion from afar many times but only met her once briefly, at our high school graduation. She always seemed vibrant and full of life, with an easy, warm smile and an infectious laugh. I could see a lot of her in Braydon. I suspected that she doted on him, him being the only child and all.

"If you don't mind, we can take lunch out in the gazebo. It's such a lovely day."

"Perfect," I said.

"Dad's study is through there." He pointed to a large carved door to our right. "Would you put the papers back in the folder on his desk? I need to attend to something for just a moment."

"Sure," I said. I broke away and pushed the huge door open.

Albert's study looked exactly as I would have imagined it. The heavy curtains were drawn. It was dark, save for one desk lamp glowing in the dim room. There was a fireplace behind the desk, but there was no fire burning at the moment. It was flanked by two taxidermied deer trophies, each at least an eight pointer. A taxidermied bobcat crouched on the fireplace mantel. I had no problem with hunting, I'm a total carnivore, but I hate taxidermy. It always gives me the creeps, dead things frozen in time with their glassy eyes.

I hurried over to Albert's desk and looked for a folder for the horse papers. It wasn't terribly cluttered, but I didn't see a folder right away. Finally, I leaned over and found it hiding under a thick manila envelope, its tab labeled "Mares." I pulled it out from under the envelope, shoved the papers inside, and carefully placed the heavy manila envelope, with the words "Township Papers" handwritten across the front, back on top of the "Mares" folder the way I found it.

I couldn't help but look for evidence of Kathleen in the house, but no matter where I looked, I couldn't see her influence. Marion's photos were still on the walls in the study and in the main hall. There were no subtle touches that I could attribute to Kathleen anywhere. I wondered how she fit into his life. I had a fleeting urge to open the desk drawers and see if I could find anything that might be a motive for murder, but I quickly dismissed it. The last thing I wanted at the moment was for Braydon to find me rifling through his dad's study. But if there was something lying out in plain sight, that would be a different thing altogether. I scanned all of the visible documents quickly, but there was nothing out of the ordinary, just a bunch of receipts for the farm, a couple of American Quarter Horse Journals, and a list of staff names and phone numbers. No one was crossed off. Maybe that meant no one had been sacked recently. I made a mental note to try and find out if that was the case.

I hurried back out into the hall, eager to get away from all the glass eyes looking at me and found Braydon already there. He led me through the house and out the back door. I had no idea that the meticulously manicured lawn extended into the old-growth forest behind the house. The gazebo was at the end of a native stone path, between two more fountains, each smaller than the one in the front. Koi swam lazily in each of them. I briefly wondered how they kept the raccoons out of the fountains, but maybe even the raccoons felt so out of place here that they avoided it.

The staff had arranged the meal on a small table that had been outfitted with a stark white tablecloth and a black runner. Our places were set, and a beautiful salad waited at each place for us. Clearly, he had planned this beyond a spur of the moment invitation. I was both impressed and annoyed. He hadn't doubted for a minute that I would accept his offer.

He pulled my chair out for me.

"I had a craving for good old chicken fried steak. I hope you don't mind."

"You can't go wrong with comfort food." I picked at my salad. It was covered in some sort of vinegar and oil dressing that I couldn't place, and it tasted dreadful. Thankfully, I didn't have to wait long for the main course, which was served by no fewer than three people in uniform. I wondered if Albert had always employed so many people or if Braydon had beefed up the staff in anticipation of his family coming in for the services. If my financial situation didn't improve soon, maybe he would think about hiring me.

I devoured the steak and coleslaw. Braydon talked about where he might sell the mares and when he was thinking about evaluating the geldings and stallions. He said he wanted my help with that too. I grunted and nodded in between bites. I was beginning to realize that Braydon didn't require much in the way of participation during our "conversations."

"That was fantastic. I can see why you would have a craving. Is that a family recipe?"

"As a matter of fact, yes. It was my grandmother's recipe. She was a great cook, especially traditional southern food. Did you leave room for dessert?" he asked as he held up the brass bell to summon the staff.

"I'm afraid not." I held up my hands in surrender.

He laughed. "Okay then."

I wanted to savor the moment, but I figured it was as good a time as any to ask what I needed to ask. "I'm so sorry to pry, but what do you know about Kathleen?"

He laughed as if I had just said something absurd. "What do you want to know?"

"Did you know she was here the night your father was killed?"

"I'm sure she was. She was like a leech he just couldn't shake. It wasn't like most people imagined, though—she had her own room."

"They weren't close?"

"I guess they were as close as you can get to a gold digger. Oh, she doesn't look like your typical gold digger, but clothes don't equal character. I don't think anyone in my family could stand to be around her. I'll never understand why Dad didn't get rid of her. I guess he could have been lonely, and he wasn't the easiest person to get along with. The fact that she hung around must've been enough for him."

"Do you think he wrote her into the will or anything like that? Made her the beneficiary of a life insurance policy?"

He laughed again. This bout shook his shoulders with the effort.

"Um, no," he said when he finally recovered. "She may have had a motive to kill him, but it wasn't because he was leaving her anything."

"I'm sorry to pry. I just can't help being curious," I said, half in honesty. My curiosity had always been one of my more annoying traits. I just didn't share the part where I was trying to clear myself of a murder charge.

A commotion toward the back porch caught our attention. Angry voices shouted words I couldn't make out, and just then a black and white blur plowed through one of the fountains and barreled toward us.

"Cooper!" Braydon shouted as the bird dog crashed into his legs under the table. "I'm so sorry. He keeps escaping from the kennel. We still aren't sure how he's doing it."

The dog couldn't be still. He circled and scooted and rubbed against our legs, occasionally looking up at us with big brown eyes and a goofy grin, tongue lolling out the side of his mouth. I can never resist a dog, so I bent down and rubbed him as he circled again. One of the uniformed staff, a young man with a crew cut, jogged over and took the dog by the collar.

"I'll put him back in the kennel," he said, gently dragging the dog away. I could tell by the way he scratched the dog's ears as they went that he had a fondness for him.

"Thank you for all of this, but I'd better head back home. I have a lot of paperwork to catch up on."

"No problem." He flashed that smile again. "I have a lot of paperwork to wade through myself. Dad was fairly organized, but I don't think he ever threw anything away."

"Oof," I said. "That's tough. I remember how awful it was to sort through Mom's stuff when she died. I'm sorry."

"Thank you," he said quietly.

He walked me back through the house and back to my truck.

"You know you're welcome here any time. We should go riding before I have to get back to the city."

"I'd like that. I don't get a chance very often to just enjoy the horses."

He leaned toward me and I got the impression he was about to kiss me—that is, until the dog nearly knocked him off his feet. I was thankful for the interruption. There was a bit more spark today than there had been on our first date, but I wasn't ready to take it further just yet.

"Cooper!" he yelled, bracing himself against my truck.

The dog tucked his tail and tore around my truck as fast as he could in a wide circle and then came to rest at my feet. He wagged his cropped tail so fast I was afraid he might take flight, like a helicopter. Forgetting any manners he might have had, if he had any at all, he reared up and planted his feet in my belly. That's when I noticed what he had in his mouth: a leather glove dyed in rainbow colors.

* * *

"How do you know it belongs to her?" Braydon turned the soggy glove over in his hands. "Is this a unique pattern or something?"

"I saw the mate at the farmers market yesterday. I watched her take it off and I've never seen gloves like that before."

He laid it down on the hood of my truck.

"She said that your dad wouldn't see her. Can you ask the staff if anyone has seen her on the property?" I picked up the glove and turned it over in my hands. "She lied about being here. What else did she lie about?"

One side of the glove was faded as if it had been lying out in the sun. I wondered how long it would have to lie out in the elements to fade and stiffen like that. Whatever the answer to that question, Heather had lied about being on Albert's property.

"She lost the glove sometime before I saw her at the farmers market since she had only had one of the rainbow gloves there," I said and put the glove back down on the hood of my truck.

"I'll ask the staff right away if anyone's seen her poking around. Do you think we should take this information to the police?"

"It might be better coming from you."

He nodded. "You may be right about that. I'll give—Grant was his name?—a call later."

"Grady," I corrected. We had all gone to school together, but they didn't exactly run in the same circles. But then I didn't either. "Will you let me know what they say?"

"Of course." He reached over and rubbed my shoulder. "It's going to be okay."

"I hope you're right."

He picked the glove up again as I climbed into my truck. He waved as I pulled through the circle drive. I waved back, watching the dog bounce along beside him, trying to get hold of the glove again.

My thoughts raced. Could Heather Rogers really be capable of murdering Albert? I had a hard time believing she was desperate enough to commit murder, but don't people always say that? People are always surprised when a murderer is found in their midst.

Banjo met me at the door carrying one of my favorite tennis shoes. Luckily, he hadn't chewed it up yet. It was soggy, but intact. I didn't even have to scold him, he looked plenty guilty when I took the shoe away.

"Yeah, you know you're not supposed to have this," I said.

I pulled my phone out of my pocket and checked the time. It was well after 2 PM. My lunch with Braydon had taken longer than I had thought. Lanie would be out of church by now.

Hey, are you busy? I have news.

I knew she would respond when she had time. In the meantime, I went to update this new development on the investigation board. I wished I had taken a photo of the glove. That was a stupid move on my part. I told myself if anything else came up, I would do better next time. I did thoroughly beat myself up about it, though.

I had gone to the kitchen to put a pot of coffee on while I waited for Lanie to respond when I heard gravel crunching in the driveway. I heard it before my crack watchdog, and it was only after I had gone to the front window to see who it was that he let out a "bork" with a question mark at the end. I didn't recognize the car. It was a black sedan with tinted windows, angled just enough that I couldn't see the driver through the windshield. I reached over and locked the door with my right hand while I pulled my phone out my pocket with my left. I dialed 9-1-1 and hovered over the green phone icon.

The driver opened the door and got out. When he turned toward the house and took off his sunglasses, I let out the breath I had been holding. My ex-husband looked toward the house and ran his fingers through his salt-and-pepper hair. He was wearing a white button-down shirt and jeans and looked like he could double for James Bond—the Daniel Craig version, not Sean Connery. He had definitely been working out, and I dare say had maybe never looked better, which instantly made me angry. Apparently the new flame had inspired him to take excellent care of himself in a way that I never had.

I shoved the phone back in my pocket and opened the door.

"What are you doing here?"

"Hello to you too." He gave me the crooked grin that makes the corners of his eyes wrinkle in the most delicious way. We may have divorced, but there was no denying how good-looking he was.

Banjo ripped past me and ran to meet him, his entire butt wagging with excitement.

"Traitor," I said, crossing my arms across my chest.

"What a warm welcome." Ethan bent to scratch Banjo's ears.

"I'll ask again, what are you doing here?"

"Well, you wouldn't respond to my messages or texts, so I got worried that you'd been arrested."

"What messages and texts?"

"I called and texted you nearly all day yesterday. The last thing I received was that you had retained a lawyer. For all I knew, they hauled you off in handcuffs right after that."

I pulled out my phone and realized I had hastily blocked his number after my meeting at the sheriff's office. I had honestly meant to unblock him that evening.

"I can't believe you drove all this way," I said, looking from my phone to Ethan. It's a five-hour drive in good traffic.

"I was worried about you, Mal." He climbed a few steps and stood just below me. "Why didn't you answer?"

"I don't know. It was really childish, but I was angry that you left me hanging and overwhelmed after talking to the sheriff and I just didn't want to deal with you, so I blocked your number."

"Ouch."

"I meant to unblock it; I really did. But I got busy and it slipped my mind," I said, looking down into pale blue eyes that had seen me at my best, my worst, and everything in between. "I feel terrible now that you've come all this way. I'll bet your girlfriend isn't very happy about this. What was her name? Diane?"

"I haven't seen Diane in a few months now."

"Well, I'm sure whoever you're seeing probably isn't thrilled," I said, wishing I would shut up.

"I'm not seeing anyone, Mal," he sighed. "Can I at least come in for a little while?"

"I don't mean to seem ungrateful, but you've just shown up out of the blue."

"In my defense, I *have* been trying to get hold of you for two days, and under the present circumstances, it didn't seem like a good idea to send law enforcement for a wellness check. I didn't want to worry Ginny, and Lanie hung up on me."

I took a step back and pulled the front door open.

"Come on in," I said. "I just put on a pot of coffee."

He walked in and took a long look around.

"It's weird being here without your parents. I like how you've made it your own, though."

"Thanks. And yes, it is. I miss Mom every day. Dad still visits a lot."

"How is Jasper?"

"He's doing okay," I said, hoping I was right. "He's on a cruise. I haven't told him about any of this. I was afraid he would cut his trip short, and this is the first vacation he's had since before Mom died."

"He probably would," Ethan said with his back to me. "He was always so fiercely protective of you."

I closed the door to the bedroom where I had put up the investigation board. It wasn't that I was embarrassed by my amateur sleuthing, I just didn't want to get into a discussion about it with Ethan, not just yet. I went to the kitchen to pour him a cup of coffee and found that he had helped himself.

"Oh, sorry. I guess old habits die hard," he said. He must've noticed the look on my face.

"Look, I do appreciate that you have come all this way just to check on me, but I'm okay. And I'm not your responsibility anymore."

He sat down heavily at the table and let out a big sigh.

"You weren't ever my *responsibility*. I'm here because I give a shit." He rubbed his eyes.

I leaned back against the doorframe and tried to figure out why I was so mad at him. Was I even mad at him, or was he just handy at the moment?

"I'm sorry," I said quietly.

"Are you okay?" He looked up at me, his brow furrowed into a V.

"Yes. No." I sat down across from him. "Maybe."

"Look," he leaned on his elbows. "I've cleared out my appointments for the next few days. Things were slow anyway. I can stay and help you get this sorted out."

"Why would you do that?"

"I don't remember you being this paranoid." He grinned again. "You're the mother of my child. At one time, I couldn't imagine spending the rest of my life with anyone else. I'm worried about you, and I can help. That's all."

"I have a lawyer."

"Two lawyers are always better than one."

"You know this can't be sorted out in a few days. The autopsy report could take weeks."

"Are you going to let me help you or not?"

"Don't make me regret this," I said, putting on my best skeptical face. "But I guess so."

"Then let's get started. I'll get my laptop out of the car."

Chapter Nine

"Good work," Ethan said. He had his arms crossed as he stood evaluating my investigation board. After trying to recount everything verbally, I decided it would be easier to just show him.

"It's not. It's just a copy of what we used to do in the office. I don't know what I'm doing."

"You know that isn't true. You've always had great instincts." He leaned closer to look at my notes on the wall. "Do you have a suspect yet?"

"I'm trying to keep an open mind, but at the moment, I'm leaning toward either Kathleen Clark or Heather Rogers."

I spent most of the next hour telling him everything I had found out up to that point, ending with Braydon's dog bringing me the glove just that afternoon.

"You're dating Braydon Cunningham?"

"I think you're focusing on the wrong part of this story."

"I'm focusing on *exactly* the right part of the story." His mouth was drawn into a thin line. I couldn't tell if he was being serious or not.

"How many women have you dated since we divorced?"

"Okay, back to the glove. You're sure it was the mate to the one you saw at the farmers market?"

"Yeah, I'm sure. It's a pretty unique pair of gloves."

"That's our best lead so far." He rubbed the stubble on his chin.

"Do you think so? I mean, I was skeptical at first, but Kathleen had the best opportunity, and as far as I know, she has no alibi whatsoever beyond her claim to have gone to bed with a migraine."

"But according to your notes," he pointed to the wall, "Heather has a stronger motive."

"Just because I haven't uncovered a motive yet doesn't mean she doesn't have one." I pointed to my note about the rainbow glove. "I'm going to talk to Heather again tomorrow. I want to see if she continues to deny ever being on Albert's property and how she acts when I confront her with it."

"It would've helped to have the glove or a photo of it, at least."

"Yes, I'm aware I screwed up."

"Do you think you could get it back from your boyfriend?"

"Okay, let's get this out of the way right now. He's not my boyfriend. I went on *one* date with him."

"I'm just teasing you," he said. "It's okay for you to have a boyfriend."

"I don't think this is a good idea. I don't know how we can work this closely together given our history."

"I'll stop. Clear boundaries, and personal life is off limits," he said, drawing an imaginary line with the toe of his sneaker.

I stared at him for a minute, trying to decide if we could adhere to boundaries. We had so much shared history, so many years together that it felt odd putting limits on our interaction. It had been much easier to just sever the ties, only coming together when we had to, like signing checks for Ginny's college tuition or selling our old house.

"I'll text him and find out," I said. The truth was, I *wanted* to work with Ethan. I pushed thoughts about *why* I wanted to work with him aside. I didn't want to look too hard at my motivations just then. I pulled out my phone and sent the text to Braydon. After deciding that he wasn't going to respond right away, I put the phone back in my pocket.

"Why don't you show me what you've done here? It looks like you've done a ton of work on the place."

"You want to see the rescue?"

"Sure. Why not?"

"You just never seemed interested in it when I talked about it, that's all."

"I was," he said, looking at his shoes. "I just didn't want to leave everything I'd worked for to do it."

"I know. Let's not rehash everything that led to our divorce." I turned and left the room. "Follow me."

I took him to the barn first, but it only took a few minutes for the real tour guide to take over. Biscuit loved him instantly and insisted on getting in the middle of everything we tried to do. Ethan was patient with him, enduring the constant nudges for attention. He escorted us as I introduced Ethan to all of my current residents and told him about the others that had passed through, either back to reformed owners or adopted into new homes.

"You've really put a lot of work into this," he said, absently patting Biscuit's shoulder.

"It may all have been for nothing," I said and leaned against the barn door.

"Why do you say that?"

"Rumors are already starting to fly," I sighed. "The feedstore owner didn't want me to charge my order because he's afraid the bill won't get paid if I go to jail. And he took down my flyers advertising riding lessons, which was a last-ditch effort to get some regular money coming in."

"I would be happy to make a donation."

"Oh no," I said, shaking my head. "I couldn't accept money from you."

"Why not?"

"It's not appropriate. It's bad enough that you're helping me with this mess. I can't take money from you too."

"Bad enough, huh?"

"That sounded worse than I meant it to."

"I should find a hotel," he said, abruptly turning back toward the house. Biscuit followed him.

"You could sleep on the sofa." I followed him, just behind the insistent donkey.

"We should keep some boundaries. I'll just grab my laptop and head into town."

I fastened the gate behind him and turned to argue, but he was already up the steps and pulling the door open. I knew I had hurt his feelings and I felt awful about it, but I told myself that maybe it was for the best. Maybe those sore feelings would help keep us at arm's length. The last thing either of us needed was to fall back into old habits because of a stressful situation.

I stood awkwardly by his car and waited for him to come back out. He seemed to be taking a long time, and I had just about decided to go in after him when he reemerged onto the porch. He was still wearing a frown and clenching his jaw.

"Ethan, I didn't mean to be hurtful," I said as he opened the back door and tossed his computer inside.

"You weren't," he said. "I was overstepping. You were right to draw a line."

"This is weird territory. It was easier when we were hours apart. I'm bound to make mistakes, but I do hope we can find a way to navigate this. I want to be friends," I said, holding onto the driver's side door. All of my previous hostility melted away.

"Me too." He folded himself into the low car. "I'll see if I can meet with your attorney tomorrow. Let me know what Heather Rogers has to say."

I nodded. "Sure thing."

*   *   *

I slapped the snooze button on my alarm for the second time Monday morning and finally decided to get up. I checked my phone again, and Braydon had never responded to my text. I hoped I had entered his number correctly into my phone. I hurried through a cup of coffee and the morning chores so I could get to Heather's as soon as possible.

I was closing the paddock gate when Tanner pulled in beside my truck.

"I wasn't expecting you today," I said as he shut the door and frowned at the yellow paint still marring the shiny black behind each wheel on the driver's side. "Did you come to work with Zeus?"

"I thought I might. Where are you going?" He gestured to my keys.

"I'm just going to run an errand." I shrugged and tried to look innocent. I have no poker face whatsoever.

"You're still investigating, aren't you?"

"Not much." I shrugged again.

"I'll go with you," he said, and crossed his arms.

"You don't even know where I'm going." I hurried around him and headed for my truck. "Besides, you don't need to get mixed up in this any more than you already are."

He beat me to my own truck and hopped into the passenger seat.

"Tanner! You *cannot* go with me!"

"Boss," he grinned, "I respect you more than most people, but you're not big enough to drag me out of this truck."

I considered that for a moment, hands on my hips, trying not to melt at the compliment and focus instead on the display of reckless stubbornness.

"Tanner, I am not going to put you in harm's way."

"Then you better just stay put, if it's all that dangerous." He buckled his seat belt. "Besides, there's safety in numbers. You're better off with me along than you would be going off alone."

Dang it. He had a point.

Tanner rode in silent satisfaction at having won that little battle of wills. I had never been to Heather's farm even though we had been neighbors for years now. To be fair, she had never been to mine either. Her drive was a windy, one-lane path that meandered through old-growth oaks and hickories, their limbs hanging over the road in a delightful canopy. I had gone maybe a quarter mile down the lane when it opened up into rolling hills, cleared and plowed. The field to my left was planted in corn and what looked like some sort of squash around the perimeter. The field to my right was bare. The dirt was dark and fertile, but had not been planted, or had been recently harvested, I didn't know which.

Her house sat on a knoll overlooking White Oak Creek, the same one I had been accused of polluting. Across the driveway was an old barn that had been restored to its former glory, painted red with white trim. The field behind her house was even more impressive than the cornfield on the way in, with row after meticulous row of assorted vegetables. It was just as beautiful as the photos at her booth made it seem. I thought to myself that she surely couldn't tend to all of this by herself, but I didn't see anyone in the fields and there weren't extra cars in the driveway. I pulled in beside a white Chevy pickup with "Heather's Happy Organics" emblazoned on the side.

"Wait here," I said as I turned off the ignition. Tanner nodded.

As I got out and prepared myself to go knock on the door, I heard a loud click followed by an unmistakable sound behind me, from the direction of the barn. If you've ever heard a pump-action shotgun before, there's no doubt in your mind when someone chambers a round. And sure enough, I turned and looked right down the barrel of one. I immediately put my hands up in front of me.

"Whoa!" I said, backing away. "You can put that up. I just want to talk to you."

"I'm calling the police," she said, still holding the shotgun with one hand and pulling out her phone with the other.

"Ma'am," Tanner said calmly and evenly as he opened the door, "please put that shotgun away."

"Tanner, get back in the truck," I said without taking my eyes off Heather. I was dumbfounded. I didn't expect her to be excited to see me, but I didn't expect this either. "I'll leave." I tried to back slowly to my truck.

"You're going to stay put until the police come and cart you off to jail where you belong," she hissed.

"In my defense, you do advertise your farm as open to the public." That got her attention. She looked up from her phone. "I'm not trespassing," I continued. "I just came to talk to you."

"After what you did last night, you have the nerve to come here and claim you want to talk?"

"What about last night? I didn't do anything last night."

She leveled the barrel at me again. I've never been afraid of guns. My dad was an avid hunter and I love a good skeet shoot, but I had never been at the business end of a weapon before, and I did not like it one bit.

"That's rich." Her lips curled into a snarl. "You, standing there denying it."

"Heather, I have no idea what you're talking about. Please believe me!" I didn't like the undignified desperate pleading in my voice, but it's hard to remain composed when you think you're about to get filled full of buckshot.

"Miss Rogers," Tanner said quietly, "please lower the gun."

I shot him a scathing Mom look, and Heather ignored him as if he wasn't even there. She watched me for a moment and then gestured with the barrel of the shotgun.

"Over there. You expect me to believe that wasn't you?" I could see now that her eyes were brimming with tears. "Or maybe you sent him!" She jerked the barrel in Tanner's direction for just a second, and I gasped before I could stop myself.

"*Tanner, get in the truck!*" I hissed between gritted teeth. This time he listened to me.

When I didn't look away from her, she took a step forward and pointed again. "Look!"

I followed her gaze to the garden beside her house, or rather what *used* to be the garden beside her house. I couldn't tell what any of the plants should have been. Everything had been hacked to bits. I couldn't imagine what could have made a mess like that. A lawnmower would have woken her. A machete, maybe?

"Heather, I didn't do that. I wouldn't do that." I shook my head and continued to hold up my hands.

"Those were my mama's heirloom seeds. I hadn't harvested the seeds for this year yet and now they're all gone. You have no idea what you've taken from me."

"I'm so sorry," I pleaded. "I don't know who would have done this, but it wasn't me."

"Just get out of here," she said, tears welling in her eyes. "And I swear to God, if I ever catch you here again, I won't hesitate to protect my property."

I took the opportunity and jumped into my truck while I could. I tried to keep from slinging gravel at her as I turned around to leave, but it took everything I had to keep from tearing out of there like a madwoman. I was back out on the paved road before I realized I was shaking like a leaf. I found one of the few wide patches of shoulder and pulled over. I took a few deep breaths to steady myself.

"That was crazy," Tanner said once we'd stopped. "I couldn't call the police. I left my stupid phone in my truck, and I don't know your passcode."

"You're not going with me anymore," I said shakily. "This is too dangerous." I shut my eyes and tried not to think of all the ways that situation could have gone horribly wrong.

"Okay, Boss," he said quietly.

I opened my eyes and jerked the truck into drive. It would suit me just fine if I never looked down the barrel of a loaded gun again in my lifetime. Once was plenty.

* * *

Back at the house, I managed to calm myself down with a good dose of wagging dog and donkey snuzzles after Tanner left to get a load of hay for the rescue. I assured him that I appreciated his intentions, but I couldn't put him in danger like that again. I leaned on the wooden fence, scratching Biscuit's perpetually itchy jaw and behind his big floppy ears and wondered how my life had gotten so complicated in a week's time. Complications were more easily put into perspective when you're standing beside a 1,200-pound animal. I left Biscuit nibbling at a flake of alfalfa hay and climbed the hill behind the barn where Zeus was grazing with River and Stormy. He raised his head and watched me warily but showed no signs that he was going to run me over again. He had such big, kind eyes. I patted his neck and moved over to River. I didn't need to get overly attached to Zeus, and I could tell it would be easy to do. I wanted Tanner to be able to adopt him when the time came.

River didn't abandon his efforts to strip the hillside of every trace of edible greenery. He was a deep red sorrel with flaxen mane and tail, a striking contrast. He was a decent size at fifteen hands. A "hand" was a measurement that originated in ancient Egypt and had come to mean four inches. So, in River's case, fifteen hands meant five feet tall at the wither, which is the spot where a horse's neck joins the back. This is also a spot that tends to be particularly itchy on most horses. I dug my nails into his tough hide and scratched. He decided that the scratches felt better than his quest for grass and raised his head, lower lip flopping in complete satisfaction. I buried my face in his neck and mane, inhaling deeply that primal, earthy scent that only horses have.

River turned slightly and wrapped me up in his neck. I try not to attribute human characteristics to the horses, but it felt very much like a hug, and in that moment, it was nice to be on the receiving end of a horse hug. I pulled out my phone and checked my messages. Braydon still hadn't responded. I started to send him a text, hesitated, but finally decided to go ahead and send it.

> Hey, haven't heard from you about the glove. Tried to talk to Heather today and almost got shot! Will fill you in later.

Biscuit gently nudged my shoulder, jealous that any attention was being paid to someone else. I scratched his wide forehead, and his lower lip hung slack.

"You're the very picture of dignity," I told him. He didn't seem to care. I needed to spend more time just *being* with the horses. It recharged my soul.

I decided to call Lanie as I descended the hill and fill her in on everything that had happened in the last twenty-four hours. River watched me walk away before returning to his grazing. I'm not sure I took a breath or even paused until I got to the disaster with Heather.

"Did you call the police?" she asked as I paused.

"No. Maybe I should have, now that I consider it in hindsight, especially since she almost accused Tanner of having something to do with it too. But at the time, I was afraid it would just make matters worse. I don't have the glove, and I can't prove we didn't trash her garden. I was here alone last night."

"Good Lord," she gasped when I finally stopped yammering. "I had no idea she was that unstable. Why did she think it was you?"

"I never got around to asking."

"And Ethan is here in town. I don't even know what to say about that," she said as she sighed.

"I'm not sure I know what to say about any of this." I turned around and leaned on the fence again. When I did, I glanced up at the Cunningham farm and noticed that there were police cars parked at the barn again.

"I think the state police have arrived," I said. "There are cruisers at the Cunningham barn again."

"Please come stay with me until this is over. I don't like the idea of you out there alone, especially now that someone is sneaking around at night as well."

"I don't want to leave the horses out here alone either."

"Well, at least come to dinner tonight. I'm supposed to meet Jennifer at the courthouse at two. I can fill you in on what she says then."

I mulled it over for a moment. "Okay, but I can't stay late. I was serious, I really don't want to leave my place unattended for long."

"You are so stubborn," she sighed again.

"You say that like it's news."

"I can come back and stay," she said.

"I know you would, and I love you for that, but I'll be fine," I said, maybe more to convince myself than Lanie.

"Okay, just dinner then. We'll start early. Be here at six."

"Thank you. I mean it. I really appreciate you."

"Aw, shucks," she laughed. "See you later, and I expect a *lot* more information about your dates."

"We'll see. Bye now," I said and hung up before she had a chance to argue. I knew it wouldn't make any difference. She was going to interrogate me like a hardened detective over dinner.

I texted Ethan and filled him in on the mess with Heather as I said I would. We went back and forth about how crazy it was, but I was in a hurry to finish the exchange, so I wrapped it up quickly and assured him I was okay.

I ran into the house and retrieved the binoculars and climbed into the barn loft to see if I could see anything from a higher vantage point. All I could really do was confirm that at least one of the cars did belong to the state police. I couldn't see much of anything else. I guessed that could explain why Braydon hadn't texted back. Maybe he was just too busy with the investigation to respond. Or maybe they had convinced him that I really was the murderer and he had turned his phone over to the police. I may not have been as attracted to him as I thought I would be, but I still didn't want him to think I'd murdered his father.

* * *

I climbed out of the shower and heard my phone ringing faintly from the kitchen. I hastily wrapped my towel around myself and sprinted for the phone. It was Lanie.

"I can't wait until dinner," she said as soon as I swiped open the phone call. "I have to tell you what I found out."

"Okay, let me dry off real quick and I'll call you right back," I said, my hair dripping onto the kitchen floor.

She didn't wait.

"Philip Atwood filed a case against Albert Cunningham trying to force a right of way across his farm." She didn't acknowledge that I had said anything. "And Albert filed a restraining order petition the Monday before he died."

"Well, that's definitely worth looking into," I said as I considered how this might fit into what we already knew. "Was she able to tell you why he filed the petition?"

"Apparently, Philip had threatened to poison Albert's horses if he didn't grant access across the farm. Philip inherited five landlocked acres from his aunt that sits a few plots behind the Cunningham farm. It overlooks the lake and Philip has grand ideas about developing it and getting rich."

"That sounds a lot like a motive." I tried not to get my hopes up too much, but this was very promising information.

"It sounds *exactly* like a motive," she said. "But I don't think you should talk to him. He's obviously as unstable as Heather, maybe more so since Albert had to file for a restraining order."

"I don't exactly have a team of detectives. I'll be fine."

"Send Ethan," she said coolly.

"I'm beginning to think that involving Ethan at all was a mistake."

"Involving your ex-husband in your legal problems? What could go wrong?"

"Yeah, okay. Point taken. Should I bring anything for dinner?" I changed the subject.

"No, I have everything."

"See you at six," I said.

She mumbled a "goodbye" and ended the call on her end. I put my phone down and ran back to the bathroom to finish drying off.

Dinner at six meant that I had a few hours to kill. There was plenty at the rescue that needed attention, but I reasoned that none of it would matter if I went to prison. I blow-dried my hair just enough to pull it into a presentable ponytail and dressed quickly. I glanced at the Cunningham farm as I climbed into my truck. The police car was still parked at the barn. They must have been going over that place with a fine-tooth comb.

My phone jingled in my pocket.

I opened it to find a message from Braydon.

Sorry, turned the glove over to police. State police here now, no idea what they think they'll find. TTYL.

I just texted a quick reply back. It didn't matter now. My confrontation with Heather had already gone disastrously wrong and the glove needed to be turned over to the police anyway. I pulled up Philip Atwood's address from the online Yellow Pages and entered it into my navigation system. According to the screen, he lived thirteen minutes from my house. That would be enough time to figure out a story that I hoped would get him to talk to me. I pulled out of the drive and followed the monotone directions, planning to make good use of the time until dinner.

I easily found Philip's house, which sat just off the main road. It was a small, red brick rectangle devoid of anything resembling personality. There was a carport to the right of the house that sheltered a black PT Cruiser. It had several bumper stickers on the back hatch, the most prominent of which was a large Arkansas Razorbacks decal in the middle. The yard was meticulously kept, but also devoid of any landscaping or decoration. After the unfortunate events of that morning, I decided that it might be prudent to pocket my pepper spray.

I knocked on the door and held my breath while I waited for a response from inside. It didn't take long.

"Can I help you?" Philip Atwood opened the door and stood behind the screen. He was a few inches taller than me. His long, thin arms were crossed, and his narrow face appeared to be permanently pulled into a sneer.

"Hello, I'm working on an op-ed piece for the paper about landowners' rights. I had hoped to talk to you about a recent dispute you've filed with a . . ."—I pulled out my phone and pretended to consult my notes—"Mr. Albert Cunningham."

"Bullshit," he half laughed, and half coughed. "I wasn't born yesterday. I know he was found dead last week. I ain't talking to no damned reporters."

"I'm not covering the death, I can assure you. I'm only interested in your dispute over a right of way. It would seem that a lot of small landowners in the county are getting the short end of the stick in favor of the larger farms. I had hoped to talk to someone who had experienced that firsthand."

He rubbed his chin as he looked me over. His white T-shirt was stained, and I couldn't tell through the screen door if it was new or old.

"I ain't saying nothing on the record. I had enough trouble with old man Cunningham. I'm hoping his heirs are more reasonable."

"Nothing on the record, got it." I made a show of putting my phone in my back pocket.

"There ain't nothing to say. I need to get access to my land. He wouldn't cooperate, so I'm taking him to court. That's all there is." He leaned on the doorframe, his face millimeters from the screen. "Or, I guess I *was* taking him to court."

"Was he hostile toward you?"

"You could say that." He rocked back on his heels. He kept the screen door between us and made no offer to invite me in.

"Could you elaborate on that?"

"Nope," he said and shut the inner door.

I knocked on the door again. "Mr. Atwood! Please, I have a few more questions for you."

"Go away!" came a muffled voice from inside.

I paused for just a moment and then turned to leave. I took the gravel path to the carport and glanced inside as I slowly passed. There wasn't anything out of the ordinary in his car, not out in plain sight anyway.

I got back in my truck before someone else had the chance to point a gun at me. I felt defeated, but at the same time, I couldn't have realistically expected either one of my suspects to just come out and admit they'd murdered Albert. Both of them had good enough reasons to murder him. People have killed for much less.

I pulled back into my driveway with no recollection of the drive home. I had been on autopilot the whole trip. Tanner's big black Dodge was parked next to the paddock, the yellow paint marring the passenger side like a wound. My phone rang as I climbed out of the truck. I expected it to be Lanie again, but when I looked at the screen it was Ashley's name and photo.

"Hello," I said.

"Mal, I have to talk to you." She sounded like she had been crying.

"What's wrong?" I instantly went into Mom mode. "Are you okay?"

"I'm okay, but I can't come back. I may be an adult, but my parents are paying my tuition and my mom has it in her head that it's too dangerous for me to come back out there until they catch the killer." She paused just long enough to catch her breath. "And I think it was that jerk at the feedstore that told her you were a suspect."

"Your mom is right," I said as gently as I could. "Someone trashed Heather Rogers's place last night. I don't know if the two are connected, but one thing's for sure—things aren't as quiet around here as they used to be. It'll be better to know you're safe."

"What if it takes months to catch the killer? I don't want to lose the progress I've made with the horses, and none of this is fair to you."

I cringed at the thought that it might take months to clear my name. There might not be a rescue to come back to if it took that long.

"Things will settle after a while. It'll be okay, Ashley. I'll work with them and make sure no one forgets what they've learned. There will always be a place for you here."

"Thank you, Mal."

"Don't worry. Take care of yourself and focus on school for a bit."

"You take care too."

When we hung up, I felt like I'd been dealt another blow. Bob Peterson was certainly making sure everyone who came through his store knew about me being a person of interest. And they say women are the ones prone to gossip. I wanted to curl up and feel sorry for myself for just a bit, but I decided it would be better to stay busy. I needed to gather the initial intake report and photos for the evidence bundle for Zeus. We would add the vet report when it came in the mail and any appropriate follow-up documents before turning it all over to the prosecuting attorney. I had been pretty clueless when I first started out, but I had worked out a smoother process now.

I went to the barn first to check on Tanner. Never one to shy away from hard work, he was stacking the load of hay in the barn. I hadn't expected him to unload the trailer, just to drive it back for me. I sighed as I looked at the stacks of fresh Bermuda bales. Another bill I would have to pay soon. I tried not to think about that.

"I'll finish that up," I said, feeling guilty that I had put him in danger. It also stung that I couldn't pay him or Ashley yet. They both worked far harder than some paid employees I'd known.

"Nah," he said, just slightly out of breath. "I got it. Besides, without football anymore, I gotta do something to keep Mama's cooking from sticking to my ribs." He grinned and patted his belly. "Look, Boss, I'm really sorry I didn't listen to you earlier. I just wanted to help."

"I know your heart was in the right place," I said. "I shouldn't have given in. You're very persuasive when you want to be." I pulled a bale of hay off the trailer, which Tanner promptly took away from me.

"I got this," he said, nodding at the trailer.

"Ashley is going to take a break for a while," I said, unsure of how to ask him if his parents felt the same way, or if he'd told them I nearly got him shot.

"Yeah, she texted me. I hate that, and I hate that they think you had anything to do with it. I can come a few more evenings this week to help make up the difference."

"Oh no," I shook my head. "That's not what I meant. You don't have to do that."

"I don't mind. And I would feel better about it if I was looking in on you more often."

"You are wonderful, and I appreciate you, but I am not your responsibility. I will be fine, I promise."

"Still." He grinned again. It didn't matter that he towered over me and was built like a tank. I still saw an adorable little boy, and I really did love him like a son.

"Your mama"—I used his term of endearment—"may not want you coming out here right now either."

"Mama's not worried," he said, slinging another bale of hay. "She agreed that I should talk to you about coming more often. She doesn't believe a word of what Bob Peterson is telling everyone."

I tried to hide the horror that I knew washed over my face. If I'd wanted to do any harm to anyone, it would have been that big-mouthed Bob Peterson. I decided then and there that I would get my account paid in full as soon as humanly possible and drive the extra half hour across the river to buy my feed elsewhere from then on. I had no intention of spending another penny that I didn't already owe in his store.

"Did you happen to tell her what happened at Heather's?" I cringed at the thought of Rachel Blake calling me about nearly getting her oldest child killed.

"I didn't tell Mama, exactly. But I did talk to Dad." He grinned sheepishly. "He said Heather is all talk and not to worry about her. He also said I'm an adult, and if I want to do stupid stuff, he can't stop me."

I laughed. I doubted his mama felt the same way.

"Tell your mama I appreciate her. Don't work too hard," I said as I turned toward the house.

He tipped his baseball cap and nodded before grabbing another bale of hay. It was as hard to think of Tanner as an adult as it was to think of Ginny that way, even though they both were.

I couldn't focus on the documentation, so I found myself standing in front of the investigation board. I added my notes about what Lanie had found out at the clerk's office and what happened when I went to talk to Philip Atwood. I also added that someone had trashed Heather Rogers's heirloom garden. I didn't have any reason to think that the garden vandalism was connected to the murder, but it was definitely a coincidence, considering the timing and all.

I tried to make the pieces fit, to determine if one of the existing suspects looked more likely than the other, but nothing stood out. The best piece of evidence so far had been finding Heather's glove at Albert's, and all that really did was prove she had lied about not being there. And I hadn't had the forethought to take a photo, which I regretted every time I thought about it. I really hoped that Grady would consider it as important as I did.

The police would have a better chance of establishing time lines and alibis than I would, and considering that I didn't have an alibi for the night of the murder myself, I knew that it wasn't a foolproof way of establishing guilt. It was a great way to rule out suspects, though, and I needed to focus my energies in the right direction.

I went to my desk and opened my laptop. I pulled up Facebook and searched for Philip Atwood. His posts were set to "private" so I couldn't see any of them, but his friends list was public and relatively small. I took some screen shots and printed the lists. It was a long shot to think that anyone would talk to me, but it was worth a try. When I had printed the most promising prospects, I pulled up Heather Rogers's page. Her personal page was locked down completely. I couldn't access any of her information or friends list, but she did have a link to her farm page, so I clicked on it.

The cover image was a beautiful shot of Heather kneeling in what I assumed was the heirloom garden before someone destroyed it. The rows of vegetables were flanked by rows of marigolds, and sunflowers grew tall and proud in the back. She was smiling and holding a huge striped squash. Even though she had threatened me with a shotgun that very morning, my heart ached for her. To lose something like that might push me over the edge too.

I started looking through the comments on her posts on her farm page and fell down a rabbit hole of cross-referencing the comments with the poster's profile and noting any potential personal connections to Heather. After exhausting that line of investigation, I searched for Kathleen's page. Her profile was wide open. I doubted she had any privacy settings turned on at all. It also appeared that she was quite active, with well over 3,000 "friends" and multiple updates every day. In fact, she had posted twelve times already that day alone. Nine of the posts tagged someone named "Maxwell Smith." I scrolled through those. One was an article about Doctors Without Borders, outlining the organization's efforts in treating HIV/AIDS in sub-Saharan Africa. She'd asked, *"Is this your group?"* The others were thinly veiled memes about long-distance relationships.

I clicked on Maxwell Smith's page. At first glance, it looked legit. But on closer inspection, there were some red flags. His "about" section was a laundry list of accomplishments that seemed suspicious, just in the sheer amount of them. His friends list was primarily women—older women, to be precise. I saved his profile picture, which was a very handsome man in scrubs standing in front of a yacht. His salt-and-pepper hair was closely cropped, and his crooked grin was reminiscent of George Clooney. I opened the Google Image search and uploaded the image. Just as I suspected, it was a stock image from an advertisement that he had cropped to exclude the identifying text. That meant he could really be anyone, anywhere.

I looked up the first few awards he was supposed to have won for various humanitarian efforts, and only one of them actually existed, the APA International Humanitarian Award. It was for extraordinary service in the field of psychology, so he hadn't even bothered to claim he'd won an *appropriate* award. The other few that I checked brought up no results on Google, but they sounded official—the Ellen Sandberg Award for Achievement in Underserved Populations and the All Coasts Humanitarian Award. I rolled my eyes at his audacity.

I had completely lost track of time when I heard Tanner's truck fire up in the driveway. I had meant to go back out and visit with him again before he left. I would have to catch him next time. I glanced at the time on my laptop and realized that I barely had enough time to get to Lanie's, and I hadn't left any time to feed the horses.

I grabbed my phone off the desk and tore out the door so fast I startled Banjo, who looked like he was trying to figure out if the house was on fire and whether or not he should flee too. I rounded the front of my truck and found all of the horses happily munching away at the feed buckets. Tanner had fed them all before he left. I had no idea how, but I vowed that I would figure out some way, come hell or high water, to start paying those kids. They were both so dependable and dedicated that I couldn't have asked for any better if I'd picked them out of a catalog.

I quickly texted a "thank you" to Tanner and ushered Banjo back in the house. My phone rang and I answered it without looking at the caller ID. I had expected Tanner, but it was Ethan's voice that greeted me on the other end.

"I tried to talk to your lawyer today, but he wouldn't see me."

"I get the impression that he's pretty busy."

"I don't know that he's the best choice to represent you in a criminal case."

"It isn't a criminal case yet, and I hope it doesn't get to that point." I found myself defending Andy, even though I'd had some of the same thoughts.

"I think you need to take it seriously, and that means hiring the right attorney."

"We can talk about this tomorrow," I said. "Right now I'm late for dinner."

There was a long pause.

"With Braydon Cunningham?"

"No. With Lanie and Bill," I sighed.

"Give them my best. Have a good night."

"You too."

I paused as I reached to open the door to my truck. There was note tucked under my windshield wiper. I looked around, having the irrational idea that whoever had left it might still be lurking nearby. I grabbed it and opened it quickly.

Sorry Boss was scrawled across the bottom of the hay bill in Tanner's messy but deliberate script. Tanner's barely legible handwriting warmed my heart, and I smiled as I tucked the bill in my console. I pulled out my phone and texted a quick note.

Nothing to be sorry about. Just want to keep you safe.
THANK YOU for everything you do, you and Ashley
mean the world to me.

It only took a few seconds to receive a "thumbs up" emoji in response.

The drive to Lanie's was a short one. She lived just inside Hillspring city limits, one street away from the grand old houses of the Historic District.

Her house itself was built just after the turn of the century. Nineteen hundred, not the turn of the last century. She and Bill had renovated it room by room until it sparkled like new, positively glowing with atmosphere and personality. The one-story Folk Victorian house (I knew the right term because Lanie told me) was circled by a large wrap-around porch. The decorative railing featured ornate gingerbread trim that matched the trim around the roof. Lanie had insisted on painting it pale robin's egg blue with white trim, like her childhood dollhouse. She told me once that she had always dreamed of having a house exactly like that dollhouse.

I pulled in close to the curb. The only parking for the house was taken up with Lanie's Challenger and Bill's truck. Did I mention that a lack of parking was the bane of our existence in Hillspring? A rock wall topped by a wrought-iron fence circled the yard. The gate in the middle was open onto the winding rock path. I loved Lanie's house almost as much as my own; it was as warm and welcoming as its owners.

I knocked on the door and heard Bill yell for me to come in.

"Hey there," I called to back to him. He grunted a friendly response.

"Come on in the kitchen," Lanie said.

I found her busily working on our dinner, which appeared to be pasta. Lanie was a firm believer in the fact that you can never go wrong with spaghetti.

"This smells amazing." I grabbed a piece of garlic bread and started munching.

"I was further behind at the shop than I anticipated, and I got a late start here."

"Can I help?"

"I'm just finishing up the sauce. You can start toting stuff to the dining room."

It was only a few minutes before Lanie joined me, carrying a huge pot of spaghetti sauce. It smelled as good as the rest of the meal.

"Come and get it," she called to Bill.

I heard the sounds from the TV stop and Bill lumbered into the dining room looking like a mountain man, or a bear. He was six foot four and nearly that broad, with a full black beard that hung down to his sternum. He rubbed his belly, which had only now started to thicken a bit.

"Looks great, hon," he said. "How you gettin' along, Mal?"

"I'm doing okay, considering." I smiled.

"Yeah, Bob Peterson has lost my business completely," he growled.

"Oh, you don't have to do that on my account."

"He's acting like you've been tried and convicted already, and it's just ridiculous. I'm not interested in doing business with someone like that. He isn't the only hardware store in the county."

I could have hugged him like the giant teddy bear he was. Bill's business likely accounted for a pretty big chunk of change for the hardware store. Bill ran one of the most successful construction and renovation companies in the area.

"I still think you should talk to Grady about Heather nearly shooting you and Tanner this morning," Lanie said in between bites of pasta.

"I'm afraid it'll backfire on me since she thinks I destroyed her garden. Grady is just looking for reasons to arrest me."

"Still, she's acting unhinged. Maybe she destroyed it herself," Bill interjected.

I hadn't considered that possibility. Sometimes I was much too trusting and naïve.

"If she had killed him, it would make sense to do something like that to throw any suspicion off," Lanie said, punctuating her point with a piece of garlic bread. "How was Philip when you talked to him?"

"Which was stupid, by the way," Bill said, never one to mince words. "You've already been threatened at gunpoint. What if one of these people really did kill that old coot? It wouldn't be a stretch to think they would kill you to keep their secret."

"I'm not even going to argue with you," I said.

"Well, it's not like law enforcement is doing much but trying to pin this on Mal," Lanie said before taking a drink of wine.

"He was weird," I said, circling back around to Lanie's question. "But I didn't see anything that would lead me to believe he's killed someone," I said.

"Albert didn't file for a restraining order for nothing," Lanie said.

"True. I'd like to find out more about why he did that. I wish Luis would talk to me, but he seems to be convinced that I killed Albert too."

"You could ask Mr. Hottie," Lanie said in a sing-song voice.

"What are we, twelve?" I shot her a dirty look.

Bill rolled his eyes and dove back into his spaghetti. Still, obnoxiousness aside, she had a point. Albert might have confided in his son.

"I'll text him later."

"It would be a better excuse to see him again."

"I'm not sure I want to." I scrunched up my nose. "We didn't really click."

"Who said anything about clicking? I said have dinner, maybe a little something else if you're lucky. You don't have to marry the guy to enjoy the scenery."

"I need a *little* click even for that," I said. "But I am definitely going to find out if he knows anything about Albert's restraining order. I did find out something odd about Kathleen this afternoon. I took a look at her Facebook page, and it looks like she's been getting pretty chummy with someone who might be a scammer."

"How so?" Lanie asked in between bites.

"His profile picture is a fake, and he claims he's a doctor working in Africa. She's been posting things, tagging him left and right."

"She may think she has a Nigerian prince on the hook and needed to bump off old Albert to make room."

I had just taken a sip and nearly did a spit take. "Lanie!"

"What? It's a possibility." She shrugged.

I mulled it over as I ate. Would having an online affair be enough to cause her to murder her real-life boyfriend?

"Maybe Albert found out about it," Lanie continued. "Or maybe she was sending him loads of Albert's money. Didn't you tell me the family didn't trust her?"

"Yeah, but that's pretty common with new girlfriends, isn't it?" I tore into another piece of garlic bread. "I wish I knew if she had access to his accounts."

"Ask your hot boyfriend."

I scoffed, but it wasn't the worst suggestion. We finished the dinner visiting about booming sales at Junk & Disorderly, and she even produced a happy surprise. My leather work pieces that she had put up for sale had turned a nice profit. It would be enough to pay off my balance at Bob's. I couldn't wait to do that and never set foot in there again. And even though I hated the inconvenience of shopping out of town for both Bill and me, I was eternally grateful for his loyalty.

True to my word, I didn't stay long. As I was leaving, Bill tried to talk me into staying, just as his wife had earlier in the day.

"I can run back out with you and get Banjo," he said, pulling me into a massive bear hug. "We can check on the horses and then I can run you back out in the morning, take a look around before you go back in."

"Thank you." I hugged him back, my arms barely reaching around the mountain of a man. "But I promise I will be okay."

"I told you she wouldn't stay," Lanie said, hands on hips.

"I had to try," Bill said, releasing me.

"I love you two."

"We love you back," Lanie said. She held the door and watched me until I got in my truck. I don't know if she thought I had been followed or what, but she had never done that before.

I got back home at a little past eight. The lights were on in the show barn on the hill, and I wondered if Braydon was already showing horses for sale. I thought about texting him, but he hadn't been great about returning those, so I decided I would just show up in the morning. He had asked me back to help catalog the other horses, after all.

I pulled out the flashlight from my glove box and shined it into the paddock. I was greeted by several sets of blinking eyes and annoyed snorts.

"Sorry, guys," I said to them. I couldn't help myself. I've always talked to the horses.

After everyone was accounted for, I went to the house. The door was still locked and secure and I could hear Banjo wagging against the wall on the other side. Everyone being concerned for my safety had made me extra paranoid. So even though the door had been secure, I checked every room and closet and the back porch before I settled down with my book.

I was just getting to a good part when I saw headlights. Banjo let out a little "boof" with a question mark at the end. Biscuit started braying in the paddock, ever my loyal, long-eared alarm. I pulled the curtain back and tried to stay out of sight. I could make out that it was a car, so that ruled out Tanner, Bill, and Braydon if he was still using the SUV. It was also definitely not bright purple, so it ruled out Lanie too. I watched the driver's door open, and a tall man unfold himself from the driver's seat. It was Andy. I stared at him for a minute before I got up and went to the door. Banjo ran past me and greeted him, his entire butt wagging.

He definitely didn't look like Mr. Rogers in jeans and a flannel shirt. His hair was a bit tousled, and he was wearing dark-rimmed glasses. There was faint five o'clock shadow darkening his angular jaws.

"What are you doing here?" I said from the doorway.

"That's not the friendliest greeting I've ever received."

"Sorry," I said. "I'm just on edge. What's going on? Everything okay? How did you know I'd be home?"

"I didn't. I've heard rumors around town that you trashed that organic farm down the road. I was just visiting my mom at Applewood Estates and thought I would drop by." He climbed the steps and stood in front of me in the doorway.

Applewood Estates was an assisted living facility just down the road from my rescue. It sat atop a craggy limestone bluff overlooking Deadwood Lake. Unlike the assisted living facilities I had toured for various cases in St. Louis, Applewood Estates featured an orchard, a community garden, and a chicken coop where residents could care for and cultivate some of their own foods.

"Seems like everyone is either sure I killed my neighbor or sure that I can't take care of myself."

"Or it could be that you have a lot of people who care about you." He shrugged and shoved his hands in his pockets.

I softened. There was just something about him that was so genuine and comforting.

"Do you want to come in for some coffee?" I stepped aside and opened the door wider. Banjo took the opportunity to dash past me.

"Sure," he said, following me inside and into the kitchen.

Banjo bounced excitedly beside him, hoping to get some attention since he never gets enough.

"Hello there." Andy crouched down and scratched his ears. Banjo regarded him with slobbery adoration.

"Banjo never meets a stranger." I shook my head.

"He's a good boy," Andy cooed as he continued petting my shameless dog.

"How bad are the rumors?" I crossed my arms and tried to brace myself for news I didn't really want to hear. "I know Bob Peterson has been telling everyone that I'm guilty and it's just a matter of time before I'm arrested. I didn't know Heather was telling everyone I trashed her garden too."

He turned around and leaned on the counter while I started the coffee maker.

"Honestly?" He shrugged. "It's pretty bad. You know how small towns love gossip. Have you been on the Hillspring Facebook page?"

"No," I said and pulled out my phone.

"Well, don't. I wouldn't recommend it. People who've never met you are speculating on the case. It's probably better if you don't look if you want to continue to live here when this is over."

I put my phone down on the table and slumped onto the chair as a wave of nausea washed over me.

"Oh, Mallory, I'm sorry," he said and sat across from me. "People just love gossip, that's all. It'll blow over soon. It's just that this is out of the ordinary here and there's nothing else to occupy the rumor mill."

"I'm going to lose everything I've worked for," I said with a shaky voice.

"No, you won't. Like I said, this will blow over."

In spite of my best efforts to keep my emotions in check, tears started streaming down my cheeks. I wiped them away angrily. He got up and came over to me, pulling me gently up from the chair and then into his arms. I sank into him, buried my head against his chest and wrapped my arms around his surprisingly firm frame. I held on long enough to make it awkward. I took what was supposed to be a kind gesture and made it weird. He stepped back and held me at arm's length. Humiliation and horror flooded over me.

"I don't know what got into me." I stepped back and held up a hand. I could feel my cheeks burning with embarrassment. "I'm sorry. I shouldn't have done that."

"You don't have to apologize," he said softly. "This has to be awful for you."

"I think you should go," I said. I hoped the light was dim enough to hide my reddening cheeks.

He looked hurt, or maybe as embarrassed as I was. I couldn't tell.

"Call me tomorrow. We need to review our approach if the state police decide to question you."

I nodded. He lingered for a moment in the doorway and then turned to leave. I heard him speak softly to Banjo on his way out. When I heard his car start up, I groaned out loud. Banjo cocked his head sideways at me, oblivious to my humiliation. What was wrong with me? I had blubbered all over a man I'd just met. I wanted to pull the covers over my head and forget this whole mess. So that's just what I did.

Chapter Ten

I sat in my truck outside Coldstone Bank and tried to gather enough courage to face people. Embarrassment from last night lingered like a hangover, and I kept inwardly cringing every time I thought about desperately clinging to a virtual stranger who was just trying to be nice. I wanted to call Lanie and tell her about it and talk it through, but that would mean I would have to admit it out loud and drag it out into the light of day.

I had no idea if the rumors had reached the bank or not, but I was afraid they had. I was afraid they would look at me like I was guilty, as Bob Peterson had. But I needed to deal with pressing and practical matters. I needed to deposit the cash Lanie had given me last night and pay off my feed bill. And I wanted to be able to write a check for it so I would have double proof that I had paid it, especially since I wasn't feeling too warm and fuzzy about Bob Peterson anymore.

The bank's new location didn't suit it as much as the old spot that now hosts the farmers market. The old bank was a small two-story Victorian-style with native stonework and manicured flower beds. The new one was a modern metal and glass building with floor-to-ceiling windows on three sides. I think they were going for sleek and clean, but it felt more like cold and impersonal to me. Thankfully, it was at the south end of town, far away from the historic buildings that gave Hillspring its personality.

I smoothed my shirt, grabbed my bag, and went inside with my head held high. The regular teller was at her station, wearing her usual bright smile. She was a small, thin woman with strawberry blonde hair and delicate features. She was always friendly and courteous, and today was no exception. If she had heard any of the rumors, she wasn't acting like it.

"Would you like a balance on the account?" she asked as I handed her the cash and deposit slip.

"Yes, please."

It only took her a few minutes to key everything in and hand me the receipt. I thanked her and looked at my balance after the deposit on my way toward the door. I stopped in my tracks. I blinked and looked at the receipt again. She had made a mistake. I took it back to the counter.

"Did you forget something?"

"I'm so sorry, but there's been a mistake." I pointed to the balance on the slip of paper.

"No, ma'am," she smiled, but looked a bit confused.

"That can't possibly be right," I said.

"I'll check again," she said, polite enough, but still with the air that she was humoring a crazy woman.

She took the slip and entered the account number again.

"This is your account number, correct?"

I confirmed that it was.

"There was a sizable deposit yesterday." She turned the monitor around so that I could see it.

"Who made the deposit?"

"I don't know, ma'am. It was a cash deposit."

"There has to be a mistake. This must have been entered into my account by mistake."

She nodded and waved over her supervisor. An older woman with perfectly coiffed, short gray hair came over and smiled at me too.

"Is there a problem?" she asked as she adjusted her scarf, revealing a name tag that read "Judy."

"I think someone mistakenly put a deposit on my account." I pointed to the monitor.

"Well, let's see, shall we?" She took over the station and started typing away. After a moment she turned the screen back around and showed me an image of the deposit slip used to add the cash to my account. On the line that would normally be for the signature it said, "Donation for Hillspring Horse Rescue."

"It doesn't look like there's been a mistake," she said. "Is there anything else I can do to help you?"

I was speechless. I blinked and looked at the screen again.

"Ms. Martin, are you okay?" Judy asked.

"Yes," I croaked. "Yes, thank you. I'm sorry for the inconvenience."

"It's no bother at all." Judy smiled again. "Is there anything else?"

"No, thank you," I said. I picked up the receipt and went back out to my truck.

I looked at the slip of paper again and started to laugh like a maniac. Just yesterday I had been sure that I was going to lose everything I had worked so hard for, and now I was set for the next several months, maybe even longer.

I started laughing. Who could possibly have donated this much money? And then it occurred to me. Ethan. Who else could it have been? He'd already offered to make a donation, and I'd turned him down. It was just like him to do it anonymously. I dialed his number. My stomach sank at this sudden turn of the emotional roller-coaster I seemed to have gotten on. I would have to return the money.

"Hello?" He sounded sleepy.

"Thank you, I really appreciate it, but I already told you, I can't accept money from you."

"What are you talking about?" he asked around a breathy yawn.

"The anonymous donation. I can't accept it."

"I didn't make a donation."

"Ethan, I really do appreciate it . . ."

"I didn't make a donation." He cut me off, sounding annoyed. "I don't know anything about a donation. I'll talk to you later when I've had a chance to wake up."

I believed him. We'd been married long enough for me to know his tells, and apparently he wasn't my mysterious benefactor. I looked at the balance slip again like it might hold some new clue I'd missed the first time I stared at it. Could it have been Braydon? I had confided in him that the rescue wasn't doing very well. He had obviously wanted to do something without putting me on the spot or in a position to turn it down. He was the only other person I knew who had the means to make a donation like this. It had to be him. Maybe he wasn't as self-absorbed as he'd seemed. Suddenly, all I wanted was to drive up to his house and throw my arms around him. And I planned to do just that as soon as I paid off my feed bill.

Thankfully, the feedstore wasn't as busy as it had been on the weekend. Bob was behind the counter again. He looked up when I walked in.

"I'm afraid this weekend was the last time I can put anything on your bill," he said the moment I reached the counter.

"That's fine, Bob. I'm here to pay off the bill." I paused for a moment to relish the look of surprise on his face. "And you won't have to worry about me charging anything here ever again. In fact, you won't have to worry about me spending a penny here ever again."

"Mallory, you don't have to be that way. I mean no disrespect, but surely you can understand I have a business to run here."

"Oh, I understand," I said, slamming the balance ticket on the counter. "I understand that you chose to listen to rumors and baseless accusations over a steady customer and that you put more stock in gossip than you do in loyalty."

"Now, just wait a minute . . ."

"You just wait a minute," I cut him off. "When this is all over, you'd better weigh your words carefully, because if you keep spreading lies about me, I'll take you to court for slander."

"Are you threatening me?"

"I'm *promising* you. Stop spreading unfounded rumors and ring up my bill."

He turned red in the face but made no further effort to speak to me. He rang up the bill, provided me with a receipt, and slammed the till.

I was shaking when I left, but it felt so good to tell that busybody off. I knew I couldn't take him to court for slander since nothing he'd said about me was actionable, but it felt good to bluff a little too. I left the feedstore and drove straight to the

Cunningham farm. Braydon was at the barn, wearing breeches and English riding boots and looking very much like a modern-day Mr. Darcy. I jumped out of my truck and hugged him before I could talk myself out of it.

"A guy could get used to a greeting like that," he said as I loosened my grip. "What brings you by today?"

I saw Luis come around the corner of the barn, pause for just a moment, and then duck inside.

"I just came from the bank," I hinted and watched his face for any signs of recognition. He must've been a very good poker player.

"I feel like I'm missing something crucial here."

"*Someone* made an anonymous donation to the rescue."

"Well, that's a very nice someone." He grinned.

"Very nice indeed." I knew I was practically gushing, but at that moment I didn't care.

"Would you like to go riding with me? I'm trying out one of the geldings before I put a price on him, and we might as well turn it into a trail ride."

"I would love to." I was glad that I had chosen jeans and boots this morning. If he was willing to be this generous so soon after his father's death, then maybe there *was* hope for a spark between us. And Lanie was right. He was eye candy in the best possible ways.

"Give me just a moment," he said and disappeared into the barn.

When he remerged, he was leading a tall bay horse tacked in English gear and a smaller, stockier sorrel with a western saddle. Both of them displayed impeccable ground manners befitting what I could only guess were stellar pedigrees. He handed me the reins for the sorrel, and I stroked the horse's broad forehead. Luis came around to stand beside Braydon and give him a leg up onto his horse, all without looking at me even once.

Since I had the benefit of both a western saddle and a shorter horse, I swung easily up into the saddle.

"There's an old logging road that winds around the mountain, if I remember correctly," Braydon said, taking the lead.

"I believe it's still there," I said, my horse easily matching strides with the big bay. "And speaking of the land up there, did your father tell you anything about the dispute he was having with Philip Atwood?"

"He may have mentioned it. I don't recall that he shared any details. I did find the paperwork in his office, though. Looks like he was working on filing a restraining order," he said as we crossed the fence line and entered the trees at the back of his property. "According to his notes, he thinks Mr. Atwood was cutting the fences at the back corner and taking some shots at the mares," he continued. "Do you think he could have killed Dad?"

"I really don't know."

"That would definitely be a motive, I would think. Dad would've made it clear that he wasn't going to back down. He would've made Mr. Atwood's life miserable."

"Did you give that information to the police?"

"Of course. They were here for hours and hours yesterday, going over everything again and asking a million questions. Whatever it takes to put the monster that did this behind bars, though."

"What did they say about the glove?"

"They didn't say much about anything, just that they would look into it."

"Yeah, I'm sure they're not giving out much information right now," I said. "But I would think they could at least update you a bit more than the rest of us."

"You would think so, wouldn't you?" he scoffed.

We easily found the old road, and while it had been overgrown with weeds and a few small bushes, it was still mostly clear of any big timber and overhanging limbs. The view from that elevation was just stunning, overlooking the valley and Deadwood Lake to the east. I could see why Philip thought it had development potential. Selfishly, I hoped that would never happen. I didn't want to share our beautiful mountain with a suburban development full of McMansions and minivans.

We rode in comfortable silence for a lot of the trip, finally circling the property and coming up the driveway from the front. When we reached the arena, the hounds had noticed our arrival and started baying from the kennels. It wasn't long before Cooper made his appearance, once again immensely proud of himself that he had escaped.

"That dog is a menace," Braydon sighed as he swung his leg over the saddle and dismounted in one fluid motion. He bent down and patted the dog's side.

"I think you might as well give up keeping him contained," I laughed.

"Yeah, it seems to be a lost cause."

One of the ranch hands I didn't recognize came and took the horses from us.

"Tomorrow is the remembrance, and my aunt is coming in tonight. I would invite you to dine with us, but I wouldn't wish that on anyone. I'd like to see you again after the memorial, or remembrance, or whatever we're calling the thing. Thursday?"

"I'd like that too," I said. "Are you sure you want me to come to the memorial?"

"I'm sure. I don't care what anyone thinks, you were his closest neighbor, and under any other circumstances you'd be there, right?"

"I would."

"Then you should go," he said and took my hand in his. "And I want you there."

"Then I'll be there," I said, although I dreaded the inevitable looks and murmurs after Bob Peterson had been telling everyone all week that I was guilty. "Eleven, right?"

"Yes. I was going to have it here, but of course Aunt Mae thought we should have it at the cathedral in town. I don't think Dad had been to mass since I was a kid, but she wants to keep up appearances, I'm sure."

"I know this has to be very stressful for you. I'm so sorry."

"Getting through tomorrow and getting Aunt Mae back to Illinois will help immensely."

"Your family isn't close?" I asked, although it should have been obvious.

"Not at all," he laughed. He bent down to pet Cooper again, who was bouncing in happy circles around his master's legs. "I'll pick you up at ten fifteen. That should be plenty of time to get there and find parking."

"Oh," I said, surprised. I had assumed we would meet at the memorial. "That sounds good. I'll see you then."

He nodded and waved as he went back to the barn. I practically floated back to my truck and then felt guilty that I was excited that he was going to pick me up to attend his father's funeral. I spent just a moment wondering if I would be willing to give this another chance after our less than stellar first date if he hadn't been so devastatingly handsome. Ultimately, I decided that I probably would have. I gave myself the benefit of the doubt, anyway.

I called Lanie on the short trip back home and filled her in on what Braydon had told me about Albert's suspicions.

"If he thought Philip was shooting at his horses and cutting his fences, that would definitely be a good reason to ask for a restraining order," she said.

"Yeah, I would think so." I rounded the last corner of my driveway and slammed on the brakes. "Lanie, I've got to go. The police are at my house."

I didn't give her time to respond. I just hung up and dialed Andy. I would have to get over my humiliation in a hurry, because I clearly needed my attorney.

"Hello?"

"The police are here. I just got home, but I think they're searching the house."

"I'll be right there. Don't say a word after you tell them your attorney is on the way."

"Okay." I hung up and I swallowed, hard. If they were searching my house, I was pretty sure that meant I had been upgraded from "person of interest" to "suspect."

I pulled in beside a state police car, and I was glad to find that Tanner's truck wasn't there. He didn't need to be involved any more than he already was. I texted him quickly and told him to steer clear of the rescue until he heard from me that the police had vacated. He responded almost immediately with his standard "K." There were three police SUVs in total, and an armed officer on the porch, who watched me with his hand on his pistol. I got out of the truck slowly, with my hands held up.

"I'm not armed," I said as he took a step toward me. I couldn't see Banjo, and I started to panic. "Where is my dog?"

"Ma'am, we're going to need you to stay outside, please." He held his hand up, the other still on his weapon.

"That's fine, but I need you to tell me where my dog is," I said firmly, my hands still held up.

"He's in the backyard," Grady said as he came out of my house behind the uniformed officer. "I locked the doggy door so he wouldn't get out."

I nodded, relieved.

"You can put your hands down," Grady said, gesturing for me to do so.

"Your buddy there seems to be a little trigger happy. I don't need to get shot in my front drive."

"Mallory," Grady sighed. "You're not doing yourself any favors acting this way."

"Be sure and tell me how to behave when I'm being accused of something I didn't do, and my house is being searched."

He pinched his eyes with the thumb and forefinger of his left hand and sighed again.

"I don't expect you to be happy about any of this, but I did expect you to realize I'm not the enemy here."

"How am I supposed to feel, Grady? You're investigating me for *murder*, for God's sake!"

"Why don't we have a seat while they finish up here?" He gestured to my bench.

I crossed my arms and looked from him to the men ransacking my house.

"I'd rather go to the barn so I don't have to watch this."

"That's fine. They've already searched there."

"They've been in the barn?" My voice rose several octaves.

"The search warrant covers all buildings on your property."

"Fine. You can give a copy of the search warrant to my attorney when he gets here."

He nodded. I opened the gate and waited for him to pass through, slamming it for effect behind him. He pretended not to notice.

I led him to the benches at the back of the barn overlooking the lower paddock. Several of the horses were grazing peacefully on the hillside, happily oblivious to the chaos at the house. Biscuit leaned on the paddock fence trying to entice someone to pay attention to him.

I sat down and turned slightly away from Grady.

"Where were you this morning?" he asked.

"I'm not saying anything else until my attorney gets here."

He sighed again. At that point, I hoped all his sighing would cause him to hyperventilate. I wanted to tell him *just* where to stick his disapproval.

"Okay, then I'll talk." He sat down on the other bench since I managed to take up all the available space on my bench by angling my body and propping up my leg.

"I understand that you went to see Heather Rogers yesterday."

I tried not to show any signs of reaction. I guessed she had made good on her threat to call the police after all.

"It looks like you're poking into the investigation. It wasn't a secret that Heather had been having a dispute with Albert over water quality. I just hope that you understand we're looking into every possible lead." He leaned forward into my line of sight. "And it won't be looked on kindly if you're found interfering."

"You can't tell a private citizen not to speak with other private citizens," Andy said from the barn door. "Good afternoon, Grady." He extended his hand.

Grady stood and shook Andy's hand.

"It's just friendly advice," Grady said. "We're going to need your cell phone, Mallory." He pulled an evidence bag out of his pocket.

I stared at him for a moment, trying to process what he had just said to me. I pulled out my phone and dumped it in the bag.

"Is there a passcode?"

"Two, one, one, eight, nine, four."

He wrote it down on the outside of the bag with a Sharpie he'd pulled out of his shirt pocket.

"Do you or the investigators have any questions for Mallory right now? Because if you don't, I think it would be in her best interest to leave until you're finished."

"I believe they would like an opportunity to speak with her."

"Why don't you go check?"

Grady nodded and excused himself. After he had gone, I stood and looked up at Andy.

"This is bad, right?"

"Not necessarily. They're not going to find anything, so it may help them rule you out faster."

"I love your optimism."

He rubbed my shoulder, and I was reminded of my humiliating behavior last night. I could feel my cheeks burning all over again.

"About last night . . ."

"Don't worry about it," he cut me off. "We'll talk about that later."

Oh good, I thought to myself. *I can look forward to reliving it again and again.*

"Go get your dog. We can go to my office while they finish here," he said, nodding toward the house.

"What if they want to talk to me?"

"Then they can make an appointment. You haven't been arrested and you're not required to accommodate their schedule."

My dog was ecstatic to see me when I opened the side gate to the backyard, alternately wagging his entire butt and yipping happily. I tried not to look inside but glanced briefly through my bedroom window to see a uniformed officer rifling through my underwear. The feeling of having your home violated by strangers is awful. I was glad that I had left a leash clipped to the back gate back when Banjo had been digging under the fence, and I snapped it onto his collar. He bounced along beside me, ready for whatever adventure awaited. He wagged at the officer on the porch as I circled my house. Sweet Banjo—he never met a stranger.

When I got to the driveway, Andy and Grady were talking beside Andy's car. Andy crossed his arms and nodded as Grady spoke, but I couldn't hear what he was saying. By the time I got close enough to hear, Andy was speaking again.

"You know that Mallory wouldn't vandalize anyone's garden or property. You have to know that," he said.

"Did Heather tell you I vandalized her garden?" I asked Grady as I approached. "If she's the killer, then it would make sense for her to keep the focus on me . . ."

"She's not the killer," Grady cut me off.

"How do you know that?"

"She has an airtight alibi," he said.

"Just how 'airtight' is it?" I made air quotes with my fingers.

"She was with me all night," Grady said, avoiding eye contact with me.

"Well, did your pillow talk include how her glove wound up on Albert's place?"

"What?"

"One of her very distinctive rainbow gloves was found on Albert's property. Braydon said he turned it in to you," I watched him closely.

"A random glove doesn't prove anything if she has an alibi for the night in question."

I couldn't argue with that. My stomach sank. The glove, the lies about not being on Albert's place, none of it mattered. My mind was reeling, and my thoughts were racing so fast I felt like I couldn't process them.

Andy reached into his back pocket and produced his business card. "You can reach me on my cell phone. And I expect a call any time you choose to speak with my client."

Grady took the card and walked past me back to the house, tipping his Stetson as he passed me.

Andy patted his thighs and "smooched" at Banjo.

"I'll follow you in my truck," I said.

"You have to leave your truck here. It's included in the search warrant."

"You've got to be kidding me."

"You can leave the keys in it."

I stood there in disbelief for a moment before I let him take Banjo's leash and load him in the car. I took my truck key off my keychain and put it in the ignition. I wasn't about to leave them my full set of keys. I paused on my way to the car and looked at the horses. How much my life had changed in a week boggled my mind.

"It's going to be okay," Andy said as he opened the passenger door.

I got in and he shut the door.

"I'm really sorry about last night," I blurted out as soon as he got into the driver's seat. "I don't know what got into me. I usually don't have trouble respecting professional boundaries." My cheeks burned again.

"Like I said last night, I know this is awful for you." He didn't look at me as he spoke, putting the gearshift into drive. "Forget about it."

As we descended the driveway and I left strangers in my house, invading my space and privacy, I turned my attention to my more pressing matters. My resolve to figure out who killed Albert was even greater after speaking to Grady, which I'm sure was not the effect he had hoped for. One of my main suspects had been ruled out, so I told myself that my focus wouldn't have to be divided anymore.

"I can focus on Kathleen and Philip Atwood now," I said aloud.

"What do you mean?" He glanced at me, brows furrowed.

"If Sheriff Sullivan isn't going to find out who really killed Albert, then someone else needs to." I crossed my arms and set my jaw.

"Maybe you should let the police handle the investigation."

"Because they're doing such a bang-up job so far? If I leave it up to them, I'll be in jail by the end of the year."

"I just don't like the idea of you putting yourself at risk like this. Plus, there's all sorts of potential legal pitfalls here."

"I appreciate your concern, but I'm not going to wait around for other people to decide my fate."

He smiled and shook his head.

"What?" I said, a bit more snappish than I really intended.

"I'm not going to talk you out of this, am I?"

"I'm not going to do anything that would compromise your defense. I just can't sit here and do nothing."

I turned back to face the front of the car as he pulled into the Hannigan Law Office parking lot. Banjo's tail thumped against the back door, signaling his excitement at the prospect of getting out and meeting new people.

"Let me just go to the office and clear my schedule," Andy said as he got out.

I nodded and stayed put. Banjo whined quietly when Andy didn't open the back door. It didn't take long for him to return.

"We're all set." He opened the door and grabbed the leash. Banjo bounded out, sniffing everything from the car to the sidewalk.

Sherry visibly recoiled from either me or my dog, or both. Banjo wagged at her, and she held a file folder up to keep him from greeting her. I wanted to ask Andy if she bites because my dog doesn't, but I figured it would be better to stay neutral in my current legal situation.

Banjo didn't hesitate to make himself at home. He jumped up on the sofa in Andy's office, turned several circles, and then nestled in next to the decorative pillow. Andy rubbed his ears. Banjo looked like he had found heaven. I reached for my phone and then remembered that Grady had taken it. I sighed and rubbed my eyes.

"I keep forgetting I don't have my phone."

"You can use my phone if you want to make a call, or my laptop if you want to do something else."

"I need to get a new phone. I don't want to be out of touch if there's an emergency at the rescue."

"Take my car. I'll stay here with Banjo."

"I need to go talk to my friend too." I hesitated. "Are you sure you don't mind me stealing your car for the afternoon?"

"Take however long you need. We'll be fine. I have plenty to work on here."

"Thank you," I said, taking the offered keys.

Sherry gave me the same look on the way out that she gave us on the way in, answering my question about which one of us she was scowling at.

It was weird driving Andy's sedan after being used to navigating the narrow streets and switchbacks around Hillspring in my big truck. I picked up a smartphone a couple of models older than mine, and it was charging in the seat next to me. I'd switched my existing number to the new phone since the police didn't need my service to check for whatever they thought they would find. They were going to subpoena my records anyway, if they hadn't already.

Lanie's shop was busy as usual, so I hurried through the crowd to the back office. Lanie was at her desk hand-writing signs for a new candle display she was planning to put in the front with the Christmas stuff. Her handwriting rivaled calligraphy.

"Well, it's about time. I've been calling and texting! You sure left me on a cliffhanger."

"The police have my phone."

"You're joking," she said and let the sign she was working on fall to the desk.

"I wish I was. They're trashing my house as we speak. They've got my truck too. I had to drive here in Andy's car."

"Your lawyer?" Her eyebrows raised.

"Yeah. Thankfully, he was able to come out to the rescue while they were rifling through all my worldly belongings. Banjo's at the office with him right now."

She made a little "huh" sound. I told her about Heather's airtight alibi and Braydon's generous gift.

"What are you going to do now?" she asked.

"I'm going to put all of my effort into figuring out who really killed Albert Cunningham. And one suspect has just conveniently been ruled out, so I'm going to focus on Philip Atwood."

Chapter Eleven

I wasn't ready to go back to the office with Andy and his disapproving assistant, so I went to the library to look into as much public information as I could access on Philip Atwood. I found that he had a history of filing land disputes around his house and the tiny piece of landlocked property behind Albert's. Before going after Albert, he had first gone after the landowners behind his parcel, and that had resulted in a ruling in favor of his opponents. They had claimed historical significance since the house and cellar on their land could be traced to Civil War documents. It was only a matter of weeks after that ruling that Philip went after Albert.

There were several court records regarding boundary disputes around Philip's house as well. It seemed that he used the courts to argue over a few feet in every direction. I jotted down the names in every single case. I hoped that his former targets could give me an idea if he had a habit of harassing behavior or made any threats of violence.

Just before the library closed, I got a wild idea. I remembered Maxwell Smith's fake account, and I googled young women's photos and picked a series that had the same person in various poses and outfits. I then quickly set up a dummy email account and Facebook profile. I decided my alias would be Mykayla Parker. I used the stock photos I had found to populate my fake account. I sent friend requests to as many people as I could think of and then locked down the privacy settings so that no one could see my friends list but me. Finally, I sent a friend request to Philip Atwood.

I shut down the computer and left the library still feeling a rush of adrenaline. If it worked, I might set up a male profile and send a request to Kathleen too. I had no idea what I hoped to find by accessing his social media posts, but it felt like I was doing something at least. I doubted he was as active on social media as Kathleen was, but I needed a window into his thoughts and movements. I had been going about my investigation all wrong. I hadn't committed myself as much as I should have, and even in the face of all evidence to the contrary, I had held out some hope that the police would clear me and find the real killer. It had become painfully clear that the police were only interested in me.

I took a chance and grabbed some takeout on my way back to the office. I was starving, and even if Andy wasn't interested, I still needed to eat. I was glad that Sherry appeared to be gone when I pulled back up to the front door and found it locked.

"I brought food," I said, knocking on the door with my foot. Banjo performed his customary duty as a dog and let out a single "bork." He was never interested in doing any actual protecting, so he seemed to feel that his dogly duties were accomplished by simply announcing that a visitor had arrived.

Andy opened the door and took the bags of takeout. "Is someone else coming?"

"I shouldn't order when I'm hungry."

He motioned for me to follow him to a break room at the back of the office. He put the bags on the counter. He pulled out some paper plates from the tiny cabinet and some plastic silverware from one of the bags. The break room was small, but cozy. A glass bistro table and three chairs occupied the corner by the door. A floral sofa sat against the back wall, and a large print of Deadwood Lake hung above it.

"I hope you like the tamales from Miguel's," I said.

"Oh wow. I love Miguel's. That sounds amazing."

We settled into an easy back-and-forth as we ate. I told him about my time as a legal nurse consultant and he told me about law school on the East Coast and why he'd chosen to settle in Hillspring. Turns out his mom's family lived in the area since the turn of the century, and when she'd needed to enter an assisted living facility she had returned to her roots, where cousins, nieces, and nephews could all easily visit.

We talked about my dad and my worry for his health and independence. While Andy said his mother was thriving in the assisted living community, I feared that my father, Jasper Hall, would wither away in a place like that. He refused to move in with me, and Andy reminded me that I had to let him make his own decisions and hope for the best.

I found myself telling him about my amazing daughter, Ginny. She had always been academically driven and had loved every animal she'd ever met, so it was no surprise when she announced her plans to go to veterinary school when she was sixteen. She never lost sight of that goal and began taking college courses her senior year in high school to get ahead on the prerequisites for the program. I was so proud of her.

After my monologue about Ginny, he mentioned an ex-wife in passing, but didn't say anything about having kids of his own. I tried to sneak glances around the office for family photos, but he very rarely looked away from me. I was about to ask when he changed the subject.

"I heard Albert's memorial was tomorrow," he said, popping the last bite of a tamale in his mouth.

"I'm dreading that a bit," I admitted.

"Would you like me to take you?"

"Um, I am, um, going with Braydon Cunningham." Smooth. I've always been *so* smooth.

"Oh," he stiffened. "Of course."

"He just asked me today. It surprised me too. I had expected to go alone, or maybe not even at all, considering."

"You don't owe me an explanation." He started clearing away the containers.

I wasn't sure what else to say, so I didn't say anything. I pulled out my new phone and downloaded the Facebook app. While I waited for it to load, I synced my account and updated all my contacts. Thank goodness for cloud storage, because I hadn't memorized a phone number in better than a decade.

I signed into the app with my fake profile. Several people had accepted my friend requests, but Philip had not. I downloaded Twitter and Instagram on the off chance that he had active accounts on either of those platforms. He did not have an Instagram account that I could find, and his Twitter account hadn't seen any activity in two years. I glanced over my shoulder a couple of times, but Andy kept his back to me as he cleaned up the takeout mess.

"Thank you for coming out to the rescue and handling the search warrant." I talked to his back. "And I really appreciate the use of your car."

"No problem."

"It's also great to have another friend to lean on through this."

He didn't respond. I excused myself to the bathroom and splashed some cold water over my face. I looked at my reflection in the mirror, curly blonde hair an absolute disaster. My life had become nearly as tangled. I had come back home for the simplicity of a life at the rescue, the quiet honesty of horse snuggles, and crisp mornings on the farm.

I smoothed down my hair as best I could and told my reflection that this was just a hurdle. Life was full of those. You just had to get over them and get back to the good stuff. The wonderful gift from Braydon would ensure that I no longer had to worry about finances in the meantime, and no matter what happened with our relationship, I would be forever grateful to him for that. I went back out and found Andy at his desk in his office.

"I meant that," I said. "I really appreciate that you've dropped everything to help me."

"I'm glad I can help." He swiveled the chair to turn and face me.

I smiled. He hesitated for just a moment and then turned back to his laptop. I picked up my phone again and checked Facebook.

"Holy crap!" I said as I clicked on the notifications. Philip Atwood had accepted Mykayla's friend request.

"What?" Andy jumped a bit and swiveled back toward me.

"I set up a fake Facebook profile and sent a friend request to Philip Atwood. He just accepted."

"What do you think you'll find out from Facebook?"

"I don't know," I said, slightly deflated. "But it's *something*. It's better than nothing."

He watched me for a moment and then turned back around to his laptop again. I pulled up Philip's page and started scrolling through his posts. He posted a *lot*. Dog memes. Dad jokes. A few political memes. But mostly it was a running commentary on everything he perceived to be wrong with our county and sometimes the country as a whole. Those were the posts I paid the most attention to, and I pulled out my notes to cross-reference his posts with the dates of his lawsuits. That's when I started to notice that he had frequent "check-ins" listed—gas stations, the grocery store, even the courthouse—on the day he filed his lawsuit against Albert.

I had been reading every post, noting the location if it was tagged, and trying to get an idea of the places he frequented when I scrolled down to a video. He was standing next to a fence, holding the camera at arm's length and just above himself so that the land behind him was visible. It was dated the day before Albert was killed. I clicked on the video and Philip instantly started talking.

"You see this fence here behind me?" he said as the video started. *"That fence prevents me from legally accessing my own property. I have acreage directly behind Cunningham Performance Horses and the landowner refuses to grant me access to my land. I am forced to cross not one, not two, not three, but four fences to get to my land."* He panned the camera around to show the fence again. *"He refuses to allow me to pay someone to establish a road. He even refuses to allow me to install gates in his fencing so I can more easily walk in. Basically, he is illegally restricting my access to my own land, and I will not stand by and let him bully me anymore."*

The video ended. There were multiple comments below the video saying that Albert thought he owned the county because he was rich, that Philip should take him to court, and several expressing anger at Philip's plight.

"He sounds angry," Andy said.

"That was uploaded the day before Albert died," I said, trying not to get my hopes up or jump to conclusions.

"I'll make sure that information gets to Sheriff Sullivan."

I didn't tell him that I planned on looking into Mr. Atwood myself. I had noted that he listed his workplace as Pine Hill Plumbing and Electric, and I planned to see if I could find him there after the memorial. There may have been rampant rumors circulating thanks to Bob Peterson, but I felt I could still get by relatively inconspicuously. Philip and I didn't travel in the same circles, and he hadn't recognized me when I showed up on his doorstep.

Philip had obviously been walking to his property undetected. It wasn't a stretch to think that he could circle around on the same logging road that Braydon and I had taken and ambush Albert in his barn and then sneak out again. And then I realized that it wouldn't be a stretch to think that he could sneak in behind *my* property undetected as well. How many times had I ignored Banjo's one bark, or Biscuit's braying? How many times had I chalked it up to coyotes or the wind? That thought sent a shudder down my spine. I quickly googled security systems and saved a few models to my favorites. I'd been thinking I needed to get something set up anyway.

"How long do you think it will take them to finish at the house? I need to feed the horses."

"I asked Grady to let me know when they were finished."

"Maybe I should go back anyway."

"I don't think that's a good idea. It's just going to make you furious, and you can't do anything about it." He spoke with his back to me this time.

"I can't wait all night," I said, even though I knew that was obvious.

"I understand."

I went back to my Facebook stalking to occupy my mind. Philip certainly didn't hold back in his comments. He used his Facebook posts almost as an online diary of what had happened and what he intended to do about it. He seemed to be angry at everyone from Albert Cunningham to his mail carrier. The posts just dating back over the last year were a litany of every perceived slight the world had dealt to him.

I was diving into a rant that was a little longer than the rest when Andy's phone rang. I could only hear Andy's side of the conversation, but I could tell from what he was saying that it was Grady. When they hung up, he turned to me again.

"They're leaving now," he said. "He can't talk about the investigation, but I didn't get the impression that they found anything they were looking for."

"Well, of course they didn't, since I didn't murder anyone."

He grinned and pushed his glasses up on his nose. "I'll take you home." He shut his laptop and grabbed his keys off the desk.

The sound of keys rattling brought Banjo to life. He jumped off the sofa and went to the door, where he turned several high-speed circles and bounced on his front legs. Andy clipped the leash onto his collar and opened the door. I watched them, each regarding the other as if they were old friends. If my dog was any judge of character, this would be adorable. But I'm pretty sure Banjo would've loved Ted Bundy too. I gathered up the few things I had brought with me and followed them.

* * *

"They took my truck," I said as we pulled in my drive.

"You knew it was included in the warrant," Andy said as he parked the car.

"I guess I thought they would search it here." I threw my hands up. "But in hindsight, I guess that was silly. I just don't know what I'm going to do now."

"I'll take you to rent a car tomorrow."

"I can't ask you to do that."

"You didn't." He got out of the car and opened the back door to let Banjo out.

I wasn't in a position to argue. I doubted that Lanie or Bill could take time off at such short notice, and I didn't want to ask Ethan. But I hated to keep monopolizing Andy's time.

I instinctively headed toward the barn, needing to make sure that the horses were calm and all the gates were secure.

"Should we take a look at the house?" Andy asked when he realized I wasn't following him.

"I need to feed and check on everyone first, then I can focus on whatever mess is waiting for me in there."

"Need some help?"

"I appreciate the offer, but I've got this routine down to a fine art. You don't have to stay."

"I don't mind. It'll make me feel better to know you're settled and safe in the house before I leave."

I smiled and nodded. "Make yourself at home, if there's any home left."

Biscuit met me at the gate. I took the time to find all of his itchy spots and rub his long ears. He was followed in turn by the rest of the herd. All of them seemed to firmly believe that they were starving to death. Some of them *had* been starved and they never forgot it.

"Okay, okay," I said to the sea of curious noses. "I'll get your supper."

I took my time feeding them, using the chores as an excuse to postpone dealing with the house. Finally, there was nothing left to do, and I had no choice but to go and find out what they had done to my home. I hated the idea of strangers rifling through my things, not because I had anything to hide, but because it was just so invasive.

I opened the front door slowly, like I expected something to jump out at me. I didn't see anything right away that looked out of place. Banjo was curled up in his bed. He lifted his head for a moment and wagged half-heartedly. Andy emerged from the hallway holding a box.

"Oh, hey," he said.

"It's not as bad as I thought it would be," I said, gesturing to the house in general.

"You should've seen it an hour ago."

"You've been in here *cleaning*?"

"Not really cleaning, just straightening. It was pretty obvious where most of it went, but there were a few things I wasn't sure about. I put them on the kitchen table. This box is the broken stuff. Luckily, there weren't many casualties. I didn't go into your bedroom, so I don't know what it's like in there."

I peeked into the box. There was a picture frame, a coffee mug, and one of my grandmother's crystal goblets. I pulled out the biggest piece. Ginny had broken one when she was little, and now the loss of this one left me with only four. I told myself it could be worse and I was lucky to still have as many as I did.

"Thank you for doing this. I certainly didn't expect cleaning my house to be part of your billable hours."

He laughed. "Cleaning is extra."

I hoped he was joking.

"I'd better get back to the office. I have a few more things to square away before I turn in tonight. What time is Braydon picking you up tomorrow?"

"Ten fifteen."

"I'll see you tomorrow afternoon then." He put the box on the coffee table.

"Andy, thank you for everything." I wanted to hug him again, but the fear of it being as awkward as it was last time kept me rooted to my spot.

He paused in the doorway and nodded. "Keep the doors locked."

I intended to do just that. When his taillights disappeared down the driveway, I picked up my phone and dialed Braydon. He didn't answer, so I left a voice mail. "Hey, Braydon, it's me, Mallory." Like most of the human population, I hate talking to voice mail. "I wanted to let you know that the police have searched my home, took my truck and phone, and I just wanted to make sure you knew before tomorrow, um, in case you want to, um, change your mind. I would understand if you did. Anyway, I'll talk to you later."

After I hung up, I wished I had texted so I could have edited it and not sounded like a babbling idiot. I had just put the phone down when it dinged with a text.

I haven't changed my mind. Pick you up at 10:15.

I smiled as I read it. I really appreciated Braydon's unwavering support, even if it mystified me. I wasn't sure I could be that understanding if the roles were reversed.

After I unlocked the doggy door for Banjo, I went to update the investigation board with the information that I had found about Philip. But it was all gone. Everything. The police had taken every scrap of paper, every note. I stared at the blank wall for a few moments and then decided that I wasn't going to let that discourage me. I went to work re-creating as much as I could remember and started over from scratch, adding in the new information as I worked.

As I reorganized my thoughts and went back through the notes that I had kept with me in my bag, I found the notes I had taken after talking to Luis in the Cunningham driveway. He had told me that he overheard Albert say that I wasn't in a position to ask for anything and that he wouldn't regret a damned thing. Only I knew that he had never said those things to me. What if he had switched over to another call and Luis hadn't heard that part? What if it had been Philip demanding that Albert give him right-of-way access and then threatening him when he refused?

I continued by listing the things that I knew. I knew Albert wasn't killed with a gun, or a knife. He wasn't robbed. The house hadn't been disturbed. None of the horses had been taken or harmed. It was likely that killing him was a spur of the moment crime of passion, or an accident and the killer panicked. It wasn't a stretch to think that Philip, who hadn't been served with the order of protection yet, would have come to try to talk Albert into seeing things his way. It also wasn't a stretch to think that

Albert had told him just where to shove his ideas, and things had gotten heated very fast.

I finished for the evening by making a list of the people I wanted to talk to next. The first one on that list was Kathleen Clark. I planned to catch her at the memorial if she showed up. Next was Philip Atwood, followed by anyone at the Cunningham farm who would talk to me. I hated that it wouldn't be Luis, but one of the other staff would likely do. I needed to know how many times Philip had shown up there and if there had been any previous confrontations between him and Albert.

I added those notes to the board and circled Philip's name. Kathleen may have had the best opportunity to commit the murder, but Philip seemed more capable of violence.

* * *

I rushed through the morning feeding and showered quickly. I had started combing my wardrobe the previous evening and still hadn't found anything that I wanted to wear to the funeral. For the second time recently, I couldn't figure out what I wanted to wear, and that wasn't usually a problem I had. I finally remembered I had stashed some of my old work clothes in a tote at the back of my closet. I performed some domestic archaeology and pulled the tote out into the middle of the floor.

As I opened the lid, I was really glad I had stuck the bundle of lavender-vanilla potpourri in there when I put them away. Instead of smelling musty and stale, the clothes had taken on a calming, clean scent. I found what I was looking for in the middle of the stack, a modest, dark gray wrap dress. I hung it on the closet door and retrieved the steamer from the laundry room. It didn't take long to bring the dress back to life.

By the time Braydon pulled into the drive, I had successfully kept my nerves at bay by focusing on perfecting my hair and makeup. I subdued my curls in a tasteful updo, and while my makeup was on the conservative side, I took my time.

I met him in the driveway. He was wearing a dark gray suit that looked like we had coordinated our outfits.

"You look lovely," he said as he circled the front of the SUV to open the door for me.

"Thank you. I'm so sorry for the circumstances."

We rode to the cathedral in silence. Braydon seemed deep in his thoughts, and my nerves had finally caught up to me. I scolded myself, being a grown woman nervous about some silly gossip when Braydon was about to have a memorial for his father. Selfishly, I hoped that arriving with Braydon might put some of those rumors to rest, especially if it hadn't gotten out that my house had just been searched.

St. Peregrine's Cathedral, named for St. Peregrine's ties to healing, a common theme in Hillspring, is one of the few older buildings that isn't limestone. The builders chose red brick for its massive arched entryway and octagonal nave, making it shine like a rose on the hillside overlooking Main Street. St. Peregrine's Spring, one of the many mineral springs to flow from the hills, opened up below the church and wound through the gardens, which were built in terraces and gentle slopes all the way to the street below. In fact, if you didn't mind a few hundred steps, you could access the church through the garden from the smaller, matching archway at street level.

When we arrived, Braydon's Aunt Mae was already holding court in front of the cathedral. She was wearing a black dress with a shiny gold shawl and gold slippers. A large group had gathered around her, and she was fanning herself with the memorial program.

"Looks like Aunt Mae didn't waste any time getting the theatrics started." Braydon clenched his jaw so hard I was afraid he would crack a tooth.

He parked in the area reserved for the immediate family and opened my door. We both took a deep breath as we walked toward the main entrance. A very pregnant young woman headed us off just before we reached the throng surrounding his Aunt Mae.

"Braydon!" She hugged him awkwardly around her belly. "I'm so sorry about Uncle Albert. It's just awful. Do they have any leads?"

I cringed.

"Not that I know of," Braydon said without missing a beat. I made a mental note to never play poker with him. "They haven't even released a cause of death yet, so we don't know what happened."

"Well, it's just terrible. Just terrible." She shook her head, sending her perfectly curled and highlighted hair swinging across her shoulders.

"What's going on over there?" He did a chin lift toward the crowd around his aunt.

"Aunt Mae almost passed out."

"Of course she did," he said with a frown.

She slapped him on the shoulder. He shrugged. She turned her attention to me and extended her hand. These were the happiest people I had ever seen at a funeral.

"I'm Kayleigh, Braydon's cousin. And you are?"

"Mallory," I said simply, unsure of what I was to Braydon exactly, especially since I hadn't figured out what he was to me either.

We shook hands; all the while the very pregnant Kayleigh was subtly looking me over.

She turned back to Braydon. "You'll have to come over and fawn over Aunt Mae or none of us will have a minute's peace."

"I'd rather be publicly whipped, KayKay."

I winced a bit at the pet name.

"Just go!" She shoved him playfully.

He rolled his eyes and took my hand. "Let's get this over with. I feel like I need to apologize for Aunt Mae before I subject you to her. She's insufferable."

"It's okay. I think all families have an Aunt Mae."

He grinned and squeezed my hand.

We made our way through the crowd to stand in front of Mae, who took up nearly the entire bench. She was leaning back, fanning her round face with the folded paper program, while another concerned-looking older lady patted her hand.

"Aunt Mae," Braydon said after we had stood there for a moment garnering a few curious sideways glances.

"Oh, Braydon, thank goodness you're finally here." She pulled her hand away from the woman and grabbed Braydon's free hand. "You have to talk to them in there. They insist that they can't do anything about the heat. It's simply sweltering, and I can't deal with the emotional ordeal and roast at the same time." She dabbed at her eyes as if she were sobbing, although they looked dry to me.

"I'll see what I can do," he said, gently trying to reclaim his hand. She held on to him for a few more moments and then finally let go.

He led me through the murmuring crowd. Thankfully, they seemed to be occupied with the spectacle Mae was making of herself. I was happy that she had the spotlight.

"Do you want me to see if I can find an usher?"

"I have no intention of talking to anyone. The temperature is just fine."

I followed him to the front row, where we took our seats. People had started to file in. I tried to keep my eyes focused forward, but I couldn't help myself. I scanned the room for anyone who seemed out of place or suspicious in any way, even though I didn't know what that would look like at a funeral. I quickly spotted Kathleen, who was dressed in a navy blue pantsuit that made her white hair even more striking. She was seated on the opposite side from the family, and I wondered if that was her decision or where she had been asked to sit.

There was a display of photos where the casket would have been. Albert wasn't smiling in a single one of them. I wondered if he had ever been happy a day in his life. Surely, at some point, he had been joyful enough to show it.

The cathedral was packed, and at one point I sneaked a peek at the back of the room and found that people were standing as well. I locked eyes with Grady, who was at the back of the crowd. He seemed surprised to see me there. The service went on for quite some time, with several family members and friends speaking about Albert's contributions to quarter horse breeding and his philanthropy in cancer research. Aunt Mae continued to fan herself throughout the service. I scanned the crowd a couple more times looking for Philip Atwood, but I never saw him. That didn't mean he wasn't there. I was sure there were a lot of people that I didn't see.

After it was over, Braydon stayed seated while nearly everyone in attendance came and paid their respects. He chatted with a few of them, reminisced with a few others. Thankfully, no one seemed to be overly interested in me—that is, until Aunt Mae's daughter Lindsay waddled over to take Braydon's hand. I knew her name because Braydon had pointed her out earlier. She wasn't an obese woman, but she had such an odd way of moving that it gave the impression of the way a duck or a penguin walks.

"Mama and I want you to know how very, very sorry we are and that you did a spectacular job in honoring your daddy," she nodded while she spoke.

"Thank you, Lindsay." Braydon flashed his dazzling white smile.

She turned her attention to me. "Who is your friend?"

"Mallory," I offered my hand. She didn't take it. I left it there long enough for it to be awkward and she finally shook it quickly.

"Always nice to meet one of Braydon's girls," she said as if she was greeting a poodle.

I opened my mouth to say something, remembered I was at Braydon's father's funeral, and clamped my mouth shut again. I gently excused myself and made my way through the crowd out to the courtyard again. It felt intrusive to be present while Braydon reminisced with his family.

I was pretending to admire the rose bushes that flanked the gate to the garden, angling myself so I could see when Kathleen left, and a shadow fell over me. I turned quickly and looked up into Grady's disapproving face.

"You and Bradyon Cunningham seem to be close," he said.

"Braydon has been very nice through this ordeal, unlike some of my older friends."

He ignored the barb. "It was a nice service."

I nodded. I wasn't ready to make small talk so soon after he had searched my house. I looked around him to make sure I hadn't missed Kathleen.

"Looking for someone?"

"What if I am?"

"You need to leave the investigating to us."

I fumed for a moment. "What exactly are you doing besides searching my house? Have you even looked into Kathleen? I mean, she was *there* when he died, with only the flimsiest of alibis. Are you even supposed to be talking to me without my lawyer present?"

He looked amused, which made me even angrier.

"You haven't been arrested, so talking to me without your lawyer is entirely up to you. As for Kathleen, she didn't kill Albert."

"How do you know?" I snapped my attention from watching the doorway to meeting Grady's gaze.

"I'm going to take a big risk here and tell you"—he leaned in and lowered his voice even though there wasn't anyone within earshot—"in the hopes that you'll leave this alone when I do. She was online all night. She was ashamed at first and didn't admit to it right away. But she has been carrying on an online affair for the last year. Her computer chat history confirms that she and her online boyfriend talked well into the morning with no more than a few minutes of inactivity."

"Maxwell Smith," I gasped.

"I'm not even going to ask how you know that," Grady said, gritting his teeth. "But now that you know it couldn't have been her, *leave it alone.*"

"I'm afraid he's scamming her, out of what I don't know, but his entire Facebook profile is a red flag. His photo is a stock image from an advertisement."

He cocked his head a bit, and I couldn't tell if it was a smile or annoyance tugging at the corners of his mouth. "I don't want to know any more. If you tell me anything else, I'm afraid I'll have to arrest you for obstruction. But I'll tell you again, stay out of this."

I started to say something, but I noticed Braydon approaching on my left.

"Shall we?" Braydon smiled as he walked up between us, extended his arm to me, and turned his back to Grady.

I took his arm and let him lead me out to the car. I didn't look back at Grady. Braydon didn't say anything until we were pulling out of the parking lot.

"If you would like to spare yourself the trial of dealing with my family any further, I can drop you off at your house." He smiled sheepishly at me. I was thankful that he didn't ask me what I was talking about with Grady.

"They're not that bad," I lied. "If you need a friendly face, I can come back to the house with you."

"You just might get nominated for sainthood with that offer," he grinned. "But I'm hoping to usher them all out fairly early."

"If you're sure then," I said, hoping I didn't sound too relieved, "I have plenty to do at the rescue and I need to rent something to drive since the police still have my truck."

* * *

He kissed me on the cheek when he dropped me off at my house. I hoped that he wasn't just being polite and that I should have insisted on accompanying him back to the house. He didn't seem to be very close with his family. I was grateful, though it felt intrusive to be there, especially considering my status as a suspect.

I shed my dress and changed into jeans and a T-shirt. I checked my phone and found I had missed a call from Ethan.

"Hey, I missed your call while I was at the memorial."

"How did that go?"

"It was awkward." I shrugged, even though he couldn't see me.

"I was just calling to see if you're okay."

"I'm fine," I lied. I didn't bother telling him that the police had searched my house and that I was even closer to jail than when I'd first called him.

"Do you want me to meet with your attorney? Do you think he's adequately representing you?"

"I think he's alright. If I need a trial lawyer, I'll let you know." I felt protective toward Andy. He had helped me far beyond the call of duty, so to speak, and I wasn't going to second guess his skills. He had given me no reason to doubt his skills either.

Ethan told me he was planning to stay a few more days and visit with some old friends since he was in the area, and he reminded me that he was available should I need him.

I followed that call with one to Andy.

"Are you sure you don't mind taking me? I can get my friend Lanie to drive me," I said awkwardly. I didn't want to seem ungrateful for everything he was doing for me, but I knew he had other clients besides me.

"It's not a problem at all." He sounded distracted, which just added to my guilt for taking up so much of his time.

"Do all of your clients need this much attention?" I joked.

Thankfully, he chuckled. "Just my VIP clients," he said, and I could almost hear the smile in his voice.

He picked me up within a few minutes of ending the call. We fell into a comfortable conversation about Hillspring history. He had developed a renewed interest since his mother's family had lived there for several generations. She sounded like someone I would really like, fierce and independent, refusing to remarry or accept help raising her two boys after their father had a fatal heart attack. I hoped I would get the opportunity to meet her someday. And when this was all over, I hoped I would get to know Andy better too. He was so easy to talk to, and I just enjoyed being with him.

Andy didn't wait for me to get through the mountain of paperwork necessary to rent a car, and I didn't mind since he was taking time out of his business day to play chauffeur for me. When I finally finished there, I drove away in a tiny black sedan, and I felt like I was driving a Flintstones pedal car after being used to my F-150.

* * *

After getting the rental car all squared away, I took the opportunity to check up on Philip Atwood. I pulled into Pine Hill Plumbing and Electric and circled around to the employee lot, wishing I had brought my coffee with me. Philip's PT Cruiser was sitting just to the left of the back door. I finished circling the building and pulled back onto the highway. I wanted to talk to Philip at work, but first I was going to see what I could find at his house.

I couldn't shake the nagging feeling that someone needed to warn Kathleen about her online boyfriend. Ideally, that would be Grady, but he hadn't given me any indication that he would talk to her. I pulled over in the parking lot at Wilson's, our locally owned grocery store. It only took a moment to find Kathleen's number online. I hoped it was a working number.

"Hello?"

I was surprised she answered. I tended not to answer numbers I didn't know because I'm not interested in talking about my truck's extended warranty.

"Kathleen?"

"Yes. Who is this?"

"It's Mallory Martin. From the rescue." As if that wasn't obvious.

"Oh." She sounded disappointed, like she had been expecting someone else. "What do you want?"

I ignored the less-than-warm greeting and decided to dive right in. "Kathleen, I'm so sorry to be the one to tell you this, but Maxwell Smith may not be telling you the truth."

The line was silent. I quickly pulled my phone away from my ear and glanced at it to make sure I hadn't dropped the call. Nope.

"Kathleen?"

"How do you know about Maxwell?" she hissed in a tight whisper.

I froze. I hadn't thought this through well enough, and I didn't expect her to ask that particular question. In my head, when I had imagined this conversation, she'd protested, and I had presented the clear and compelling evidence to convince her of his deception.

I started talking to try to jerk my brain into action. "I didn't mean to pry. But . . . I looked you up on Facebook to . . . send a friend request because I would hate to lose touch after all of this." I rolled my eyes at my own excuse. "And I recognized Maxwell's photo from an advertisement I'd seen before. It's a fake photo. The awards he claimed don't exist. I'm worried that he's trying to deceive you."

There was another bout of silence.

"I'm really sorry, I'm sure this is awkward," I said, *knowing* it was awkward.

"I saw you at the memorial, buddying up to the family. Did Braydon put you up to this?" Her voice was still a hissing whisper.

"What? No!" My voice rose several octaves.

"Well, one of them did. Who was it?"

"Honestly, no one, Kathleen. I'm just concerned. I don't want someone to prey on you when you're vulnerable."

She hung up on me before I could say anything else. I debated whether or not to call her back, but finally decided against it. I hoped that I had planted enough of a seed to keep her from sending her life's savings to some random internet crook.

*   *   *

I pulled into Philip's carport like I belonged there and quickly scanned for any visible cameras or security systems. I'm not an expert by any means, but I didn't see anything I thought might be a surveillance system. I got out and looked around carefully to see if any of the neighbors could see me. The only house that was visible from Philip's was across the road and it didn't appear that anyone was living there. The grass looked unkempt and there was no evidence that anyone was coming and going from the untouched driveway.

Speaking of evidence, I started my search by looking through his front windows. The newspaper sat folded on the round kitchen table, but I couldn't see any further into the house from there. I didn't think the front door would be open, but I used the bottom of my shirt to cover my hand and checked it anyway. It was locked. I froze when I heard movement inside the house.

I *knew* Philip was at work. So who was that in his house? I had the sudden irrational thought that it was the police, waiting to catch me creeping around. I dismissed it quickly and decided to knock on the door before I lost my nerve. I couldn't have been more surprised at who opened the door. In the few seconds I had been frozen on the porch, I had decided that Philip must either be married or have a girlfriend. So when a small, elderly woman opened the door and pulled her robe tighter around herself, I wasn't sure what to say.

"Can I help you?" she asked and pushed her glasses back up on her nose. Her silver hair was pinned into a loose but neat bun on top of her head. She looked like she'd walked out of a Mother Goose rhyme.

"I'm so sorry to bother you," I said, finally snapping into action. "I was hoping to speak with Philip Atwood. I spoke to him the other day about a piece I'm writing for the paper. I would love to hear his thoughts about property owner's rights." I gambled that she hadn't overheard my previous exchange with Philip and hoped that he hadn't talked to her about it.

"Oh my, yes," she said, her face brightening. "I'm sure he'd love to talk to you about that, he's been treated so poorly. But he's at work right now."

"I have the worst timing," I laughed nervously. "I only have a few minutes today. Would you be willing to share your thoughts? Since I'm already here."

"I don't know if I could add anything. My Philip is the expert." She beamed with pride. I wondered if she knew he had been trespassing and cutting other people's fences.

"I love to get all perspectives. It helps shape the piece to see how conflicts have affected everyone involved."

"In that case, come on in." She stepped aside and opened the door for me to enter. "What did you say your name was?"

"I didn't," I said, floundering for a moment. "Mykayla," I said, using my Facebook alias.

"Pleased to meet you. I'm Thelma."

There were no photos on the walls or on any of the end tables. There was a clock on the living room wall and a mirror by the front door. The counters were entirely clutter-free. In fact, the place barely looked lived in at all. The only signs that anyone lived there were the newspaper on the table and a coffee cup beside the sink. There wasn't even a coffee maker. Maybe he drank that awful instant stuff, which would confirm my suspicions about him, because anyone who drinks that on purpose is capable of anything.

"Make yourself at home," she said and gestured toward the sofa. "Want some coffee?"

"Oh no, thank you." I took a seat and smiled warmly. I was glad that I had an unconscious habit of grabbing my bag when I got out of the car. I pulled out the little notebook I used for feed and grocery lists and opened it to a clean page. She sat in the rocking chair opposite me, completing the Mother Goose image perfectly.

Philip looked nothing like his mother. She was small and round, with rosy apple cheeks and bright, honey-brown eyes. Philip was dark and angular and seemed permanently unhappy. It was a stark contrast to his sweet elderly mother sitting across from me.

"I'll just jump right in, if you don't mind," I said, pen poised above my notepad.

"Go right ahead."

"How has Mr. Atwood's dispute with Albert Cunningham affected your family?"

"It's been awful, just awful." She shook her head as she spoke. "He's treated my Philip like a common criminal, calling the police any time he tries to get to his own land!" She pronounced it "poe-lease."

She went on for several minutes about all of the various ways the world had done her son wrong and how he had been targeted by neighbors, coworkers, and especially Albert Cunningham. I took notes as she talked and sneaked glances around the house when she wasn't watching me. The house was almost entirely impersonal, like a staged property or a hotel room. The only things that seemed to be sentimental were the rocking chair that Thelma occupied and a crocheted doily under the lamp on the table by the door.

"I'm so sorry to ask, but would you mind if I used your restroom?" I asked, hoping to get a quick look at the rest of the house.

"No bother." She waved off my apology. "It's the last door on the left."

I smiled and put my notebook back in my bag. I left the bag on the sofa because I thought she might be suspicious if I took it with me. I stopped just before I entered the short hallway and turned back to Thelma.

"I think I'll take that coffee, if it's not too much trouble."

"It's no trouble. I'd fancy a cup myself." She hopped out of the chair with an ease that belied her apparent age.

I quickly went to the end of the hall and opened the door I assumed belonged to the master bedroom. I did a quick once-over and found it to be just as sterile as the rest of the house. The bed was made, complete with hospital corners. There was nothing but an alarm clock on the bedside table, and again, the walls were completely bare and starkly white.

I crept back out into the hall and passed the bathroom again. There were two more doors besides the bathroom door, making Philip's house a three-bedroom. I padded quietly down the hall and peeked around the corner. Thelma was still busy in the kitchen. I took a few steps back and found the door to the first bedroom slightly ajar. It creaked when I pushed it open, and I froze. I waited, holding my breath, for her to appear in the hallway, but she never did. The curtains were open, allowing in plenty of light to see that this was clearly Thelma's room. It was the most "homey" place in the entire house, with an antique vanity and a handmade quilt on the bed.

I hurried to the last room, opened the door, and audibly gasped.

Chapter Twelve

The door hit against something about two-thirds of the way open, but it was enough to see inside. I clamped my hand over my mouth, hoping Thelma hadn't heard my gasp since she hadn't heard the creaky door. There were boxes stacked nearly to the ceiling against the back wall. The desk that sat against the wall to my right was covered in loose papers and debris. Loose papers on the floor surrounded the desk. Newspapers were piled in several stacks beside the desk at least a foot deep. It was one of those piles that prevented the door from opening fully.

I flipped on the light and stepped inside. The corkboard above the desk was just as littered with papers but one toward the bottom caught my attention. It was an article from the local newspaper about Cunningham Performance Horses from several years ago. Albert's photo was circled in red marker and several passages in the article were underlined. I took my phone out of my pocket and snapped a few pictures of the corkboard and the article. I didn't understand the significance of the parts he had underlined, but I took careful photos of them anyway. The first was a description of the farm and the second was a reference to how long the Cunninghams had been in the county.

With the light on, I could see that the boxes were labeled and numbered: *Back Border, Highway Property 1–3, Dead Wood Lake Property 1 and 2, Highway Frontage 1 and 2, NE Corner and Fence 1–4,* and so on. It appeared that he had kept and catalogued every scrap of paper from every dispute he had ever filed, and there were a *lot* of them. I took photos of the boxes as well, but I only opened the ones labeled "Dead Wood Lake Property." I rifled through the papers, but they were just copies of the court filings, property maps, and multiple folders labeled "research" that appeared to be copies of similar property disputes that he had printed and filed.

I closed the boxes and put them back exactly where I had found them, using the photos I had taken to make sure. I knew I had to work quickly, since it wouldn't take her forever to make two cups of coffee, but I didn't want to miss anything either. I took photos of the desk before I started peeling back the layers. Near the top I found a copy of the protective order summons. It had been wadded up and smoothed back out. I could understand that impulse. I had wanted to do the same thing to the search warrant. I had been *angry*. Maybe Philip had been angry enough to murder. The summons was dated, but I didn't know when it had been served. It could have come after Albert had been killed, and if so, that wouldn't have been the last straw I was looking for. The court date would have been next week.

All the speculating in the world wouldn't take the spotlight off me, though, so I continued to dig. The computer was asleep, so it came to life as soon as I pushed the power button. It wasn't password-protected, which astonished me. I guess, living with just your mom, you wouldn't need that kind of security, but it was still hard to believe in this day and age.

The last page he had been looking at was still minimized at the bottom of the screen. It was the article about Albert's death. I pulled up his search history. Unfortunately, there was no search for "how to kill a cantankerous old man and frame his neighbor" in the history, but there were plenty of searches that featured Albert. He had searched for the Cunningham Performance Horses website too and had clicked on a good many of the links on that site.

The most recent search for the farm had been the afternoon of the day Albert was killed. Philip had searched for "horses for sale" on Albert's website. Could that have been what he did? Could Philip have made an appointment late in the day and killed Albert in a fit of rage? I took photos of the everything and closed the browser. I clicked on the email icon, but he hadn't set up the default email on the computer. That meant he used a web-based email account, and I wasn't sure which one. That information hadn't been in his recent history.

Once I decided I had gotten all the information from the computer that I could, I selected "sleep mode" and left the laptop where I found it. I could hear Thelma in the kitchen and the tinkling of a spoon in a cup, so I was running out of time. Still, I wanted to take another look through his bedroom when I caught my reflection in the mirror on the bureau. Standing there, looking at myself, I suddenly became very ashamed. I had nearly broken into someone's home and had been rifling through his belongings. As bad as that felt, I told myself that I was doing it to prove myself innocent and ensure that the real killer was caught. If it turned out to be Philip, maybe the end justified the means. I didn't let myself think about the fact that Philip might not have done it and I was violating the privacy of an innocent man.

I looked away from the mirror and tried to ignore my shame. There was one chest of drawers and an end table on either side of the bed with one drawer each. I opened the first drawer, and it was nearly empty, save for a flashlight and a pair of fingernail clippers. The second end table was the one that held the alarm clock, so I assumed that was the side of the bed that Philip slept on. I pulled the drawer open and lying right on top was my flyer. It had been folded in half so that all that showed on top was the *Now Offering Riding Lessons!* announcement and a photo of Ashley's cousin on our palomino mare.

I took a photo of the flyer in the drawer, then carefully removed it. I opened it up to see if there were any notes written on it. There weren't. The rest of the contents were pretty much what you would expect to be in a bedside table—a few paperback spy novels, some lip balm, some loose keys. I put the flyer back and opened the closet.

His closet was as neat as his bedroom. His shirts were organized by sleeve length and color. His pants were also organized by color. His shoes were lined up like little soldiers on the floor. There were sweaters and blankets stacked on the upper shelves. Save for the bedroom with the boxes of legal documents, it was all just so painfully *ordinary*. I suddenly felt the need to get out of there, and in a hurry. I shut the closet door and looked over the room. I hadn't left anything out of place. I ran through the hall and met Thelma as she was sitting back down. She had placed my cup on the coffee table in front of the sofa.

"Thank you," I said and picked up the cup to take a sip. I was feeling queasy after snooping through their house, but I didn't want to be rude after asking for the coffee.

"Feeling okay?" She did a chin lift in my general direction. "You're a bit flushed."

"Yes," I lied. "Thank you so much for the coffee and for your time. Everything you've told me will help a great deal."

"Oh, good."

I made some polite chitchat and then told her that I was late for an appointment. She saw me to the door and waved as I pulled out of the drive. The pang of guilt at deceiving her felt like a brick in my belly.

I felt the same uneasy urgency all the way back into town. I'd love to say that my apprehension was due to some innate sense of intuition or instinct, but it was more about me just being disgusted with myself. I tried to shake it off as I pulled into the Pine Hill Plumbing and Electric parking lot. I circled to make sure he was still there and then parked in the front with the other customers.

I hovered around the counter for a few minutes and didn't see Philip, so I decided to wander around a bit. That paid off, because he was stocking shelves toward the back of store. As I looked at his back, I panicked. I ducked into an adjacent aisle and pretended to be fascinated with pipe fittings. I suddenly had the ridiculous idea that he could tell I had been snooping around in his house, that somehow he could see my guilt written all over my face.

I picked up a metal fitting that was bent at a curvy ninety degrees, with no clue what it was or what it was used for, and tried to steady my nerves. I shook off the stupid notion that he could tell I had been in his house, smoothed down my shirt, and took my notebook out of my bag. If I was going to play the reporter again, I was going to need to look the part.

I rounded the corner and found Philip was still stocking some sort of electrical component onto the shelves.

"Mr. Atwood?"

He turned and looked me up and down, then rocked back on his heels as a nasty grin pulled the corners of his mouth.

"I know who you are now, *Mallory Martin*." He practically spat out my name. "I thought you looked familiar when you showed up on my doorstep. And sure enough, I found your picture next to an article about your little rescue in the paper."

I tried not to let my face betray my surprise. That article had run in the local paper two years before. I wondered if he had dug back through the piles and piles of papers to find that article, and then felt my cheeks flush as I thought about being in his house.

"You're right." I tried to sound as warm and friendly as possible. "I should have been honest from the beginning."

"Damn right you should've."

"I'm sorry." I weighed the idea of apologizing to a potential murderer against getting the information I needed to prove it.

"What is it that you really want?"

"I need to talk to you about Albert Cunningham."

"I ain't interested in talking about him." He crossed his arms.

I hadn't expected him to clam up, especially considering how vocal he had been on Facebook. "I just have a few questions."

He shook his head and went back to work.

"Did you know he filed for a protective order against you?" I hoped that would prod him into saying something—anything. I knew the answer, of course, but he didn't know that.

He froze. He straightened up but kept his back to me. "What did you say?"

"I don't guess you've been served yet then." I took a step back as he stiffened.

"What are you playing at?" He turned to face me. There was something about his body language that seemed menacing.

"Albert wasn't very fond of me either." I scrambled for some common ground. "I just thought you should know."

He looked me up and down again. It made me really uncomfortable.

"I don't know what game you think you're playing, but you need to leave."

"I'm not playing any games, Mr. Atwood."

"Go on." He pointed to the front of the store. "Git."

I hesitated for just a moment and he pointed again, like he was kicking out a stray dog. I put the big, friendly smile back on my face.

"Let's visit when you have more time."

"I've said all I'm saying to you," he said with a sneer.

I nodded, still smiling. "We'll see." I turned and left before he had a chance to say anything else.

I almost ran to my car, but I didn't want to draw any attention on my way out. I was breathing as hard when I got in as if I *had* run. I pulled my notebook out of my bag and wrote everything down before it left me when the adrenaline faded. I didn't stop to think about whether any of it meant anything or not, just furiously wrote it all down before I forgot the look on his face or the way he had stiffened when I told him about the petition for a restraining order. He'd known about it already, so I had to wonder why he had reacted the way he did.

As I was pulling out of the parking space, I glanced in my rearview mirror. I could have sworn I saw Philip in the front window watching me. By the time I got turned around to see the window clearly, no one was there. I shuddered and left the parking lot in such a hurry that my tires squealed.

I went straight home and distracted myself with the evening chores. I texted Tanner and told him that it would be better for him to stay away for a little while longer. The thought of either of my volunteers getting more caught up in the mess made me sick to my stomach. He gently protested at first, but finally agreed. I sent a text to Ethan too, but he didn't respond. I went to bed that night feeling uneasy and anxious.

* * *

Sunlight shined through my bedroom window onto my face and stirred me from unsettled sleep. I had forgotten to set my alarm, but a quick check of my phone told me that it was still very early. I didn't feel like I had slept at all. Ethan still hadn't responded.

As I finished up at the barn, I found myself craning my head trying to see the Cunningham mansion, which was stupid since I knew I couldn't see the house from my place. I wondered if Braydon still had company. I wanted to talk to some of the staff to see if they had seen Philip or anything out of the ordinary the day Albert died, but I didn't want to show up in the middle of more family drama. And the more I thought about it, I didn't want to talk to them with Braydon around either. They might be more comfortable talking to me if he wasn't there.

I pulled my phone out and sent a quick text to Braydon.

I hope things went well (considering) with your family.
If you need to talk, I'm here. Let me know when you're
ready to sort the geldings. I'm happy to help.

I called Lanie and told her about searching Philip's house and
confronting him at work.

"You're crazy," she said when I was finished. "And why didn't
you take me with you? What if he had come home and found
you in his house?"

"He was at work. I checked before I went to his house.
Besides, I didn't want to get you mixed up in this."

"You don't know when his shift ends! I could have at least
kept watch for you!"

She was right. I could easily have been caught, and then the
police would have a concrete reason to arrest me, even if I hadn't
broken in. It was still a gray area, snooping around in an active
investigation.

"I'm not going to do something that stupid again," I said.

"What do you make of the flyer? It's not like he would be
interested in kids' riding lessons."

"I don't know, but I do know that Albert was found with one
of my flyers in his hand."

"That's quite a coincidence, don't you think?"

"It's less than circumstantial in the eyes of the law, though.
It isn't even a tangible connection since I put them out in several
public places. But it's definitely weird. And there's just something
off about him."

"If he really did murder Albert, you need to be careful."

"I will."

She used the rest of the call to try to prod me into giving her details about Braydon and refused to believe me when I told her there weren't any details to share. She called me a liar right before she hung up and, smiling, I put my phone in my back pocket. Biscuit nuzzled me for more scratches, and I was happy to oblige. He snorted when my phone dinged with a text message.

Managed to talk them all into leaving last night. I'll let you know when I'm ready for the geldings, have some business in town today.

I sent him a "thumbs up" emoji, borrowing Tanner's habit of responding in emojis, and then felt more than a little awkward. On the one hand, he had been very practical and pragmatic in dealing with his father's death. On the other hand, I didn't want to ignore the fact that he had, in fact, just lost his father under horrible circumstances.

This *did* give me the perfect opportunity to talk to his staff. I could tell them that I was there to see if he was ready for the horses, and if he came to find out I had been there, I could tell him that I had hoped to catch him before he left. The thought of more lying and sneaking around made me feel . . . *icky*, but I told myself that investigators had to use deception sometimes to get to the truth.

I pushed that feeling aside and ran up to the barn loft, so I could see when Braydon left. It was a short wait. I watched the Escalade disappear behind the barn and then emerge on the other side before disappearing again into the trees at the top of the driveway. I waited a few more moments just to make sure he didn't double back.

Biscuit was waiting for me when I left the barn. I stopped for a moment to scratch him behind the ears when I noticed something about one of the mares. I don't know why I hadn't seen it when I fed her, but I suspected it was a combination of being preoccupied and the fact that Molly had a long, bushy mane true to her potentially Shetland heritage. She was also smaller than the others, and I kept her and Goldie, another of the more timid residents, together in the lower paddock where they wouldn't get bullied.

"What have you gotten into?" I rubbed her narrow chest with one hand, while I pulled her mane back with the other one.

It looked like she had snagged something, a piece of a feed sack or thin white cardboard. I tugged on it and found it was just thick paper, like card stock or poster board.

But I also found that it had been *tied* into her mane.

I stumbled a few steps backward as I stared at the paper in my hands. Molly sniffed at it, likely hoping it was something good to eat. I, however, looked at it like I had just pulled a venomous snake out of her mane. The block letters were scrawled in dark black marker.

I got this close. How close next time?

I tried to force my hands to stop shaking and my breathing to slow. It wouldn't help me at all to have a panic attack. I patted Molly hastily on the rump and ran to the house. I called Grady immediately, but not before I took a photo of the note.

"If I wasn't clear before, let me be crystal clear now. Stop *investigating*." He said it in a way that made me envision him using air quotes. "Or whatever you think you're doing."

"Fine," I hissed, anger replacing the panic. "But the fact remains that *someone* trespassed on my place to leave the note. Can you at least take that part seriously?"

"I am absolutely taking this seriously," he said. "I'm taking it so seriously that I'm formally warning you to stay out of this investigation. The intent of that note is pretty clear, even if it isn't directly spelled out as a threat. I have one dead body in my county, and I don't want you to be the next one." He sighed heavily. "I'll send someone out right away to get a statement."

"Thank you," I said, biting back what I really wanted to say. Another statement. Fantastic.

After I hung up, I ducked into the house and put the note in a plastic zipper bag. It may have been silly, but if there were any fingerprints on it besides mine, I wanted to preserve them.

Keeping to my original plan, I drove my rental car up to the Cunningham house. If I was being stalked by the real killer, it was even more important to speed things along. Up until the note, I thought my biggest threat was losing my freedom. Now I was afraid it might be losing my life, or the life of my beloved horses. Grady's warning hadn't been lost on me, and the note definitely had the intended effect. I was scared. But instead of scaring me into submission, it stoked my resolve to make sure that the real killer was brought to justice.

I was immediately greeted by the young man with the crew cut who had recaptured Cooper the day I had helped Braydon sort the mares.

"May I help you, Miss Mallory?" he asked as I rounded the front of the car. "Mr. Cunningham isn't here right now."

"Oh shoot," I said, attempting to sound natural and surprised. "I had hoped to catch him before he left and nail down the details about sorting the rest of the horses."

"You just missed him."

"I'm sorry, I didn't catch your name the other day."

"Jeremy. I'm impressed you remember me at all."

"I never forget a face," I bragged. "I had also hoped to talk to him about something else, but maybe you can help me with that."

He looked at me and raised one eyebrow ever so slightly. I guessed he was used to hiding how he really felt if he had worked for Albert for very long.

"I doubt that I could help you with anything."

"I was wondering if you or anyone else had seen Philip Atwood around here recently?"

"Who?"

"Philip Atwood." I pulled out my phone and found his profile picture on Facebook.

"Oh, yeah, that nutjob," he said and then immediately flushed. "I just mean that he caused a lot of problems for Mr. Cunningham. He was always cutting fences and showing up here to yell about his rights. And Mr. Cunningham was convinced that he had been shooting at the horses from the back fences."

"Do you remember the last time he came here?"

"It was . . ." His voice trailed off. "Maybe two, three weeks ago."

"Did he yell at Albert then?"

"Not at first. I couldn't hear what they talked about at first. They were in the driveway and I was trimming the hedges. But it escalated quickly and they started yelling at each other before Mr. Atwood jumped in his car and sped away. He slung gravel all over the front walk."

"What were they yelling about?"

"I'm pretty sure that Mr. Atwood served him with a lawsuit." He smoothed down his shirt. "As you know, that wouldn't have made Mr. Cunningham very happy."

"Oh, I can imagine."

"Why do you want to know all this?"

I considered that question for a second. I had no idea how close the Cunningham staff were or whether Luis had shared his suspicions about me to anyone but the police.

"To be perfectly honest, the police suspect me of murdering Albert. And since I know it wasn't me who did it, I'm trying to figure out who did. Braydon has been incredibly supportive."

"Wow," he said and ran a hand through his short hair. "That sucks."

"It certainly does. Do you know who was the last one to leave the day Albert was killed?"

"Sure. It was Caroline, the housekeeper. The police have talked to her a couple of times now. She's been a wreck."

"Do you think she would be willing to talk to me?"

"Probably. I think she would do just about anything to help."

"Is she working today?"

"Yes, she's inside." He hooked a thumb toward the house and took a few steps up the walk.

"Would you mind asking her if she would come out here? I feel weird about going in with Braydon gone."

"Sure. I'll just be a minute."

He jogged up the stone walkway and disappeared into the mansion. I looked up at the imposing structure and tried to guess how many rooms it contained. The yearly electric bill probably came to more than my place was worth. I was lost in my thoughts when Jeremy came back down the walkway with Caroline in tow.

Caroline was a squat woman with a hard, unsmiling face. I would have taken her for a stern, unsympathetic person if not for her bright, mischievous blue eyes. Her ash blonde hair was pulled back in a loose bun that bounced when she walked. She was wearing a dark blue polo shirt and khaki pants, which I took to be the Cunningham Estate uniform, since it matched Jeremy's attire as well. It was also the same uniform she'd worn when Tanner and I brought the food.

"Hello," I extended my hand, "I'm Mallory Martin."

"Caroline Lannister." She pronounced it "Caro-line" instead of "Caro-lynn."

"Thank you for talking to me."

"Jeremy said you wanted to talk about the night Albert died, God rest his soul."

"You were the last one here that day?"

"Yes, ma'am." She nodded emphatically. "It took longer than usual that day because I was getting young Mr. Cunningham's room ready."

"Braydon?"

"That's right. Mr. Cunningham told me that afternoon that he would be coming to visit the following day, on Thursday."

I wondered why Braydon hadn't mentioned that earlier. Of course, it hadn't come up in conversation either.

"Did you notice anything out of the ordinary that day?"

"No. Like I told the police, it was just another day except for getting the spare room ready."

"How about in the days leading up to his death? Does anything stand out?"

"No, not really." She shrugged.

"Albert filed for an order of protection against Philip Atwood. Do you know anything about that?"

"Oh, that awful man was always causing problems for Mr. Cunningham. Do you think he's the one that . . . did it?"

"I don't know. Right now, all I'm sure about is that I didn't."

"I told the police the same thing. You were always so kind and patient with Mr. Cunningham. Even when he was yelling at you in the driveway, when your horse got out. You were just apologetic and respectful." For the first time in our conversation, she smiled.

That had been over a year ago. I was surprised she remembered it so well.

"Thank you. I appreciate that."

She nodded, the stern expression replacing the brief softness. "Is that all? I have a lot to do after Miss Kayleigh's hooligans nearly destroyed the house yesterday."

"I just have one more question." I smiled sympathetically. "Has anyone on staff been dismissed recently?"

"No," she shook her head. "We're a pretty tight-knit group. I would know if anyone had been let go."

"Of course, yes. Thank you so much for your time." Another motive dead end.

She nodded again. I hadn't had the pleasure of meeting the "hooligans" at the memorial. I could imagine that children turned loose in that house would be a nightmare, though. It was set up like a museum. I wondered what it must have been like for Braydon to grow up there, if Marion had softened Albert some. It was weird to get this glimpse into Braydon's life. He had been larger than life in high school. None of us ever wondered what his home life was like.

"Thank you," I said to Jeremy as he turned to follow Caroline.

"Do you think he'll sell?" Jeremy said quietly as he turned to make sure Caroline hadn't heard him. "Has he said anything to you? It's bad enough knowing he's going to get rid of the horses, but I don't know what some of us will do if he sells out. It may not seem like much, but the staff here, we're like a family."

My heart sank, and I felt like a complete jerk. I hadn't even considered how Albert's death would affect his staff. I didn't even know how many people he employed.

"He mentioned selling some of the horses, but that's all he's said. Have you talked to him about it?"

"It's different for you, ma'am. That isn't a question he would appreciate from me."

"Surely he would understand your need to know," I said, hoping my words were true.

"Yeah, maybe I'll give it a shot." He didn't seem convinced as he turned and took the same route Caroline had taken just a few moments ago.

It had become a habit now to write my notes as soon after an interview as possible, so I hurried back home and added my latest observations to my ever-growing file. I tried to justify Jeremy's response as I worked. Braydon obviously didn't visit very much, or Caroline wouldn't have had to ready a room. So it was within reason to think that Jeremy just didn't know him well enough to ask. The Braydon I had come to know over the last week wouldn't be offended by a simple question, would he? But I had to admit, I really didn't know him that well.

I added index cards with bits of information to my new investigation board and stood back to look at it as a whole. All of the bits pointed in one direction: right toward Philip Atwood. The investigators I worked with in St. Louis always talked about motive, means, and opportunity. Philip had all three.

His motive was clear. He had been in the middle of a contentious court battle over a right of way to his tiny piece of property.

Everyone I had talked to confirmed that he'd had angry confrontations with Albert on more than one occasion. The murder didn't require any special means since it looked like Albert had been killed with a blunt force object or pushed so hard that he fell and hit his head. Either way, anyone had access to the means necessary to commit the crime. And he obviously had opportunity, since he had been hiking onto Albert's property unnoticed and cutting the fences for some time.

As I was trying to decide if I had anything concrete to take to Grady, I heard Biscuit start frantically braying. It was so intense that even Banjo sat up and paid attention, adding a half-hearted bark of his own. I cursed under my breath that I hadn't dug Dad's shotgun out of storage yet. I glanced around the room for anything that could be used as a weapon and found that my household was sadly lacking in baseball bats and hockey sticks.

I settled for a mop and went from window to window to see if I could figure out what Biscuit had decided was a threat. There were no strange cars in the driveway and nothing I could see from the windows. I listened closely, but I couldn't hear anything over the braying donkey, who had started to pace up and down the paddock fence as he sounded the alarm.

I eased out onto the porch, mop first. I didn't see anything in the driveway, but Biscuit was looking up the hill, behind my house. He had pinned his long ears back and was swishing his stubby little tail angrily, still braying with every breath.

"Biscuit, hush," I said in a hoarse whisper. Not that I thought it would make any difference.

I hurried down the steps, pointed my mop up the hill, and tiptoed around the corner of the house. I came face to face with Philip Atwood.

Chapter Thirteen

Philip looked me up and down with a smirk that made my skin crawl.

"What are you doing here?" I said, my voice several octaves higher than I would have liked.

"I guess we have a habit of showing up where we aren't wanted, don't we?"

"You're crazy," I said, backing up several steps. I pulled my phone out of my pocket and dialed 9-1-1. It felt like it took forever for the dispatcher to pick up.

"There's someone trespassing on my property and I feel threatened," I said, willing my voice to stop shaking.

"That's rich," he said, laughing. "You show up at my job asking all sorts of questions. Well, I'm right here. Where are your questions now?" He spread his arms.

I recited my address to the dispatcher and added, "Please hurry."

She told me to stay on the line with her, which was fine because I had no intention of hanging up.

"That old logging road took me right to your house, just as I suspected it would. If I can't work out a deal with Junior over there," he motioned to the Cunningham farm, "then I'll see what the judge has to say about your place. I'll bet you have a lot less pull in the county than the Cunninghams."

"What makes you think you can just waltz up on private property?" I pointed my mop at him, feeling anger rising in my belly. I knew he had been the one who tied the note into Molly's mane.

"Ma'am, don't engage with the trespasser," I heard in my ear.

"Private property? What a joke. You people think you can just fence out anyone you want, keep them from using their own land. Well, I've got news for you."

He took a step toward me and there was a loud crash behind me. Philip looked past me toward the noise, and I couldn't help but follow his gaze. Biscuit was trying his level best to fit himself through the boards of the paddock fence, sending one of the boards slapping the post on one loose end, all the while emitting a noise that sounded more like a roar than a bray.

I quickly turned my attention back to Philip, who seemed less amused than he had been previously. And after what felt like hours, I heard a siren in the distance. For the first time in over a week, I was glad to see Grady pull into my drive. He got out with his hand on his holster, a deputy following him. I recognized the deputy as Corporal Darrin Bailey.

"Mallory, put the mop down," Grady said with a crooked grin.

"He showed up in my backyard." I pointed toward Philip. "He's lucky it's only a mop." In hindsight, that statement probably didn't make me look innocent, but I was shaken and angry.

"I have every right to be here," Philip crossed his arms.

"And he's crazy," I said as I tossed the mop back toward the porch.

"Why don't you both come back to the station and we'll sort through this." Grady looked from me to Philip.

"I'm not going anywhere unless I'm under arrest." Philip gave Grady that same smirk he gave to me earlier.

"So arrest him!"

"Everyone calm down." Grady raised his voice slightly. He nodded toward Corporal Bailey, who took the hint and went to speak with Philip. Grady stayed with me.

"I want to press charges."

"And that is certainly your right," Grady said, glancing back at the deputy. "Tell me what happened."

I recounted the events and tried to be as factual and unemotional as possible, which was difficult since I was so angry and upset I was shaking. I had almost finished when Corporal Bailey waved Grady over.

"He says she harassed him at work." Corporal Bailey looked at me while he spoke. "Asked him all kinds of questions about Albert Cunningham."

"Even so," Grady looked at me, obvious disappointment on his face. "She wants to press charges for trespassing, so go inform him of his rights."

Amazingly, Philip didn't put up a fight at all. Corporal Bailey led him to the SUV and Philip smiled at me the whole way, causing a shiver to run up my spine.

"You can come by in the morning, sign your statement, and make it official."

"How will I know he won't come back? He hiked in from the woods like a maniac."

"Philip is noisy, but harmless."

"Well, I feel completely safe now," I said, hands on my hips. "Can you at least take the note and take a look around? It was obviously Philip who trespassed last night too."

Grady rubbed his eyes, a gesture that he seemed to do pretty often in my presence anymore. "I'll speak to him, tell him to steer clear."

"Did that work for Albert?" I put my hands on my hips. "And speaking of Albert, where was Philip Atwood the night he was killed?"

"I'm not discussing an open investigation with you, especially since I've told you over and over to stay out of this."

"With the main suspect, you mean?"

He didn't respond. He followed me to the paddock, looked at Molly, and walked the perimeter of the paddock she shared with Goldie. He didn't find anything—no telltale fabric snagged in the fence, no obvious footprints in the dirt, nothing. He took the note with him and suggested that I stay with Lanie for a few nights.

As if I would leave my horses unprotected, I thought to myself.

"Good evening, Mallory. I'll see you in the morning." He turned and got into the SUV without looking back at me.

I was even more furious and had nowhere to point it, so I kicked a rock into the bushes. Biscuit snorted from the paddock. I went over and scratched behind his long ears.

"Who's a good boy?" I cooed. "You're the best burglar alarm ever."

After scratching Biscuit until I thought my fingers might fall off, I went back inside and made sure all my doors and windows were locked. I tried, and failed, to convince myself that I was a strong, independent woman and I didn't need anyone to make me feel safe. The truth was that I was really anxious after Philip showed up in my backyard. He was just so . . . *weird*, claiming that he had a right to be on *my* property. And while Grady didn't seem to see the threat in the note, I certainly did.

I gave in and texted Lanie.

Hey, up for a girl's night? I need to unwind.

That was true—not the whole truth, but definitely part of it. It didn't take her long to respond.

Sorry, can't tonight, going to dinner & a movie. Maybe tomorrow?

I hesitated for just a moment before I typed my answer. I didn't want to guilt her into leaving her date night.

Sure. Talk later.

I thought about calling Braydon, but I didn't feel like we were far enough into whatever it was we were doing to play the damsel-in-distress card. That left one choice if I didn't want to spend the night jumping at every little noise and bump. I sighed and dialed Ethan.

"Hello?"

"Are you busy?"

"Not at the moment. Why?"

I launched right into telling him what had just happened. "And I just don't want to be alone tonight. Lanie's busy."

"Always good to be the second choice."

"I hate to have to ask my ex-husband at all," I snapped and then instantly regretted it.

"With an invitation like that, how can I refuse?"

"I'm sorry. I appreciate your help."

"I'll be there in a few minutes."

*   *   *

True to his word, he pulled into my driveway about twenty minutes later. Biscuit announced his arrival and Banjo met him at the door. After I had time to calm down and reflect, I regretted calling him.

"I shouldn't have called," I said as soon as he closed the door. "I shouldn't have dragged you into any of this."

"I could have said 'no.'"

He bent down to rub Banjo's ears.

"I just want you to know you don't have to be here." I felt awkward and guilty all at once.

"Are we going to do this every time you ask for help?"

"Probably."

He stifled a laugh. "Well, let's just agree that if I don't want to help, I won't."

"Okay, deal." I stood there watching him pet my dog, and wondered where we had gone so wrong.

"I'll camp out here in the living room. Point me toward the extra linens."

It was awkward setting Ethan up on the sofa when we had shared the same bed for so many years, and for about the millionth time in the last week I wished I hadn't called him. I wondered if it was just habit to lean on him. But if I was going to cultivate anything with Braydon, it was a habit I was going to have to break. And that led me down a whole other path of self-reflection. Did I even *want* to cultivate something with Braydon? He was infuriating in his inconsistency, being self-absorbed and generally clueless during our dinner and then turning around and leaving me an anonymous donation that I desperately needed. As I tucked myself in that night, my head spun. I alternated between my weird and awkward personal situation and how uneasy Philip had made me. I was sure he had murdered Albert, especially now, especially after he had shown up in my backyard. I just had to figure out how to prove it. How had my life gotten so complicated?

I thought having Ethan in the house would make me feel better, more secure. But I still found myself jumping at every bump in the night and jerking awake at every snort and whinny from the horses. Every noise sent me into a spiral of imagining Philip's sneering face creeping through the woods and into the paddocks.

*   *   *

It had taken some doing, but I had managed to talk Ethan into staying at the house while I went to the sheriff's office to sign my statement. He told me that I shouldn't go without representation, and I told him I wasn't going to leave the horses alone. In the end, I had won. For the first time since Andy had agreed to represent me, he couldn't drop everything and accompany me to the sheriff's office. He had, however, sternly cautioned me not to answer questions or say anything about the investigation.

I sighed as I pushed open the doors. I was getting tired of coming in to give and sign statements not related to the rescue, and just tired in general. My anxiety and paranoia-filled night had not been restful. Grady met me before anyone asked if I had an appointment. It didn't take long to go over my statement, which I deemed entirely accurate, and I signed it without any fuss.

Grady was seeing me out of his office when Philip came bursting through the front doors. My eyes locked with his just in time to see that grotesque sneer come over his face.

"Better get used to seeing me, Missy. You'll be seeing me a lot as I drive through your so-called *rescue*."

"Is that what you said to Albert too? But he managed to get you stopped, didn't he?" I fought back a shiver. Something about that man gave me the all-overs.

"Oh, but he didn't, did he? Didn't stop me at all," he said in a hoarse whisper as he leaned toward me.

"We all know you killed him!" I couldn't fight the shudder that time. In fact, I was nearly vibrating with rage. "You murdered Albert when he shut you down!"

"Mallory!" Grady said, taking me by the arm and ushering me back into his office. I noticed that we had caught the attention of the entire department as he shut the door behind him.

"What is wrong with you?" His voice was still raised, and I was almost certain that it would have carried through the closed door.

"What's wrong with me?" I was breathless with rage and my voice was shakier than I would have liked. "What's wrong with *you*? Why are you so focused on me that you can't see the evidence right in front of you?"

"Just stop it!" he roared, his face getting red and splotchy. "You are making absolutely everything worse! You can't go around accusing people of murder!"

"Just taking a page out of your book," I snapped.

He started to say something else, but snapped his mouth shut and leaned heavily against the door.

"Have you even taken a look at Philip?"

"Of course we have," he sighed. "You have got to trust that we are investigating every possible lead."

"And?"

"And he was out of town the night Albert died." He pushed himself off the door, his anger rising again. "He was with his bowling team competing in the regional finals. He checked into the Best Western in Russellville and checked out the next day. And I shouldn't tell you any of that, but damn it, Mallory, I'm hoping if you understand that the people you keep focusing on are innocent, you'll stop speculating and let us do our jobs."

"He could've driven back and killed Albert with plenty of time to check out the next day."

"Mallory, you have got to stop. Just stop."

"And just quietly let you pin this on me?"

He rubbed his eyes again. I was getting really tired of his acting like I was exhausting him when I was fighting for my innocence.

"Your behavior certainly isn't helping. I'm not the enemy here."

"Well, it *feels* like it, Grady." I crossed my arms against the vulnerability that was creeping in. "It feels like I'm going to get railroaded for something I didn't do by one of my oldest friends."

And there it was. I had inadvertently blurted out the reason I had been so hostile, and it surprised both of us.

He softened. "I'm not trying to railroad you. I promise you that. I've already told you more than I should have, but please know that I'm on the side of the truth. And I'm doing my level best to keep you safe."

I wasn't sure I believed him, but I also knew he was in a terrible spot.

"Can I go?" I asked quietly.

"Of course." He stepped back from the door.

I wasn't sure how to respond, so I just left without saying anything else. I opened the front door to the department and Philip jumped up from the bench to the right of the door. He shoved his phone in my face.

"You see this woman here? This is Mallory Martin. She owns the shitty little horse rescue next to the Cunningham estate. She's the next tyrant trying to keep me from accessing my land."

I held my hand up in front of the camera and backed away.

"She just accused me of murdering old Albert and then I come to find out that she's suspect number one. Trying to deflect the heat off yourself? Think it'll keep me from getting access to my property?"

I nearly fell off the curb as Grady burst through the door and took the phone from Philip.

"Hey! You can't take that!" Philip looked genuinely surprised.

"Do you want to add harassment to your trespassing charge?" Grady was incredibly imposing, all squared up and looming over Philip. He punched the screen on Philip's phone with his index finger a couple of times.

"You can't delete that!"

"I just did. Get your ass out of here before I arrest you."

"You don't . . ."

"Leave now, Philip, this is your last chance."

Philip apparently finally got the hint. Grady handed him the phone back and he climbed into his PT Cruiser, glaring at me the whole time.

"Thank you," I said, still shaking. "But how did he know I was a suspect?"

"What?"

"He told me that he just found out I was 'suspect number one.'"

Grady turned slowly and glared at a middle-aged woman watching the commotion from her desk. I knew immediately that it was Janet's cousin. I still didn't know her name, but I knew from the way the color drained from her face that she was the one who had told Bob and now Philip too.

"I'll handle it," Grady said with gritted teeth.

I was happy to get out of there. Every interaction with Philip Atwood left me feeling even more uneasy and suspicious. I didn't care if he had checked into a Best Western two and a half hours away. He could have easily done just what I told Grady—driven home and killed Albert with plenty of time to get back and check out the next day.

I debated spilling the beans to Ethan, but I figured he would just try to talk me out of it. I texted and asked him if he could stay the day if I ran an errand with Lanie. He said he didn't mind, so I quickly texted Lanie and told her I needed an alibi, just in case.

Oooooh, what sort of alibi? Am I covering for you and Mr. Hottie?

Ugh, no Lanie, I have to check something out, about Albert's murder. I don't want Ethan to talk me out of it.

She responded in just a few seconds.

If I'm your alibi, let's do this right. Pick me up in 10 minutes.

There was no use in arguing, so I turned my rental car south and hoped that Ethan would forgive me.

Chapter Fourteen

The two-and-a-half-hour drive felt much longer, even though I had driven straight through. It was nice to have Lanie to chat with on the way, though. My shoulders and back ached as I got out in the Best Western parking lot. The long drive hadn't diminished my resolve, and after stretching I marched inside like I was supposed to be there. I was greeted immediately by a young brunette behind the counter.

"Can you tell me who was working the night of the Northwest Regional Bowling Tournament? The team from Hillspring stayed here."

She hesitated, looking from me to Lanie, who was uncharacteristically quiet. "We aren't allowed to give out that kind of information."

"I'm investigating a homicide and I need to know if this man stayed here on the night in question." I held up my cell phone with Philip Atwood's Facebook profile photo displayed.

"I wasn't working that day." She looked at the photo and then back to me.

"Can you tell me who was?"

"Rachel," she said without hesitation. I was relieved that she hadn't asked for any identification. I wasn't sure how I would have handled it if she had.

"Rachel?"

"Davis. Rachel Davis."

"Can you give me her phone number?"

"No, I don't think I can I do that," she said, shaking her head.

"Can you tell me when she works again?"

She bit her lip. "Who did you say you were again?"

"I'm investigating a homicide." I dodged the question. "How about an email address? I can contact her, and she can decide if she wants to meet me."

She chewed her lip again and shifted her weight from one foot to the other. "Okay."

She typed in something on the computer and then wrote the email address on a Post-it note. She hesitated again before handing it over to me.

"Thank you," I said and left quickly before she had a chance to change her mind.

I emailed Rachel as soon as I got back to the car. I hoped she was one of those people who had their email pushed to their phones. I put my phone back in my bag and pulled out into the street. I drove around and listened for the email alert on my phone while Lanie took a phone call from Eve about an inventory issue. I knew I couldn't wait very long for her to respond, and thankfully, I didn't have to.

Dear Ms. Martin,

I do not remember the man in the photo. I'm sure you can imagine that I see hundreds of customers and there was nothing to make that one stand out. I vaguely remember some people checking in and talking about the bowling league, but I don't remember that man specifically. We do not record entry/exit times for the rooms, although security footage should still be available with a warrant. Hope that helps.

Sincerely,

Rachel Davis

I'm not sure what I expected, but whatever it was, that wasn't it. I felt defeated all over again. Heather had the best alibi in the county, a night with the sheriff. Kathleen had been online with someone who was likely scamming her or would be soon if he wasn't already. And now it would seem that Philip had an alibi too. Even I was beginning to think I was guilty.

After indulging my self-pity for a few minutes, I filled up the gas tank and started the trip home. I had plenty of time on the drive to decide my next move, which I told myself would be to take this information to Grady. I had no power to get a warrant for the security videos, so if that was what it took to prove that Philip had driven back to Hillspring that night, so be it.

"I need to make one more stop if you don't have to get back too soon."

"Nope, I'm good." She shrugged. "Who are we investigating next?"

"No investigating this time. I need to get a security camera," I said, and when she gave me a puzzled look, I filled her in about Philip sneaking onto my property not once, but twice. That I knew of.

We stopped at a big box hardware store on the way home and bought a security camera. The salesman assured me that I would have no trouble setting up the wireless system. I was away from the horses far more than I wanted to be, and with a wireless system that fed to my phone and computer, at least I would be alerted if Philip decided to do something when I wasn't there. I tried not to think up nightmare scenarios in my head as I drove the rest of the way home.

I was about five miles from my hometown when my cell phone rang. I was so used to answering with the Bluetooth in my truck that I fumbled with my phone and dropped it on the floor. I was able to slow down and retrieve it without pulling over or killing myself.

"Hello?" It came out as a question and I'm sure I sounded more than a little annoyed.

"Mallory? Are you alright?"

I recognized Andy's voice, and his worried tone set me on edge.

"Sorry, dropped my phone. What's up?"

"I have been notified by a reliable source that the state police are going to ask you for an interview. I think it would be prudent to go in the morning and get it out of the way. I've cleared my day to accompany you."

"On a Saturday?" My stomach sank.

"Yes. I've made arrangements to meet the lead detective."

I told him what I just done. "Should I give the email to them tomorrow?"

"I don't think we need to tell them that you're investigating on your own. It might look like you're trying to deflect the blame or worse, frame someone." He sighed. "And while we're on the subject, I don't think it's a great idea for you to be investigating on your own anyway."

"You and everyone else."

"Well, maybe if everyone is telling you the same thing, there's something to it."

"What time?" I changed the subject.

"Meet me at the sheriff's department at nine, or I can pick you up and we can talk on the way."

"I'll meet you there," I said, and we ended the call.

Lanie spent the rest of the drive to her antique store where we had left her car telling me how stupid it was for me to be a suspect. She gave me the biggest hug she could manage with both of us still in the car and told me not to worry before she got out and went inside. She turned at the door and waved enthusiastically. Her optimism was comforting.

As I pulled into my driveway, I found Ethan on the porch with Banjo. He looked up from his iPad and Banjo wagged.

"How is Lanie?"

"She's fine." I avoided looking him in the eyes by leaning down and scratching Banjo's ears.

"I know you weren't with her," he said quietly. "At least not at the shop."

"What?"

"Please stop playing games. I don't know why you're lying to me, but I don't really appreciate it."

I couldn't avoid looking at him any longer and wished I hadn't. He looked genuinely hurt.

"I went into town for lunch at Griff's," he continued. "Bill and his crew came in. Imagine my surprise when I asked how the inventory was going and he said Lanie had gone on a road trip with you."

"I went to Russellville to try to poke holes in Philip Atwood's alibi for the night that Albert was killed."

"Why didn't you just tell me?"

"I didn't want you to talk me out of it."

He stared at me for a moment, and I tried to read his expression. I couldn't tell what he was thinking.

"My lawyer called. He said that he heard from a 'reliable source'"—I used my fingers for air quotes—"that the state police want to go over my statement. He thought it would be a good idea to go in the morning and meet them before they summon me."

"Probably a good move. That way you can appear helpful and open."

"I *am* helpful and open."

He scoffed.

"I'd like to go with you," he said as he stood and opened the door. "Andy seems like he's a decent enough attorney, but he hasn't had any criminal experience in recent history."

"He's doing a good job," I said. "I appreciate your concern, but I think we're okay."

He looked skeptical but didn't argue with me. I fed the horses while my stomach growled. After I was finished, I gave in to my cravings and fixed my favorite comfort food for supper: grilled cheese. Ever since I was a kid, grilled cheese sandwiches meant security and happiness, probably because that was what Mom always fixed for me when I was sick or when I had friends over. I sat down at the table across from Ethan and dug in unceremoniously.

"I'll have to admit, I've missed your grilled cheese sandwiches."

"How can you mess up a grilled cheese?" I said around a giant bite of my own.

"I don't mess them up," he laughed. "They're just not as good as yours . . . I have to give you credit, you've made a nice life here," he said in between bites.

"It's not all fun and games. I'm struggling most of the time. Money is always tight."

"But you're happy, right?"

"Yeah." I smiled over my sandwich. "I am. I hated my job, and I hated the city."

"And you hated me."

"Is that what you think?" I gasped. "I've never hated you, Ethan. We just wanted different things out of life. You know that it wasn't working."

"I shouldn't bring up ancient history."

"Do you really think I hate you?" I wasn't letting that one go.

"Mallory, you packed your stuff and moved out without so much as a discussion."

"What was there to discuss? Our marriage was over."

"I don't know, maybe discuss marriage counseling?" he said, pushing himself back from the table. "Maybe discuss if we even wanted to end the marriage? But no! You just decided for the both of us."

I stared at him for a moment. I couldn't believe he was angry after all this time, especially since he had seemed to move on to Diane so easily.

"We discussed it to death! I remember discussing it nearly every time we were in the same room together! Only it was more yelling than discussing, if I remember correctly."

"I knew you were unhappy. You made that abundantly clear. But I was floored when you left. I had been harboring the illusion that we could work through it together."

"Would you have left the city? Would you have moved back down here with me and gone all-in on the rescue?" I tossed the rest of my sandwich onto my plate and crossed my arms.

"I honestly don't know. You didn't give me a chance to decide."

"Are you kidding me?" I could feel my face flush and my chest tighten. "You act like we hadn't been fighting about that *exact thing* for months before I left!"

"I don't want to do this again." He held up his hands, as if in surrender.

"Just like the good ol' days," I snarled. "When the going gets tough, you shut down."

"I just don't want to fight anymore. I didn't mean to dredge up all the old resentments."

"What *did* you hope to accomplish?"

"I guess I just finally wanted to tell you that I hadn't wanted our marriage to end. I know we had a rough year, or maybe couple of years if I'm being honest. But I hadn't wanted a divorce."

"You never contested anything. You just signed the papers like you were relieved."

"I wasn't relieved. But I also wasn't going to stand in the way of your happiness." He stood and took our plates to the sink. "You're right. I wouldn't have left the city and my job. I've always loved the law. I can't imagine giving that up. I know divorce was really the only answer, but I wanted you to know that it wasn't a relief."

"Maybe we're better as friends," I said, willing myself not to get misty-eyed.

"I hope so." He smiled.

We retired to our opposite sides of the house, me in my bedroom and Ethan on the sofa again. I pulled up the Notes app on my phone and entered all my questions. I thought about what might have driven Philip to murder Albert and wondered if he was unhinged enough to kill me too. He'd certainly been unhinged enough to sneak around and leave creepy, threatening notes. Normal, law-abiding citizens didn't do things like that. I shuddered as I thought about the note, *I got this close. How close next time?* It was pretty close, I guess, since he had walked right up in my yard. I heard one of the horses whinny, and I sat bolt upright in bed before the logical part of my brain kicked in, and I realized it was a whinny and not a bray. Biscuit wasn't sounding the alarm.

When my alarm went off the next morning, it took a few moments for me to realize why I had set it so early. I had only slept a few hours, and not consecutively. Brooding over Ethan kept me from worrying myself sick over my impending appointment with the state police and whether or not Philip was planning to murder me like he had Albert. I dressed quickly and braced myself to face the man in my living room. But when I hurried in, I found the living room was empty. The only male was Banjo, wagging his whole butt in his enthusiasm to see me.

"Where did Daddy go?" I asked and then inwardly cursed myself for referring to Ethan as Daddy. Old habits die hard.

I moved toward the window to check for his car, and that's when I noticed the note taped to the door.

Mallory,

In light of recent events, I think it's best that we establish some clear boundaries. I'm going home, but the offer remains that if you need anything you can call me. I've asked Lanie and Bill to stay at the rescue with you.

Ethan

I ripped it off the door and pulled my phone out of my pocket.

I never meant to make you leave. I'm grateful for everything you've done for me.

I followed that by calling Lanie and telling her that I didn't need her and Bill to stay with me. She protested a bit, but finally agreed to stay home if I promised to finally dig Dad's shotgun out of storage. Ethan texted back while I was on the phone with Lanie and I tapped the notification when I ended the call.

No worries. Call me and let me know how you are. I still care.

I smiled at the text. Ethan was a good man, and I was glad that he was Ginny's father. It would have been nice to grow old with him, but it would have meant giving up who I really was, and that wouldn't have done either of us any favors. It would have been inevitable for me to come to resent him for that.

Before I headed to the barn, I opened up my wireless security camera and set it up. The salesman hadn't lied, it was relatively easy to set up and only required a moderate amount of swearing to get it to sync with my phone. It took longer to mount it on the corner of my porch than it did to set up, because it took me ten forevers to capture *just* the right angle to see both the yard and the barn at the same time. When I was finally satisfied with its field of vision, I pulled on my boots and went to the barn.

I tried to slip into autopilot while I was feeding the horses, to just find comfort in the routine. But worry and anger kept creeping in, and after I had fumbled buckets and tripped over the water hose, I had a proper hissy fit. I took everything out on an unsuspecting bale of hay, and when I had exhausted myself, I sat down on the bale to catch my breath. I had only permitted a few minutes of self-indulgent pity when Biscuit nosed the barn door open and joined me.

Velvet donkey nose nuzzled my cheek, and I stroked his soft neck. I buried my face in his soft coat and wrapped my arms around his neck. That in itself was almost miraculous—he had been such a skittish and frightened creature when he first came to me. But once he decided people weren't all bad, he became our resident ambassador and therapist. I was certain that he had comforted me many more times than I had comforted him.

I took longer than I should have with Biscuit, so by the time I crawled into my car, I was afraid I was going to be late. But I pulled into the sheriff's parking lot with five whole minutes to spare. Andy was already waiting for me.

"I was beginning to wonder if you'd left the country," Andy said, laughing at his own joke.

I smiled at him. Andy opened the door for us, and I tried not to throw up. The office was nearly empty, which wasn't surprising on a Saturday. We were shown to the same stuffy interview room where I had given my first statement. The deputy who had shown us in returned, accompanied by two state police officers who introduced themselves as Sergeants Fenwick and West. Sergeant Fenwick seemed to defer to Sergeant West, a middle-aged woman whose black hair was captured in a severe bun on top of her head.

"Mallory Martin, I presume?" Sergeant West extended a perfectly manicured hand to me and shook it with just the right amount of practiced strength. "Who is your friend here?"

"Andrew Hannigan, my attorney."

"Attorney?" She cocked her head to the side and smiled. "Do you anticipate needing legal advice?"

"I understood you had some questions about my statement," I said, ignoring her barb. I guessed that she was trying out the "bad cop" part of their duo.

"We do." She continued to smile, even though it made her seem colder than she had been before she started showing her teeth. "When was the last time you talked to Albert Cunningham before your conversation with him on the day he died?" she continued.

"I have no idea. We didn't talk regularly." I shrugged. That question caught me off guard, as I'm sure it was meant to.

"I'm sure that can be verified with phone records," Andy said, leaning back in his chair. He looked even more like Mr. Rogers this morning in his pale blue cardigan. He'd switched back to contacts and his dark hair was slicked back in a stylish Harvard clip.

"Sure, sure." Sergeant West nodded and then she leaned over and pulled out a thick file from her bag. "The meeting I'm talking about, though, wouldn't have happened over the phone. It would have been in person."

"Well, that was even more rare," I said.

"Was it?" She opened the file and started thumbing through the contents. "When did Mr. Cunningham tell you about his plans regarding the township?"

"What?" I had no clue what she was talking about. I looked at Andy, who shrugged.

"The township, Ms. Martin," she repeated slowly. "When did Mr. Cunningham tell you about it?"

"I don't have any idea what you're talking about."

"Are you sure about that? Do you want to take a minute and think about that?" She pulled a manila envelope out of the stack with a handwritten label across the front. I could just make out the word "Township."

"I don't need a minute. I've never talked to Albert about a township." I stared at the envelope. I felt as if I had seen it before, but I couldn't remember ever having a conversation with Albert about anything other than his disdain for my rescue.

"How do you explain that your fingerprints are all over this envelope then?" Sergeant West held up the thick manila envelope and then let it fall loudly down on the table. I jumped.

"I can't." I could hear my heart pounding in my ears, and it felt like the room had gotten several degrees hotter. "All I know is that I never talked to Albert about much of anything but my rescue, certainly not any townships."

"What are you getting at, Sergeant? What does this have to do with Mr. Cunningham's death?" Andy asked, still leaned back casually in his chair.

She regarded Andy with a cool expression for just a moment before she took out another set of papers from her folder. I looked over at Sergeant Fenwick, who was apparently just there for decoration.

"Mr. Cunningham had big plans," Sergeant West said as she slid the papers over to Andy. "He was laying the groundwork to reestablish the old Oak Valley Township. You're aware of the old township, Ms. Martin?" She didn't wait for me to respond. "He had done quite a lot of work toward that goal. He had researched the previous boundaries, put together a petition, proposed charter, proposed local government, and added a clause that would give you even more motive to get rid of him." She leaned over the table and tapped the bottom of one of the pages she had slid over to Andy with her pen.

"I need a moment with my client, please." Andy suddenly looked very serious, and my stomach tied itself in knots.

"Of course." Sergeant West rose quickly and gathered up everything she had laid out on the table. Her mute colleague followed her lead and they both left the room.

"What is going on?" I asked as soon as the door closed.

"Mr. Cunningham added a clause to his petition for incorporation that essentially would have eliminated your rescue. In the simplest terms, it would grandfather in older farms that could be traced back to the original township, namely his, but would outlaw newer farms like yours. They're suggesting that this was your motive for killing him."

"Could he do that?" I suddenly felt breathless. "I mean, what were his chances of actually getting that to pass?"

"It doesn't matter if they can establish beyond a reasonable doubt that you knew about it and that you believed he would be successful," Andy said, looking grim.

"But they don't have any physical evidence that ties me to the murder," I pleaded.

"You know as well as I do that there have been plenty of people convicted on circumstantial evidence alone. Scott Peterson, for one." Andy didn't seem fazed by my comment at all; he just continued to lay out the worst-case scenario for me in his calm, friendly manner. "And they have circumstantial evidence in spades. Plus, there's the matter of the long-standing feud and the easy access to the scene."

The only thing keeping me from hyperventilating was sheer will. I don't know how much time had passed when Sergeant West poked her head back through the door.

"We just have a few more questions, if you're finished."

Andy looked at me and then nodded for her to come back in. She left the quiet partner outside this time.

"How long ago did you cut the fence between your rescue and the Cunningham farm?" she asked as soon as she sat down.

"I didn't cut the fence," I said, shaking my head. Even with everything going on, I worried that the horses would get out before I got home to fix it. "But I'll tell you who did. Philip Atwood, that's who. He had a habit of cutting the Cunningham fences."

"We talked to Mr. Atwood. He has a different story. He said that you showed up on his doorstep and lied about who you were. He said he thought you might try to plant evidence against him, so he was trying to keep an eye on you."

"He uploaded videos of himself cutting the fences." I pulled out my phone and opened my Facebook app. It took a few minutes to log into my fake account, and my hands were shaking so badly that I entered the password wrong twice.

I scrolled through Philip's time line to find the videos, only they weren't there. My breathing became rapid and shallow as I clicked on the "video" tab. Nothing.

"He deleted them," I said, my eyes burning as they threatened tears. I looked at Andy, desperate for a lifeline.

"I would expect there to be a search warrant for Mr. Atwood's computer and phone history. The videos in question can easily be verified."

"Mr. Atwood isn't a suspect."

"And I am?" My voice squeaked pitifully.

"Yes," Sergeant West looked me right in the eyes, no smile this time.

"I think we're done here." Andy stood and extended his hand to Sergeant West. "We'll be in touch."

"We're not finished." She stayed seated.

"Unless I've missed something, you haven't charged my client with anything."

"Not yet." And there was that icy smile again. "We can clear this up pretty quick if your client will consent to a polygraph test."

"Absolutely not," Andy said as he took hold of my arm. He practically dragged me out of the room, leaving the Ice Queen in the depressing bare room. Grady opened the door to his office as we passed, and the expression on his face confirmed my fears.

I was going to be charged with Albert's murder.

Chapter Fifteen

" Take some deep breaths." Andy patted my shoulder. We sat in his car at the back of the sheriff's department parking lot since he didn't think I could drive in my current state. He was probably right.

I tried to do as Andy suggested, but I ended up panting like a dog in July.

"They haven't charged you yet," he said calmly. "That may be a good sign."

"You're a lousy liar for a lawyer," I said, tears welling in my eyes. He laughed and continued to pat my shoulder. "What do I do now?"

"I'm not entitled to see their evidence at this point, so I don't know what sort of case they're building against you, other than what they've told you. But I can start investigating what we do know."

"Okay."

"Don't repair that fence," Andy said, staring off into the middle distance. "We need to thoroughly document the area. If it's rusty we can prove it was done a long time ago."

"I don't think it was or the horses would've gotten out."

"Still, just move them around or something until we can get in there," Andy said.

"Philip did this," I said. I fought back the tears and tried to stoke the little flame of anger that was building in my belly. "He deleted those videos. He creeped up in my backyard and turned the whole thing around."

"What about the township?" Andy asked.

"I don't have any idea about that." I shook my head, which must have knocked something loose, because I finally remembered where I had seen that envelope before. "Oh my God," I gasped. "That envelope was on the folder."

"What folder?" he asked.

"I helped Braydon sort some mares to sell, and he asked me to put their registration papers back in his dad's study. That envelope was on top of the folder for the papers. That's why my fingerprints are on it!" I whirled around in my seat to face Andy. "We have to go back in and tell them."

"I don't think that's a good idea right now," Andy said.

"Why not? If that's the biggest smoking gun they have, so to speak, then why wouldn't we go back and tell them why my fingerprints are on it?"

"Because it looks like we came out here and cooked up a reason," Andy said. "It would be better if you got your boyfriend to explain why your fingerprints are on it."

"He's not my boyfriend." I turned in the seat to face him.

"Entanglements aside, we need him to make the statement," Andy pulled out a notebook and pen. "But let me make the call."

I wrote Braydon's number down on the blank page, although I had every intention of contacting him myself. We said our goodbyes after Andy was sure I was calm enough to drive. I drove myself straight to Junk & Disorderly, where I knew Lanie was working the morning shift.

"Whoa," she said as I finished recounting my disaster of a morning.

"Yeah."

"Get your butt over to Mr. Hottie's house and tell him you need him to get his sculpted abs up to the sheriff's office and clear your name."

"I texted him on the way here, but he hasn't responded."

"I didn't say 'text him.' I said, 'get your butt over to his house.'" She pointed at me for emphasis.

"I don't know if he's home." I leaned back in my chair and wrapped my arms around myself. "Plus, I just need to sit here and talk to my friend and forget that I'm living in a nightmare, for just a little while."

"Okay then," she slapped the desk. "I'll order takeout from Minnie's Munchies and we'll forget the world."

Lanie is one of the best distractions ever created, and not for the first time recently, I counted myself grateful that she was my friend.

* * *

Driving home after a few hours with Lanie, I realized all over again how lucky I was to have a best friend like her. She had asked several more times if I was sure I didn't want her and Bill to stay with me as Ethan had asked. I assured her that I was safe, and that Philip would be really stupid to eliminate the one person who was taking the heat off him. She remained skeptical, but finally quit asking. I wished I believed what I'd told her.

Driving through the town where I had grown up, the town that I had always associated with comfort and a sense of belonging, suddenly felt cold and unfriendly. The shadows seemed darker, and it felt like there was an undercurrent of betrayal. I knew it was a stupid notion, but I felt like my acquaintances and neighbors should just *know* that I couldn't murder anyone.

I slowed my rental car as I approached the Cunningham driveway. I had suddenly lost my nerve and I almost drove right past to my own driveway. But I forced myself to turn into the manicured drive and turn up the hill. I had a pretty good idea of why I felt apprehensive. I hadn't heard from Braydon since the memorial, and I was afraid that the police had convinced him that I was guilty of killing his father. It's not like we were established enough in our relationship, if you could even call it that, for him to know me well enough to know I wasn't capable of murder.

I topped the hill and saw Braydon's Escalade parked in front of the house. Well, I guess technically it was Albert's Escalade, but Braydon had driven it since that first day back. I briefly wondered why he didn't use the garage, but I also had no idea if the garage was full of Albert's other cars or not. Albert seemed like the type to have an assortment of luxury vehicles.

I got out of my car just as Braydon was walking down the front walkway, holding his phone to his ear. His jaw was clenched and his nostrils flared. I couldn't hear what he was saying, but he ended the call with an angry jab at his screen.

"I'm so sorry to ambush you like this," I said as soon as he was close enough.

"Don't be silly. You're welcome here anytime." He flashed that dazzling smile, and the anger I had observed melted away.

"I take it you haven't spoken to the police then," I said, leaning against my car.

"Not today."

"Look," I gulped. "The state police are even more convinced than Grady that I killed your dad. I didn't, I want you to know that. I would never hurt your dad for any reason. I would never hurt anyone."

"Mallory, I know that. They're grasping at straws. If you need me to speak with them, I'll be happy to."

I smiled back at him. Even though I knew I was innocent, I felt like I didn't deserve his intense loyalty.

"Now that you mention it, that's what I came here to ask. I know I have no right to ask for favors . . ."

"Just stop." He cut me off and put his hands on my shoulders. That close I could smell his earthy cologne, a woodsy scent that suited him perfectly. "What do you need?"

"When we sorted the mares, I put the papers back in your dad's study. The folder for the papers was under a manila envelope. Apparently, your dad had started the process to reestablish the old township here to put my rescue out of business."

"That sounds like dear old Dad."

"Well, the petition and research were in that manila envelope. My fingerprints are all over it because I moved it to put the registration papers up. The police think that I knew about it since my fingerprints are on the envelope. They think that's my motive."

"That should be easy enough to clear up." He rubbed my shoulders reassuringly. "I'll just tell them what happened. And quite frankly, I'm getting tired of all the focus on you, and meanwhile the actual killer is just out there, free and unbothered."

"I don't know what I'd do if you believed them." I looked up into his eyes and silently hoped he would kiss me. I'm pretty sure I blushed at that silly thought.

"I don't mean to be rude, but I was on my way out." He rubbed my shoulder again.

"Oh, of course. I'm so sorry." I fumbled around with my keys and opened the car door.

"No problem. How about we have dinner again? Tonight?"

I almost jumped to say "yes" before I remembered that Philip Atwood could walk onto my property from the woods at any time. And the police thought he was innocent.

"As much as I would love to, I'm afraid to leave the rescue unattended. Philip tied a creepy note in one of my horses' manes and then he walked up in my backyard last night and acted very threatening. Not that the police seem to care."

"Why didn't you call me?"

"You just lost your father. I didn't want to burden you with my problems."

"Honestly, it's nice to have a distraction." He shrugged. "I'll call you when I get back. We can do something closer to home."

"Talk to you later," I said and got in my car, a little more gracefully on the second try. He followed me down the driveway.

When I got back to the rescue, I decided to work outside for a while. I was hoping the physical activity would keep me from thinking. About anything. I started by closing the gates to the paddock that joined the Cunningham farm since I wasn't supposed to repair the fence. All of the beasts were accounted for, grazing in the upper pasture behind the barn and lower paddock for the mares, so it was just a matter of shutting off access.

I pulled out some chain and my bolt cutters and chained every gate on the rescue. I realize that Philip had a habit of cutting fences, but I wasn't going to make it easy to steal the horses or let them out. I had purchased a set of locks that were all keyed the same years ago with the intention of padlocking the gates, but I had never gotten around to actually doing it. This seemed as good a time as any.

Banjo had finally had enough of watching me from the backyard and yipped loudly, so I went to retrieve him before I went to check the rest of the fences. He wasn't much on guard dog duties, but I still felt better having him with me. It took longer than it should have to check the fences since I had neglected clearing them as I should have, and I cursed myself every time I got tangled in briars or tripped over a sapling. If I stayed out of jail, I was going to get the fence rows cleaned out ASAP.

None of them had been cut other than the one between the rescue and the Cunningham farm. I appreciated Andy's train of thought about when the fence had been cut, but there was no rust on the shiny end pieces of wire. It had been relatively recent. I stood in the tree line and looked up at the huge show barn clearly visible in the powerline clearing. I was deep in thought when my phone rang, and I jumped like I'd been shot.

"Hello?" I said, realizing I had answered without paying any attention to the caller ID.

"Mom?"

"Oh hi, Ginny," I said. It *was* Saturday. I was really glad she didn't call while I was being interrogated.

"Is everything okay? You sound funny."

"I'm good." I choked back tears. For some reason, it was harder to pretend with my sweet daughter. "I'm just out checking fences."

"Ashley told me about everything that's going on," she said quietly.

Ashley doesn't know the half of it, I thought. "Nothing you need to worry about," I said. "How are your classes going?"

"Of course I worry, Mom. I can come home and stay with you for a while, until all this gets sorted out."

"It's okay. Your dad is here." *Was* here. She didn't need to know he'd gone home.

"Dad? There?" Her voice cracked.

"Yeah, he's been helping with the legal issues and helping me at the rescue."

"Neither of you ever tell me anything."

"There's nothing to tell," I said, out of breath as I climbed the hill to go home. "This is all going to blow over. It's nothing, really."

"It's nice that you and Dad are in the same state again."

"Yeah." That was all I could muster.

"Please let me know before he leaves, I would love to have lunch or dinner with the both of you."

"That sounds wonderful." I didn't add that we should do it soon, before I'm arrested, or that it would be hard since he wasn't here anymore.

She launched into telling me about her odd chemistry professor who always smelled like pickles and how hard she thought Statistics 101 was turning out to be. I was thankful that our conversation turned to what was occupying her, instead of my potential incarceration.

I made a mental note not to tell Ashley anything I didn't want passed on. Ashley was such an old soul it was easy to forget that she and my daughter were the same age and had become close friends over the last few years. Ashley had been part of a different crowd than my artistic, academically driven daughter, choosing instead to focus on sports and cheerleading. When they graduated, albeit from different high schools, Ginny had gone straight to college, and Ashley had worked in her family's bed and breakfast for a year before figuring out what she wanted to do with her life.

Ginny talked excitedly about her plans to open a veterinary practice after college and how she could help at the rescue. I was glad that she was talking a mile a minute because I choked again. I had no idea if the rescue would still be around when she graduated. I knew I had to refocus my efforts and prove that Philip had killed Albert, but at that moment I had no idea how to do that.

* * *

I felt my resolve renewed after I got off the phone with Ginny. I wasn't about to let the likes of Philip Atwood take everything away from me. I looked over my investigation board again. I added a note about Philip deleting his videos, which prompted me to check his Facebook page. I pulled out my phone since I was still logged into my fake account on it. I typed in Philip's name and received a list of Philip Atwoods in the area, except none of them were the Philip Atwood who walked up in my yard. He'd unfriended Mykayla Parker. I cursed under my breath and then noticed the little icon that showed a message. I clicked on it and quickly signed into the fake account on Messenger as well. The message was from Philip. I clicked on it.

I know this is you, Miss Martin. You're not nearly as smart as you think you are.

I closed the app and pushed my phone to the other side of the desk like it had somehow been contaminated by Philip's message. It wasn't a stretch to figure out that Mykayla wasn't a real person, but I had no idea how he could figure out it was me behind the profile. I had only told Andy about setting up the fake account, and he wouldn't have told Philip anything, even if he had thought I was wrong to do it. Maybe I had underestimated Philip after all.

I needed to clear my head and figure out what to do next. And I needed to remind myself why I was fighting so hard to find the real killer, beyond the obvious reason that I was innocent, of course. River met me at the gate, almost as if he'd known I needed him. I stroked the white snip on his chestnut nose. Zeus whinnied after him from his grazing spot on the hill, a sound that Dad had always called a "nicker."

I slipped the halter over his nose and buckled it behind his jaw. Biscuit escorted us to the barn, where I took my time saddling and tacking up. River waited patiently while I dusted off all of my rarely used tack. I would remedy that. After all, this was a big part of what had been missing from my life in St. Louis. Not that I couldn't have had a horse there, boarded it somewhere, and ridden any time I was free. The problem was that I hadn't been free. I'd been tethered to the job even when I was supposed to be off, taking calls, reviewing records, doing research. Those were the things that energized Vera, the other legal nurse consultant at my firm. She lived for it. I didn't.

As I swung my leg over River's back and settled into the saddle, I knew in my bones that *this* was what I lived for. I took up the slack in the reins and asked River to side pass to the gate.

I opened it, rode through, and then closed it again with River never making a mistake. Whoever abandoned him missed out on one of the best horses I'd ever had the pleasure of working with.

I rode him down the steep driveway, to a chorus of whinnies and braying from the herd we were leaving behind, and onto the grassy shoulder alongside the pavement. Normally, I would have headed into the woods, taking some of the same old logging roads that Braydon and I had taken. But those were the same roads Philip was using to sneak around, and I didn't want to run into him when I wasn't prepared.

We settled into an easy rhythm. River was content to walk on a slack rein, not too fast, not too slow. He looked around like he was enjoying the scenery, but he didn't look for horse-eating logs or deadly shadows the way some horses do. I reached down and gently patted his neck. I'm not sure how long I rode, but it was long enough that I figured I would feel it in the morning. I didn't want to overdo it for River, though, since he hadn't been ridden in . . . well, I wasn't really sure the last time he'd been ridden.

We ascended the driveway to another chorus of excited whinnies and Biscuit, who sounded like a foghorn, louder and more obnoxious than the horses. He trotted along the fence beside us. River didn't seem fazed by any of it. I felt a lump in my throat at the thought of losing this little piece of heaven.

"If I make it through this," I told him as I stroked his neck again, "you're going to make a great lesson horse."

I took my time untacking him as well. I brushed him down, though he hadn't even broken a sweat. I finished by picking out his hooves. I took him back out to the others and they greeted him like he'd been gone for days, squealing and biting at each other. Horse affection tends to be on the rough side.

Even though I was pleasantly tired by the time I got to the house, I couldn't shake the weird, uneasy feeling that started after I read Philip's message. Taking the time for a ride helped, but only for a little while. I didn't turn on the TV for fear that it would mask Biscuit's alarm. I couldn't concentrate to read, so I ate in silence. I showered quickly, also afraid that I couldn't hear someone sneaking up on me while I was in there. That stupid movie scene from *Psycho* kept replaying in my mind, making me even more paranoid than I already was.

I checked all the doors and windows and made sure they were locked and secure again, and went to bed early with the hope that my sweet long-eared watch donkey would let me know if Philip walked up in my yard. It didn't matter how early I turned in. I still jumped at every noise. Banjo, not used to having the doggy door locked, also came to get me several times to relieve himself in the backyard. I doubted that a full-grown man could fit through the doggy door, but I was also paranoid enough that I wasn't taking any chances.

Sometime around three AM I gave up and decided to upload some of my newer photos to the amateur photography group on Facebook, but I couldn't concentrate on that either. I really wanted to call Dad. No matter how old you get, you never stop needing your parents. There wasn't anything he could do from his Alaskan cruise, so I fought the urge to call him in the middle of the night.

I rummaged around in my closet and found my trekking poles. I hadn't had time to take a good hiking trip since I'd officially opened the rescue, but I was glad I'd kept the gear. Having two potential weapons leaned up against the bedside table finally helped me drift into a fitful sleep.

* * *

I woke with a start the next morning after an unsettling dream. I couldn't remember the details of the dream, but it left me feeling off and uneasy. It took several moments of frantic searching before I remembered I had left my phone in my bedroom/office. I delayed going to get it until I had started the coffee. I knew it was irrational, but I didn't want to get my phone after I had found that message from Philip.

The nagging feeling that I wanted to talk to Andy kept creeping in while I made my breakfast, while I cleaned up after breakfast, and while I fed the horses. Having Ethan here dredged up old hurts and insecurities I thought I had overcome. I was still shaken by what he had said. I had thought, or maybe I had just convinced myself, that we had mutually grown apart. I had been floored when he had moved on and started dating Diane. And hadn't that been further proof that he was ready for our marriage to end? My thoughts were on a continuous loop of convincing myself to stop thinking about Ethan, and then following that loop with the desire to call my attorney, of all people. He had just been so easy to talk to that evening we spent at his office.

After finally finishing the morning feeding, I retrieved my abandoned phone to find that the battery had died overnight. I put it on the charger and pulled out my book to occupy my brain for a while. I had plenty to do. I needed to work on the budget and books for the rescue, which would entail cataloguing all of the feed and medical receipts, and I still hadn't finished the report on Zeus. But I needed a mindless distraction since I couldn't focus on anything that required me to string two thoughts together.

When my phone charged enough to come on, it started alerting almost continuously. Deciding that I might have missed something important, I got up and checked. There were two missed calls from Andy. Crap. There was also a missed call from Ethan and two texts from Braydon. I opened those first, delaying whatever bad news the others were going to give me.

Hey, sorry I didn't call last night. I'm free today if you want to get together.

And the next one was sent about an hour after the first.

If I don't hear from you before noon, I'm just going to come on over. You can always tell me to leave (smiley emoji).

I checked the time. I still had a couple of hours before noon. Taking a deep, steadying breath, I called Andy back first.

"Mallory, I was beginning to get worried," he said as soon as he picked up.

"Sorry, my battery died." I didn't tell him about my stupid notions about Philip's creepy message.

"They're likely going to charge you, if not today, then first thing Monday."

It didn't immediately register what he was talking about. When he said "charge me" my first thought went to making me pay for services or something.

"Mallory?" he said when I didn't respond. "You need to make arrangements for your animals because I can't guarantee I'll be able to negotiate bail."

That's when it hit me. They were going to *charge me* with Albert's murder.

Chapter Sixteen

I felt like all of the air had been sucked out of the room. I sat down on the floor next to the end table where I had plugged in my phone. Banjo came over and licked my face, worried about my odd behavior and hyperventilation.

"Are you still there?"

"I'm . . . here . . . ," I gasped in between my rapid, shallow breaths.

"I'm going to do everything I can to get you out of this," he said. And I believed him, but I wasn't sure it would be enough.

"I . . . can't . . . breathe," I whispered. Banjo licked my face again. I gently pushed him back and put the phone down. I needed to get everything away from my face. As a nurse, I knew I was having a panic attack. But as a person having a panic attack, it felt like I was dying. I could hear Andy yelling something and I quickly tapped the speaker function. "Panic . . . attack," I croaked.

"Deep breaths," he coached from my phone on the floor beside me. I tried to follow his advice, but my body wasn't cooperating. "Do you need me to call someone for you? Do you need me to come over?"

"No," I said through my hyperventilation, although I was marginally successful at slowing my breathing. "How do . . . you know?"

"That they're going to charge you?"

I made an affirmative noise.

"It's a small town. I have my connections," he said. "I can't betray my source's confidence, but I can assure you it's accurate information."

"I just . . . need . . . to go. I'll call . . . later."

I didn't wait for him to respond. I punched the red "end call" icon and tried not to pass out. My rapid-fire thoughts were a torturous hurricane in my head. I don't know how long it took for me to slow my breathing and calm my pounding heart. My chest felt so tight, and I was so breathless, that I understood why people thought they were having a heart attack when they were having a panic attack.

My head was still swimming, and I felt like I might throw up, but I pulled myself to my feet and told Banjo, who had never left me, that he was a good boy. Grasping at straws, I stumbled into my office and stared at the investigation board. I had to be missing something, some crucial clue that Philip forgot to hide.

I called Lanie to bounce ideas around. I decided not to tell her about Andy's call. There would be plenty of time for that.

"What am I missing?"

"I have no idea, Mal. I'm not a private investigator."

"No one watches more crime documentaries than you do. What would the investigators in your shows do?"

"Most of those crimes are solved with forensics. We can't exactly check Philip's house and car for trace evidence."

I sighed. "True. But surely not all cases are solved with forensics alone."

"I'll think on it and get back to you."

"Okay. Thanks, Lanie."

Andy texted several times to check on me, and I kept assuring him that I was okay, just keeping myself busy. After another round of telling him I had stopped hyperventilating, I decided I couldn't put off calling Ethan any longer. He started talking the minute he picked up.

"I regret leaving with just the note. I wanted you to know that I hope we can still be friends. It was nice seeing you again, but it's just not good for either of us to rehash old wounds."

"I agree," I said. I meant it. We worked pretty well as long-distance friends. "I appreciate that you drove all the way down here to make sure I was okay. Have a safe trip home."

We said our goodbyes and I ended the call quickly. There was work that needed to be done. And another call I had to make before noon.

"Hey, I was beginning to think you were dodging me." I could hear the smile in Braydon's voice.

"Not exactly. I do have to tell you something, though, and I'm not really sure how to say it."

"That sounds ominous," he said. "Just tell me."

"My attorney called this morning. They're going to charge me with murdering your dad."

He didn't respond right away.

"I will understand if you want to distance yourself," I continued. "No one would blame you for staying away from me, including me."

"I was afraid of that," he sighed. "That sheriff didn't seem even remotely interested in my statement about how your fingerprints ended up on that envelope."

My stomach sank. Why was Grady so sure I'd committed murder? Why wouldn't he listen to such a credible witness?

'They've made up their minds." I fought back the damned tears that stung my eyes again. "They seem to be ignoring anything that doesn't fit with me being guilty."

"I'm not interested in distancing myself from you. Even Luis says that he doesn't believe you could have done this, and he's supposed to be their star witness."

"Luis doesn't think I'm guilty?" The tears I'd been fighting back broke through and streamed down my cheeks.

"Not at all. He told me that he felt terrible for causing the police to suspect you to begin with. That's why he's been avoiding you."

I laughed like a maniac. It was such a relief to know that at least one other person could see through this mess.

"I'm coming over at noon and I'm bringing a picnic lunch," Braydon said cheerfully. "We can talk about your defense strategy. Or we can talk about *anything* else, if you'd rather."

"I do have one favor to ask." I hesitated for a second. "And believe me, I know I have no right to ask you for anything."

"Just ask, Mallory," he said, friendly impatience creeping into his voice.

"My attorney advised that I make arrangements for the horses in case he can't negotiate bail. I need someone to oversee getting them into foster homes if I'm . . ."—I could hardly say the word—". . . incarcerated for an extended period of time. I don't want to pile that on my volunteers. They're just kids." Technically, they were both adults, but I still didn't want to saddle either of them with the responsibility. I didn't want to saddle Braydon with it either, but I didn't have a lot of options.

"That's not going to happen, but if it makes you feel better, I'm happy to help. I'm sure I could talk Luis into overseeing everything, on the remote chance that you need it. I have no doubt he would jump at the opportunity to make it up to you."

"Thank you so much. I can show you where all the records are, where the keys to everything are kept, and a few other details when you come over. It would make me feel better to know someone will look after them if I'm suddenly not in the picture."

"I have a bit of a favor to ask of you as well."

"Name it," I said.

"I need to drop my car off this evening for a few repairs and I need a ride back to the house. Would you mind?"

"Not at all. After what I'm asking of you, that hardly seems like a favor."

"You're not asking that much. I'll see you soon."

After we hung up, I took a long, steadying breath. I decided it would be best not to dwell on "what ifs" and to focus on the immediate tasks I needed to complete. Taking advantage of the few hours before his visit, I organized all of the pertinent records on the horses and Biscuit. I made notes on each horse's record as to who I thought might take them in as fosters, ending with Zeus and Biscuit. I thought both would be a good fit with Tanner. It was a lot to ask of anyone to take on a half-ton animal, but I also made notes on the financial impact of each one and how much of the rescue's funds could be allotted to the foster family.

When I was finished, I felt like I had laid out a solid plan to take care of everyone if I was not around to do it myself. It would be easy enough to have Andy draw up a contract for Braydon or Luis to take over the accounts and make the arrangements to foster.

As I put everything together in a document box, I heard the doggy door slam. Banjo burst into the room proudly brandishing a stick that he had managed to fit through the door. I didn't have the heart to take it away from him, even though I knew I would have to sweep up the million pieces he would chew it into. I bent down to rub his head, and he ran away, sure that I was trying to steal his treasure. I smiled at his silly antics. I really hoped that Ethan would take him, if needed. Banjo loved him, and while he generally loved everyone, I knew he would be happy with Ethan.

I heard gravel crunching in the driveway and Biscuit brayed from his grazing spot on the hill behind the barn. I went through the house to the front door and recognized Braydon's BMW pulling in beside my car. My stomach sank. I knew I had asked him here, but for him to actually be here made it all real. I took a deep breath and met him on the porch.

"Hello." He smiled as he spoke. He held up a picnic basket. I took it and put it on the accent table just inside the door.

"Do you mind if we go to the barn first?" I felt like I needed to get the unpleasantness out of the way.

"Not at all."

"None of them are pedigreed like you're used to. Like I said on the phone, I just need to make sure that someone can oversee getting them into homes if . . . well, you know. If I'm convicted of killing your dad."

"You're not going to be convicted." He ran his hand up and down my arm. "But I'm happy to look things over if it makes you feel better."

I nodded as he took my hand and led me into the driveway. I pulled my keys out of my pocket since I'd locked all the gates, and I fumbled with them, dropped them in gravel. I released his hand and bent down to pick them up. That's when I noticed the splattered paint behind the wheels on the passenger side of Braydon's BMW, the yellow road paint marring the shiny white.

I held my breath, just on the edge of realization. I knew immediately that it was important, but my brain hadn't yet caught up with my intuition. Like gears clicking into place, the pieces started to fit. Tanner left the rescue the evening of Albert's death and got yellow paint on his truck because there were no signs. Braydon was supposed to have arrived the morning after when he had been notified of Albert's death, when the paint would have already been dry.

"Oh God," I gasped and looked up at Braydon. I have absolutely no poker face whatsoever, so everything I had just realized was written all over my face.

He caught on a lot quicker than I had.

"I really wish you hadn't seen that, Mallory." He lunged forward, grabbed me by the hair, and knocked me off balance. "I just haven't had time to get it removed yet. We were supposed to drop it off today, but you just *had* to notice it, didn't you?"

I reached up and grabbed his wrist with both hands and scrambled in the dirt. He easily pulled me along. I seemed to be barely an inconvenience.

"It would've been great for you to have been convicted of good ol' Dad's death, but I suppose killing you in self-defense will be just as good," he spat between gritted teeth.

I twisted as hard as I could in his grip, against the pain as he ripped out a chunk of my hair. I managed to get to my knees and then pull free. I started screaming, not words, just a guttural, primal cry to survive. It startled him for the fraction of a second it took to pull away. I scrambled on my hands and knees under the paddock fence, which slowed him down enough for me to get my feet underneath me. I sprinted into the barn and slammed the doors behind me. I pulled the primitive latch down and secured the doors, but I knew it wasn't the only way in and I only had a few moments.

I pulled out my phone and dialed 9-1-1. The barn doors shook violently.

"Mallory!" Braydon taunted. "Come out, come out, or I'll blow your barn down."

"What's your emergency?" a female voice asked in my ear.

"This is Mallory Martin, 98 County Road 233. Braydon Cunningham is trying to kill me," I whispered as loudly as I dared.

"Is he there now?"

"Yes, send help. Please hurry."

I couldn't hear him outside anymore and I held my breath. I turned around just in time to see him climbing through one of the stall windows. I screamed again in spite of myself. My heart was pounding in my ears. I threw the latch open and shoved the barn doors, but it was too late. He was too fast. He grabbed me by the throat from behind, and I dropped the phone as my hands instinctively pawed at his grip. We both stumbled out into the paddock.

"You're not making this easy," he hissed in my ear.

I remembered the self-defense course I had insisted Ginny take before she left for college. She'd agreed only if I took the class with her. I dropped to the ground, breaking Braydon's grip on my throat. I tried to scream again, my throat raw and aching; the sound came out in a hoarse squall. I crab-crawled away from him as he loomed over me.

It didn't register right away—the noise that I was hearing— because my heart was pounding in my ears. Braydon was yelling something at me, but the words weren't sinking in. And the other noise, an alternating high and low roar, finally filtered in and I recognized it as braying just as a small gray missile hit Braydon and knocked him off his feet. The missile turned out to be one very angry donkey, who didn't stop at just knocking Braydon down. He continued the attack, pawing and biting ferociously as Braydon put up his arms in defense and tried to scramble away the same way I had just tried to get away from him.

It was Braydon's turn to scream as the assault continued. No matter how hard he tried to deflect the blows of the donkey's little hooves, it was no use. Biscuit just fought harder, striking him with such force that I winced in sympathy. Not enough sympathy to try to help my would-be killer, but still, it was hard to watch.

I finally got to my feet and ran into the barn to get a halter and lead rope. I wasn't sure how much time had passed since I had dialed 9-1-1, and I wanted to make sure Biscuit was safely secured before the police arrived. While I was in there, I grabbed the pitchfork. I would rather have had Dad's shotgun, but I figured the pitchfork was better than nothing. When I returned, Biscuit was still pawing at Braydon, who had curled into the fetal position. I put a hand on Biscuit's round rump, and he stopped his assault. Braydon moaned, but didn't try to move.

I slipped the halter over Biscuit's head and fastened the buckle quickly. He kept his eyes on Braydon and his ears pinned back threateningly. I led him over to the paddock fence and looped the rope around the post. I tried to tell him he was a good boy, but my voice was just a squeak. My throat ached, and I hoped that Braydon hadn't done permanent damage.

I heard the sirens long before they reached us. As they pulled in, sirens still blaring, I sank to the ground beside my fuzzy little savior. Grady was the first one to the gate, and finding it still locked, swung easily over the fence. He came to me while the deputies secured Braydon.

"He's going to need an ambulance," I croaked.

"Good." Grady pulled me to my feet. His reaction surprised me. I thought he was certain of my guilt. "Looks like you do too," he said.

"I'm fine, but I want a vet to check out Biscuit. He saved my life." I patted the donkey again. He seemed none the worse for wear, however, already nuzzling Grady's pockets to see if he had treats hidden in there.

"She's crazy," Braydon whined as two deputies rolled him over to handcuff him. "She tried to kill me just like she did my dad!"

"He came home the night Albert was murdered," I said, my voice getting more hoarse by the moment. "He killed his dad, and I can prove it."

* * *

281

Grady accompanied me in the ambulance. At first, I was afraid he didn't want to let me out of his sight because I was still a suspect, but he offered to call Tanner or Ashley to tend to Biscuit and offered to accompany me to the hospital. I took him up on both offers. I also asked him to let Andy know about the recent developments. By the time we got to the hospital it felt like I had swallowed a baseball. No, scratch that. It felt like I had been *hit* with a baseball. It hurt to talk, and it hurt to swallow, but the doctor assured me that the soft tissue damage would heal and I would be "as good as new."

When the ER doctor left the room, Grady pulled out his notepad and pen.

"Do you feel like you can give me a statement?"

"Yes," I croaked.

"Okay." He pulled up a chair beside my gurney. "Start at the beginning,"

I told him about Tanner getting road paint on his pretty black pickup and how I had made the connection that Braydon must have come home the night before he claimed to have arrived.

"You might be able to get phone records to prove where he was when you called him about his dad," I added helpfully, still croaking.

"We'll do that," he smirked. I ignored his amusement.

"I didn't put it together at the time, but he orchestrated getting my fingerprints on that envelope that contained the township information too," I said and chewed a few ice chips to soothe my throat. "Now I don't even think he intended to sell the horses. He just wanted me there so he could provide a motive to make me look even guiltier. And I played right into his hands."

"Don't beat yourself up about it. He had clearly planned it pretty well," Grady said, his pen poised above his notebook. "But he didn't plan well enough to fool you forever."

I smiled and then immediately winced when my throat protested.

"He's going to say that he got the paint on his car some other time, you know that."

"He's going to have a hard time explaining the security footage," I said, my voice a hoarse whisper.

"Albert Cunningham didn't have a security system." He shook his head. "We looked and interviewed his staff. He didn't trust technology."

"Not Albert's. Mine."

"When did you get a security system?"

"It's not really a 'system.' I put in a camera after Philip creeped up in my yard. I've got his entire attack on video. Well, except for the few seconds in the barn." I opened my phone, clicked on the app, and then handed it over to him.

He winced as he watched it. "Remind me not to get in a fight with your donkey." He smiled. "Or you either, for that matter."

"Me? Braydon would've killed me if it wasn't for Biscuit."

"It looks like you gave him a run for his money."

The ER doctor told me I should spend the rest of that night at the little Hillspring Hospital to make sure the swelling in my throat didn't occlude my airway. Grady followed me to my hospital room and bade me goodnight after they had settled me in.

"I'll be talking to Mr. Cunningham now," he said as he paused in the doorway.

"I'm sorry, Grady."

"For what?"

"For being such a pain in your butt." I tried to smile again. "I know I wasn't easy to deal with through all this."

"No apology necessary. I don't think I would be very excited to be a person of interest in a murder investigation either." He put his Stetson back on and shut the door behind him.

Grady was followed by Sergeant West, who was every bit as chilly as she had been the first time I'd met her. She was skeptical of my account as usual. It was harder to argue with the video evidence of his attack. I thanked my lucky stars that I had purchased that camera and set it up when I did.

Andy burst into the room just as Sergeant West was leaving. He gasped as soon as he saw my battered face and neck.

"It looks worse than it is," I said, my voice alternating between a croak and a squeak.

"I'm so sorry I didn't check on you in person." He pulled one of the two chairs up to my bedside and took my hand in his.

I looked at him for a moment, maybe seeing him really for the first time. His chiseled jaw was covered in stubble and his brown eyes glinted with gold behind his dark-rimmed glasses. He was handsome, but not in the conventional knock-you-off-your-feet way that Braydon was handsome. His appeal was more subtle and gentle.

"None of this is your fault." I squeezed his hand. "I was an idiot for believing him, and I was an idiot for falling for everything he threw at me, hook, line, and sinker."

"Well, none of this is your fault either." He reached up and pulled some hay out of my hair. "Grady was pretty thin on details, but you can fill me in later. It sounds like it hurts to talk."

I nodded, thankful I didn't have to recount the whole thing yet again that night. I went to sleep still holding his hand.

* * *

The next few days were a blur of further interviews with both the police and the local newspapers. After I was discharged from the hospital, Andy surprised me and brought the prosecuting attorney, Dana Steinwick, with him. She was a quiet, stern woman, with an all-business demeanor. I liked her. She seemed driven and focused and completely unimpressed with Braydon Cunningham. Luis came by that same day. He must have apologized a hundred times during his short visit and offered to help at the rescue after work. I assured him that there were no hard feelings, and I meant it.

Ashley and Tanner picked up more than their share of the work at the rescue while I recuperated, and Lanie had been nearly a constant fixture at the rescue since I'd been released from the hospital. She fussed over me and insisted that I let her "take care of everything." She smoothed everything over with Ginny, for which I was eternally grateful. And she took to teasing me incessantly about Andy, who also became somewhat of a fixture in the days after my release. She made sure Biscuit was featured on the front page of the newspaper. He was heralded as a local hero, which drove some much-needed publicity and donations to the rescue. Biscuit was more than happy to soak up the attention anywhere he could get it, and even days later we had a steady stream of visitors who wanted to meet him in person.

"It's your boyfriend," Lanie said as she pulled back the curtain.

"I don't have a boyfriend," I croaked. "And the last one tried to kill me," I protested and hoped that she didn't notice my cheeks brightening.

Lanie met Andy at the door and looked at me like the cat that ate the canary as he passed her. I rolled my eyes at her. He had been here so often lately that Biscuit didn't announce his arrival anymore. He'd been accepted into the herd.

"How are you feeling?" He sat on the end of the sofa closest to my chair.

I had still felt pretty rough when he brought the prosecuting attorney out.

"Every day is a little better," I smiled. At least it didn't hurt to do that anymore.

"I'm going to run in to the shop," Lanie announced as she grabbed her purse. "I need to make sure Eve prices the new inventory. Mal is joining us for dinner tonight. You should come too." She winked at me as she closed the door behind her.

"You don't have to keep checking on me. And you don't have to come to dinner either." I said, and then instantly regretted it as his smile faltered a bit. I'd meant to let him off the hook, but I think he took it to mean I didn't want him there.

"I just had an update I wanted to deliver in person," he said before I had the chance to correct myself. "Braydon Cunningham wasn't able to make his bail. His family has cut ties and he barely has a penny to his name."

"That's a relief." I took a deep breath. "I was surprised bail was set at all. I mean, he tried to kill me and it's all on video."

"Don't underestimate the influence the Cunningham name has in a small town. The prosecuting attorney, Dana, is planning to ask for a change of venue for the trial. But that's months down the road. Right now, what's important is that he's in jail and he's going to stay there."

I nodded. "Look, I didn't mean to sound so ungrateful. I'm glad you're here and you're welcome to come to dinner. I just don't want you to feel like you *have* to."

"I'm here because I want to be." He shifted in his seat.

I reached for his hand and squeezed it tightly. "You've been such a good friend through all of this."

He opened his mouth like he was going to say something but closed it again before getting to his feet. He held onto my hand and patted it with his other one.

"I'll see you tonight. Text me the address." He squeezed my hand again before turning for the door.

He stopped and scratched Banjo's ears on the way and told him what a good dog he was. Banjo's tail thumped on the hardwood floor. Andy paused in the doorway and glanced back at me, his broad, square shoulders framed in light from the clear, bright afternoon. He looked again like he wanted to say something, but he just smiled and left.

Chapter Seventeen

I pulled my chair up to Lanie's table and couldn't wait to fill my plate, and then my belly, with her should-be-famous fried chicken. The bruising on my throat had turned a sickly shade of purple, but the swelling had gone down, and my voice was almost back to normal. Lanie had seated Andy next to me, and I couldn't tell if he was overwhelmed by the massive amount of southern comfort foods or if he was as excited as I was to dig in.

"Look," Bill said, leaning on his elbows, his beard nearly touching his empty plate. "I know things have been crazy and you're probably tired of talking about it, but I'm gonna need details."

"Bill!" Lanie smacked him on the shoulder as she put the plate of homemade rolls on the table. "You agreed to leave her be!"

"No, *you* agreed to leave her be. I need to know what happened. The newspaper has been sadly lacking in the details department."

"It's okay," I said, even though I thought I could eat the whole chicken. "What do you want to know?"

Andy smiled from his seat next to me with a "here we go again" expression.

"Grady told us that it was the road paint on his car that made you realize Braydon Cunningham had come in the night before Albert died, and not the morning he pretended to come home."

"Yeah, my volunteer, Tanner, spattered it on his black truck, or I probably never would've put it together."

"Don't sell yourself short," Andy said. "I think you would've figured it out."

"Maybe. But I should have caught on sooner, especially after the police told me about my fingerprints on that envelope. He orchestrated the whole thing, and he was always one step ahead of me. He trashed Heather's garden. He put the note in my horse's mane. He played up my assumptions without ever pushing me."

"He never counted on you putting it together at all," Andy countered. "He's a con man. And he underestimated you."

I smiled at him, and I appreciated his unwavering support. Lanie kept looking at us and trying to get my attention, but I pretended not to catch on. I was not ready for the incessant teasing to start.

"*Why* did he do it?" Bill ignored Andy's vote of confidence.

"Let everyone eat before it gets cold," Lanie scolded.

Taking the cue, I dove for the breast that I had been eyeing since I sat down. Andy followed suit and we started to pass all the fixin's around the table.

"He's in debt up to his eyeballs," I said when I had shoved a few bites of chicken down. "He had just lost another job. Albert refused to give him any more money since he had blown through his trust fund, so he cooked up some wild story about an investment opportunity. We figured out that's the conversation Luis overheard that made the police initially suspect me. When the phone records came in, they showed that Braydon had called Albert during our call and he must have switched over without Luis realizing it. The best the police can figure is that they fought over money and it got heated." I paused to take a huge bite of chicken.

"Braydon has been pretty tight-lipped," I continued. "But the prosecuting attorney says she's confident that the evidence is enough to convict him."

"Yeah, and she offered Mal a job," Andy laughed. "Grady may have wanted her to stay out of the investigation, but she thought she could use someone like Mal on her team."

"Are you considering it?" Bill asked.

"No!" I said, more loudly than I meant to. Bill held up his hands in surrender. "Sorry, I just do *not* want to go back to consulting."

"Grady figures Braydon put it all together that it would be really easy to nudge the police along in suspecting Mal," Andy said, inching his hand toward mine on the table. "And positioned himself as close to her as he could to plant more evidence against her. He even made sure her fingerprints were on an envelope that provided a motive for her to kill him."

"I thought Braydon was behind the anonymous donation to the rescue, but it turned out it was Andy." I smiled at him. "Braydon didn't even have enough in his bank account to cover the rental on his car. You remember the BMW?"

Lanie nodded.

"He was flat broke."

"Wow," Bill said, leaning back in his chair. "This sounds like one of your documentaries, Lane."

"Right?" She looked at me from across the table. "I keep telling Mal that she needs to talk to a reporter or something. This could totally be a Netflix series."

"I have absolutely no desire to talk to any more reporters." I pushed the homemade coleslaw around my plate. "This has been a nightmare I just want to put behind me."

"Where does Philip Atwood fit into all of this?" Bill asked, determined not to let me put it behind me until he had satisfied his curiosity.

"He's just a creepy troublemaker," Andy said. "And Judge Barrett had no problem issuing a restraining order for Mal after all of the Cunningham staff provided statements about his antics. And Mal apparently has a trained attack donkey if he decides to violate the order."

I couldn't help but laugh at that. I owed my life to that little donkey. All this time, I'd thought I'd rescued him.

"Braydon even trashed that organic farmer's garden to try to put more suspicion on Mal," Andy said.

"Yeah, and I've still got her lawsuit to deal with," I groaned. "But at least she hasn't pointed any shotguns at me since Braydon was arrested."

The rest of the conversation strayed into normal chitchat about the rescue and Lanie's plans to expand Junk & Disorderly. I helped Lanie clean up after dinner while Bill and Andy retired to Bill's workshop to discuss whatever men talk about in workshops. It was well after ten when Andy and I walked out to our cars, or rather to his car and my truck, which I was grateful to have back.

"You're going to have quite a story to tell your dad when he gets back," Andy said as he finally got up enough courage to reach for my hand.

"I hope he scolds me a little less than Ginny did," I laughed. My daughter had not held back as she told me how unhappy she'd been that I kept her in the dark. Someday, when she had children of her own, she'd understand why I did.

"Come by the office tomorrow. I'd love to have lunch," he said as he opened my truck door for me.

"I'll grab tamales from Miguel's on the way." I climbed in and turned back to him. "This was nice."

"It was." He lingered beside me. He took a deep breath. "Remember when you said I'd been a good friend through all of this?"

"Yes."

"I don't want that." He leaned in and met my gaze, his golden-brown eyes glinting in the faint light. "I want so much more."

The butterflies in my stomach fluttered like a hurricane. He paused just a moment to allow me to refuse, and when I didn't, he gently cupped the back of my neck and drew me in for a kiss. My body responded to him in ways that hadn't been awakened in *years*. I was suddenly way too hot but shivered with anticipation and desire.

My attraction to Andy had simmered quietly and caught me by surprise. Being a suspect in a murder investigation had been disorienting to say the least, and even that isn't a strong enough word to describe the foundation-shaking turmoil of the last few weeks. But I knew in that hospital room, with my hand in his, how comforting it had felt, and how I hadn't wanted anyone else by my side.

"I want more too," I said breathlessly, and this time, I pulled him in for a kiss.

I'm not sure how long it took us to finish saying goodnight, but once we did, I couldn't wait to see him again.

Acknowledgments

First and foremost, I would like to thank my agent extraordinaire, Jill Marsal, for making a lifelong dream come true, and for being endlessly patient with me. I will always be grateful for your guidance and support.

Special thanks to the team at Crooked Lane for giving my book a chance. I am so excited to be working with all of you and look forward to seeing what lies ahead. Thank you to Terri Bischoff and Emily Rapoport for your editorial expertise in making this book the best it could be. No one could ask for better editors.

Thank you to Kathy Ver Eecke and her amazing team at Pitch to Published for breaking down the querying process in a way that finally made sense and for teaching me things I didn't even know I needed.

A heartfelt thank you to my wonderful husband, Warren, for being my biggest fan and for letting me lean on you when my confidence failed. Huge props to my daughter, Madison, for being the best beta reader in the world and making sure that no one in *this* book took a week-long shower.

Acknowledgments

I am eternally grateful for my loving and supportive network of friends. Thank you to Jodi Lasky who pushed me to expect more. Hugs and gratitude to Pennie Malotte and Carolyn Bosshardt for being my personal cheering section throughout this journey. Much love and thanks to April Ledbetter for talking me off the ledge more times than I care to admit. And a big thank you to Erin Conard for always being my 'one friend.'

Special thanks to my writing groups, Pitch Perfect, Writers Win, Pitch to Published, and A Writer's Journey. The members in those groups have propped me up and celebrated with me, although maybe not in equal measure.

And last, but certainly not least, thank you, Reader. I hope we meet again.